HE CLOSED HIS EYES, tightened his hold on her, and kissed her hungrily. For a long, delicious moment he pushed away his awareness that he was behaving like a cad . . . that this was the girl he'd pledged to his brother, that she was a mere child—seventeen years his junior—and that he was supposed to be convinced that she was a servant in his employ. Even while surrendering to the sweet intoxication of the experience, he hated himself. After much too brief a wallow in depravity, he forced himself to regain his self-control. He released her and loosened her hold on him.

Kitty, overwhelmed, emitted a tremulous sigh . . .

THE MAGNIFICENT MASQUERADE
A Regency Love Story by
ELIZABETH MANSFIELD

Elizabeth Mansfield
The Magnificent Masquerade

CHARTER BOOKS, NEW YORK

THE MAGNIFICENT MASQUERADE

A Charter Book / published by arrangement with
the author

PRINTING HISTORY
Charter edition / September 1987

ISBN: 0-515-51568-1

Charter Books are published by The Berkley Publishing Group,
200 Madison Avenue, New York, NY 10016.
The name "Charter" and the "C" logo
are trademarks belonging to Charter Communications, Inc.

PRINTED IN THE UNITED STATES OF AMERICA

10 9 8 7 6 5 4 3 2 1

prologue

One day, without any apparent provocation, Lord Birkinshaw decided to marry off his daughter. This decision was astonishing, for the girl hadn't reached her eighteenth birthday and was not yet "out." However, the idea did not, as his wife later accused, come to him "out of the clear blue sky"—in fact, he'd retorted, the sky hadn't shown a scintilla of blue that whole dank day—but was the result of the confluence of several minor incidents which seemed to him to lead inexorably to that rather major decision. "And if you want the truth," he told his wife roundly, in strong defense of a position which, no matter how insupportable, would not be changed once he'd taken it, "that row we had this morning might well have been the incident that touched off the entire matter."

This was not quite the truth. Although the argument with his wife had been somewhere in the back of his mind, the incident that triggered his astounding decision had occurred later that afternoon, at his club. It started with, of all things, the loud, clear ejaculation of a curse. Someone had shouted "Oh, damnation!" and the sound had reverberated shockingly throughout the club's high-ceilinged rooms. It was not that the words themselves were shocking (for many more-salacious epithets had been uttered thousands of times over the gaming tables), but that the rooms had been so remarkably still a moment before.

Afternoons were always rather quiet at the gentlemen's clubs on St. James Street. Although one could find gamesters at their play at any hour of the day or night, their numbers were few in the afternoons, most gentlemen reserving themselves for the headier excitement that filled the gaming rooms during the evening hours. In the afternoons, there were often

1

more gentlemen dozing in easy chairs in the clubs' lounges than could be found at the gaming tables.

This was certainly true that rainy January afternoon at White's, the formidably fashionable club at Number 37. The famous bow windows (which Raggett, the proprietor, had installed five years before, in 1811, and in which the Dandies of London so frequently exhibited themselves while they eyed the female strollers on the street below) were on this day completely deserted. The dining rooms were also empty, and only one table was in use in the gaming rooms. So unpleasant was the weather that only a handful of gentlemen could be found snoozing in the lounges. One of these was Thomas Jessup, Viscount Birkinshaw. He'd folded his hands over his protuberant stomach, stretched his legs out before him, covered his face with a handkerchief to indicate to anyone who wished to converse with him that he was not to be disturbed, and had gone to sleep.

If one is to understand fully the progression of events, one must realize that Lord Birkinshaw was not *compelled* to venture out in the rain to nap at his club; he had a perfectly satisfactory town house in Curzon Street in which to make himself comfortable. His town house contained a perfectly satisfactory sitting room which in turn contained a perfectly satisfactory armchair in which he could quite comfortably snooze. But his town house also contained his wife, and it was to escape her carping that he'd taken himself out in the rain and made his way to his club.

On this day the subject of his wife's diatribe had been their daughter. The chit was in her fourth year at Miss Marchmont's Academy for Young Ladies and evidently causing as much commotion there as she had when she'd been living at home. Just the other day, he'd received a bill from Berry Brothers for a half case of French wine and several dozen pastries which had been delivered to the school. His wife, puzzled by the bill, had sent a letter of inquiry to the headmistress of the school, a horsey-faced female named Marchmont. The reply had come this morning. His daughter, it seemed, was the culprit who'd ordered the wine and the sweets. The minx had managed to smuggle them into the school in a laundry basket! Then she and her cronies had held a midnight party up in the school's attic and had become quite boisterous. They were, of course, promptly discovered, but by that time they were all tipsy, and even as they were led off to bed they could not be prevented from singing bawdy songs at the tops of their voices.

However, in her letter, the headmistress had assured the parents that they had no cause to upset themselves over the incident. The matter was not of any serious concern. They should not, she warned, make too much of it, such as deluding themselves that the incident signified in their daughter an incipient addiction to alcohol. There was nothing more significant in the incident than an outbreak of youthful high spirits. The girls had been appropriately reprimanded, their daughter in particular, and she'd accepted her punishment in a spirit of good sportsmanship. The letter concluded with the statement that their daughter's tendency to youthful prankishness did not in any way keep her from ranking above average in her scholastic standing.

As far as Lord Birkinshaw was concerned, that should have been that. The end of the story. To him, the matter was nothing more than a rather good joke. But his wife did not agree. She'd spent the morning nagging at him about it. "The girl has to be taken in *hand*," she insisted. "Youthful prankishness, indeed! She's almost eighteen. It's time for her to put by that sort of nonsense! Do you know what will happen when word gets out that Kitty is the sort of creature who tempts her friends to drink and carouse? No bachelor worth a fig will come *near* her! Do you want your daughter to end her days a dotty old maid?"

But Lord Birkinshaw didn't see what *he* could do about it. What did his wife expect of him? Did she want him to take a *whip* to the girl? After more than an hour of such haranguing, he did what any man of sense would do—he banged out of the house.

His wife, he told himself as he walked to his club through an icy rain, had an uncanny knack of cutting up his peace. The disturbing feelings she'd generated remained with him all through his walk and even after his arrival at White's. It took him several minutes to unwind before he was able to sleep. And even then he found no peace—his dreams, too, were affected. He found himself immersed in a nightmare in which he was hosting an enormous wedding feast at which the guests were gorging on unbelievably huge quantities of Berry Brothers' pastry and the most expensive French champagne, his wife was glaring at him from the far end of a table a half-mile long, his daughter (the bride) was swinging drunkenly from the chandelier, and, worst of all, he himself, having forgotten to put on his britches, was parading around the room in his smalls. It was then that he heard someone say, quite loudly and from very close by, "Oh, damnation!"

He sat up with a start. That voice had certainly not emanated from his dream. He pulled the handkerchief from his face and found himself staring at Lord Edgerton, seated just opposite him. "What's that?" he asked, the last vestiges of his dream dissipating into the air. "Did you say something, Greg?"

Gregory William Wishart, Earl of Edgerton, was another regular member of White's easy-chair set, although he was much younger than most of them. Only five-and-thirty, Edgerton was the head of a household even more troublesome than Birkinshaw's. With a dithery mother, a brother who was always getting into scrapes, and a sister who was convinced she teetered on the brink of serious illness, Edgerton, too, used the club to escape the tensions of his household, at least whenever he came to town from his Suffolk estate. At this moment, he was holding a letter clutched in his right hand, while his left supported his forehead, the fingers buried in a mass of dark, gray-streaked hair. "I'm sorry for waking you, Birkinshaw," he apologized. "It's just this deuced message I've received from Cambridge. My brother's been sent down again."

"You don't mean it! What's the boy done this time?"

"They don't say. But it must have been deplorable. The last time Toby was sent down, he'd been found running a gambling den in a room right behind the chapel! This must have been worse, for this message informs me that it's for good this time. I'm afraid the Honorable Tobias Wishart's muffed his last chance. Dash it all, I'd like to give my deuced brother a good thrashing!"

"I know how you feel, old fellow. My wife was saying the same thing about our daughter. Practically suggested I take a whip to the girl."

"Oh?"

"Yes, a whip! What a wild, trouble-making minx she is, to be sure. Seems the chit bought champagne, had it smuggled into the school somehow, and then she and her cronies all got drunk as lords."

"Good God! Did they send her down, too?"

"No, they didn't, for which I thank my lucky stars. Don't know what life'd be like if she were sent home. We'd scarcely pass a day without a crisis. Last time our Kitty was home the to-do she stirred up was unbelievable. First she made eyes at one of the footmen, who promptly lost his head over her and had to be sacked. Then she ran up a bill at Hoby's for nine— *nine*, mind you!—pairs of boots. Then she decided she wanted to prepare a *Charlotte Americaine* with her own hands and caused such a stir in the kitchen that we almost lost our cook. And, finally, she borrowed her mother's emerald brooch and then sold it to a cent-per-cent and gave the money to help a friend elope to Scotland, which brought the friend's parents to our house in such a state that I feared they would commit murder—and all this, mind you, in a mere three days' time!"

Lord Edgerton grinned, although he shook his head in sympathy. "Amazing, isn't it, the mischief youngsters can concoct these days? I sometimes feel, when I compare myself with my brother, that I and my generation must have lacked imagination. I don't think we were *capable* of concocting such scrapes. Toby, when he was home for his school holiday, ran up a bill at Tattersall's for over a thousand pounds, made some poor young lady fall into hysterics at the dinner table by telling her that the wine she'd just drunk was really a love potion, and scandalized Lady Jersey by appearing at Almack's in his riding clothes. And, I may add, that's the week he believed himself to have been a model of good behavior!"

Birkinshaw snorted. "Young scamp! He needs to be leg-shackled, that's what he needs. Once a fellow's leg-shackled, you know, he's less likely to carry on. Responsibilities, you know. Marital duties. Having to please someone besides himself. Having someone who'll call him to account—who'll demand to know where he spent his time or his money. Having someone who'll expect him to show his face at dinner and all that. You ought to find him someone, Greg. Someone who . . . good God! Oh, I *say!* Greg, my boy, I think I'm about to give birth to a splendid idea! A really splendid idea!"

"Are you indeed?" Lord Edgerton laughed. "And what idea is that?"

"Marry your brother to my daughter! It'd be the answer for both of them. Each one has enough spirit to tame the other!"

"Come now, Birkinshaw, you can't be serious. Your daughter's just a child! A mere schoolgirl, isn't she?"

"Turning eighteen this week. Her mother's planning a come-out for her next season. We can make it a wedding instead."

Edgerton eyed the other man thoughtfully. "What do you mean? Are you suggesting that we arrange the whole thing ourselves? Without consulting the parties involved?"

"If we consult them, it'll never come to pass. Youngsters like ours don't ever agree to do what's good for 'em. We elders know best about these things. I've never approved of offspring making their own decisions on the subject of marriage anyway. All they do when one broaches the subject with them is moon on about finding someone who engages their affections. Affections, indeed! As if falling in love is anything more than a temporary fit of insanity! Stuff and nonsense, all of that love rot. When it comes to wedlock, anyone under the age of thirty should be made to follow parental instructions."

Lord Edgerton looked dubious. "I don't know, Birkinshaw. It's something I'd have to think over . . ."

"Think over? What can you want to think over? I tell you, Greg, it'd be the making of both of them. A perfect solution to our problems. Even my wife would agree that it's an ideal cure for her worries about . . ." But at that moment Lord Birkinshaw's expression clouded over, for an important objection suddenly occurred to him. "Hang it all, now I think of it, I don't suppose she *would* . . . ! Oh, well, perhaps the idea *is* a bit hasty."

"Hasty? Have you thought of some impediment?"

"It suddenly occurred to me that my wife might not see the matter as I do. She has great plans for Kitty, you know. Expects her to make an advantageous match. These women don't think a fellow's even *eligible* unless he's very well to pass. Hate to say it, my boy, but I don't think she'd consider your brother—what's his name? Toby?—I don't think she'd think Toby a promising prospect, his being a second son and all that . . ."

"As to that, Birkinshaw, I've given the second-son problem a good deal of thought. I don't approve of the practice of settling one's entire fortune on the eldest son and letting the younger ones drift off without a penny. It's a downright crime to ingrain in the younger sons the habits of luxury and then abruptly cut them off from the wherewithall to indulge them. I won't do that to my brother. I intend to deal fairly by him. I plan to settle twenty thousand pounds on him. That would give him a quite satisfactory income, and, in addition, he'll some day come into a very substantial estate from his mother."

"Twenty thousand pounds!" This information brightened Lord Birkinshaw's brow considerably. "That *is* generous of you, Greg, I must say. My wife couldn't say twenty thousand isn't a bright prospect! In that case, I see no impediment at all to my little plan. None at all. So what say you, my boy? Shall we come to an agreement?"

Lord Edgerton remained hesitant. "Just like that? Settle two people's lives without further ado?"

"Exactly. Without further ado."

"I don't know, Birkinshaw. It's a bit high-handed, isn't it, to conclude a matter of such moment in so cavalier a fashion?"

"And how would you describe your brother's and my daughter's behavior, eh? High-handed and cavalier hardly covers it. The fact remains, my boy, that the two of 'em have been causing us all sorts of difficulty, and my plan will relieve us of a heavy burden. Marry 'em off, I say, and give 'em the burden themselves. Let *them* have the delight of dealing with each other."

Lord Edgerton felt his grin break out again. "Rather like the pair in 'The Taming of the Shrew,' eh?"

"Now you mention it, it *will* be rather like that. Except that in this case each will tame the other. Well? Is it agreed?"

Edgerton, sorely tempted despite the voice of his conscience whispering that there was something morally questionable about meddling in people's lives behind their backs even if it was for their own good, rubbed his chin with the tips of his long fingers while he considered the proposition. He couldn't deny that making such an agreement was reprehensible. But reprehensible as it was, his brother deserved it. The letter still crushed in his hand was tangible proof that the boy was indeed incorrigible. Not having known a father, he'd been too much coddled by a weak mother and too much indulged by an overly fond brother. Toby had never been forced to pay the penalties for his misdeeds. Perhaps marriage *was* a solution for the fellow. It was time he was forced to face some of life's responsibilities.

Edgerton lifted his eyes to Lord Birkinshaw's face. "Very well," he said with a sigh. "Why not?"

"Oh, splendid!" chortled Lord Birkinshaw. "Absolutely splendid! Then we have a bargain!"

"Yes, it's a bargain."

And the two men, without further ado, took the only step considered necessary to make the bargain utterly binding: they shook hands on it.

chapter one

An undersized eight-year-old girl in an oversized white pinafore opened the door of the music room of the Marchmont Academy for Young Ladies and peered inside. What she saw made her want to laugh, but she stifled the impulse by clapping her hand over her mouth. Even though the sight before her was quite ridiculous, she knew it would go ill for her if she laughed aloud.

The six students of the upper school had formed a queue across the middle of the floor of the music room and were practicing the steps of the gavotte. Dressed in a similar fashion to their observer, in white pinafores and black stockings, they looked like a row of clumsy penguins. Each was standing at arm's length from the next girl, each had a book on her head, each had extended a right hand as if it rested on a partner's arm, and each had pinned up her skirts so that Miss Hemming, the dance instructress, could see if the steps were being properly executed. Miss Hemming herself was pounding out the Gossec "Gavotte in D" on an ancient pianoforte while counting out the beat in a shrill soprano. "STEP and STEP and three and four and TURN, CROSS, seven, eight! STEP and BACK and three and four and TURN . . . hold your right arm UP, Clara! . . . seven, eight!"

Clara, the plumpest and most penguinlike of the five young dancers, while trying to comply with the instruction to lift her arm, unfortunately moved her head. This, of course, caused her book to slide to the floor with a thud. The noise distracted the others, two other heads turned, two more books slid down, and all the dancers' bodily discipline evaporated in a confusion of missteps and giggles.

"Young ladies, *really!*" Miss Hemming scolded, slamming her hands down on the keys in disgust and rising angrily. "You

9

must move with a LIFT! An inner LIFT! Smoothly! With
grace! You must think Up, Up, *Up!* How will you ever
make your marks in a tonnish ballroom if you persist in this
giddy—? Good gracious, child, what do *you* want?"

This last was addressed to the little black-stockinged inter-
loper in the doorway. The child's grin died away at once.
"Mith Marchmont thent me," she lisped, dropping the dance
instructress a quick curtsey. "She wanth to thee Mith Jethup."

"Me?" Miss Katherine (but always called Kitty) Jessup,
one of the six young dancers, had knelt down to retrieve the
book she'd dropped, but her head came up in instant alarm at
the sound of her name. "Miss Marchmont wants to see *me?*"

The girl in question was not the most beautiful of the
group—plump Clara had more perfect features and Bella, the
tallest, had a more perfect form—but Kitty was the one a
stranger would notice first. Her hazel eyes seemed at first
glance to be almost green, her upturned nose was covered
with a sprinkling of charming freckles, and her hair was not
only wildly disheveled but a unique shade of orange-red. If
she were not the daughter of the very British Thomas Jessup,
Viscount Birkinshaw, and his equally British wife, one might
have taken her for a little Irish lass.

"Of course it's you," Miss Hemming sighed, sitting down
on the piano bench and shaking her head in a gesture of hopelessness. "Who on earth else?"

"Egad, Kitty, not again!" muttered one of the girls, not
quite under her breath.

"Miss Marchmont warned you that there'd be drastic punishment if you got into another scrape," Clara reminded Kitty
in a worried whisper. "She *warned* you! This time it'll be
Coventry, and we won't even be able to *speak—!*"

"It must be a mistake," Kitty declared firmly to the child in
the doorway. "I haven't done anything wrong in . . . in
weeks!"

The child stuck her chin out pugnaciously. "I didn't make
no mithtake. The name I wath told wath Kitty Jethup."

"Kitty Jessup, you sly-boots," tall Bella demanded, "have
you been up to some mischief that you've kept from us?"

Kitty stood erect, her reddish eyebrows drawing together
over a pair of offended eyes. "I haven't been up to anything
that could remotely be called mischief."

"Oh, that's very likely, isn't it?" Bella sneered. "Listen to Miss Innocence Incarnate!"

"Don't be a clunch," Clara said, putting a protective arm about Kitty's shoulders. "If Kitty says she didn't make any mischief, she didn't."

"Then why is Miss Marchmont summoning—"

"That will be *enough!*" Miss Hemming rose from her bench again with magisterial authority and clapped her hands for order. "Stop this babble at once! Kitty, Miss Marchmont awaits you. You are excused." She was about to turn her attention to her other charges when a final glimpse of Kitty's appearance brought her up short. "Wait a moment, miss! You can't go to our headmistress looking like that. Unpin your skirts, if you please, and put on your half-boots. You can't run through the corridors in those dancing slippers. And good God, girl, do something about your hair before you go down. You look like a Zulu! As for the rest of you, back to your positions, please. Books in place? Good. Now then, once again: WALK and two and three and four and TURN, CROSS, seven, eight. One and BACK and three and TURN and COME TOGETHER, seven . . ."

Kitty picked up her half-boots from the row of shoes lined up against the wall, tiptoed across the room, and let herself out. She closed the door behind her carefully, expelled a breath, and leaned against the corridor wall to change her shoes. When this was done, her eye fell on the little messenger who still remained in the corridor watching her with an expression of fiendish delight. "Well, what are you waiting for?" she asked the child coldly.

"I'm thuppothed to ethcort you."

"I don't need an escort, thank you. Besides, I have to straighten my hair. So you may run along. Go back to your spelling class, to your geography book, or to whatever was occupying you before you came barging into my life."

"Mith Marchmont'll be livid for keeping her waiting," the child predicted gleefully.

Kitty frowned at her. "You needn't enjoy this quite so much, you little toady," she hissed.

The child felt a twinge of shame. "I'm thorry. I'm really not a toady. I didn't athk to go on thith errand."

"Mmm. Are you willing to help me, then?"

"Yeth, I thuppothe I can. But you ain't going to athk me to tell Mith Marchmont I couldn't find you, are you?"

"No, it's nothing like that. Just find Emily and send her to me. She's the only one who can fix my hair properly. She's probably making the beds in the fourth-floor dormitory."

"I can do that, all right," the child agreed.

"Good. Run along, then, quickly. And then go back to Miss Marchmont and explain that I had to change. Say that I'll be right along."

The child nodded and ran off. It soon became evident that she'd followed the instructions to the letter, for Emily, the school's most valuable maid-of-all-work, appeared in the corridor even before Kitty had finished unpinning her skirts. "Ah, there you are," Kitty greeted the maid in relief. "Sorry to take you from your chores, but Miss Hemming said my hair looked like a Zulu's."

The maid bobbed a curtsey. "I don't mind, Miss Jessup," she said in her soft voice. "I'd rather do hair than beds."

The maid, Emily Pratt, was a fixture at the school. Whenever a youngster needed buttoning, whenever a girl felt sick, whenever an upper school young lady needed a confidante, Emily was there. Every one of the students felt an attachment to her, though she never crossed over the invisible boundaries that separated maids from their mistresses. She was always unassuming, always serious, always eagerly helpful. Her appearance seemed to fit her character: modest, unobtrusive, and pleasant. Her face was pale and full-moon round, leading one to expect that her figure, too, would be full and rounded, but it was surprisingly slim. She had a pair of wide, intelligent brown eyes, silky brown hair that (when not pinned up in a knot as it was now) was long and lovely, and a smile that, in its rare appearances, would etch an unexpected pair of vertical dimples in those full cheeks. She was two years older than Kitty, but the round cheeks and wide eyes made her seem two years younger.

It was rumored that Emily had been a pupil of the school many years ago but that her parents had died in a coaching accident and left her without a penny. Miss Marchmont had kept her on, permitting her to continue with her music studies (for she showed outstanding talent at the pianoforte) and letting her earn her way by doing chores and occasionally helping to teach the pupils of the lower school. Kitty not only liked but admired Emily; the maid seemed to handle adversity with a shy, unobtrusive courage.

While Emily smoothed Kitty's flyaway tresses with a comb she conveniently kept in a pocket of her apron, Kitty told the maid what had happened. "What do you suppose Miss Marchmont wants with me this time?" she asked, fidgeting nervously.

The maid struggled to untangle the hair on the bobbing head. "I'm sure I've no idea, Miss Jessup. Have you been up to some mischief again?"

"No, I haven't done anything wrong. At least . . . not anything I can remember."

Emily managed to twist Kitty's locks into a neat braid. "If you can't remember, miss, then it couldn't possibly be something as shocking as the last time."

"You mean when I and my friends went up to the attic and were caught having a party? I never heard such a fuss! We were only a little tiddly."

"Weren't you just!" The maid grinned in recollection. "I don't think I've heard such wicked songs in all my life! You can't blame Miss Marchmont for being put out with you."

"'Put out' is hardly an adequate way to describe it," Kitty muttered, the sound of Miss Marchmont's tongue-lashing still ringing in her ears. "I wonder what she'll do to me this time."

"Miss Marchmont always says that a punishment should fit the nature of the infraction," the maid quoted, winding Kitty's braid into a neat coil at the nape of her neck.

"That's just it," Kitty sighed, "I don't know what the nature of the infraction *is*."

But Emily couldn't solve the problem. She could only do up the hair. "There, Miss Jessup, that's done," she said, pinning the bun in place with a few hairpins from her well-supplied pocket. "It seems to me that you look quite presentable."

"Oh, thank 'ee," Kitty mocked. "Quite ready for the hanging, eh?"

"Oh, I don't think it will go as badly as all *that*." Emily was too serious to recognize the other girl's irony. "Miss Marchmont is nothing if not kind."

"*Kind!* How can you, of all people, call her kind? She's made a veritable slave of you!"

The maid's wide eyes widened even more. "Slave, miss? Oh, no, not at all! You mustn't think such a thing! She doesn't overwork me. And I'm paid a fair wage, you know. I have no complaints. Miss Marchmont's been more than good to me. I don't know what I should have done without her, you see. I've had no one else since I was nine."

"Well, I suppose she likes you. She *must*, if she's so kind to you. I think she *detests* me."

"Oh, no, Miss Jessup, I'm sure she doesn't."

"We'll find out soon enough," Kitty muttered apprehensively. "Walk me down to the office, will you, Emily? If I go alone, I shall feel as if I'm marching to the guillotine."

They started down the corridor toward the stairs, Kitty trying to remember what transgression she'd committed that Miss Marchmont could have discovered. She was sure she hadn't done anything very terrible lately, mainly because Miss Marchmont's isolated and well-guarded school did not provide even a young lady of her fertile imagination many opportunities for wrongdoing. There were no young men in the vicinity; there were no hours of the day when the pupils were unsupervised (for even when they slept they were subject to bi-hourly bed-check); there were few unguarded doors (and those few were always locked), and even if one could manage to steal out, one could find no means of transportation to convey one to the more exciting sections of London. With such limited opportunities for naughtiness, what else could one be at Miss Marchmont's Academy but a good—well, almost good—girl?

So why on earth had she been sent for? Kitty wondered. The dyed hair episode (when she'd persuaded all five upper-school girls to wash their hair with henna dye, and all six had appeared at morning prayers with identical red heads) had already been atoned. (She'd been forced to spend the weekend writing the history of the War of the Roses in original blank verse, while the others were made to wash their hair every morning and evening for ten days. And Miss Marchmont couldn't possibly have discovered the little puppy she'd hidden away in the tool shed at the back of the rose garden. Had someone shown the headmistress the manuscript for the play Kitty had written, which mocked the mannerism of all the teachers—including Miss Marchmont herself—quite unmercifully? It wasn't very likely; it was not yet in rehearsal, and very few people knew of its existence. Besides, there was only one copy, and *that*, she was sure, was safely locked in her bed-chest. "I can't imagine what I've done that she could've discovered," she said as they approached Miss Marchmont's office door, "but I'm certainly in the suds." She glanced over her shoulder at Emily in unaccustomed humility. "Are you sure I look presentable?"

"Neat as wax, miss, on my honor," Emily assured her.

"Thank you." Kitty stared nervously at the gold letters on the door which read MISS MARCHMONT, HEADMISTRESS.

"You're not frightened, are you, miss?" Emily asked. "You needn't be, you know. Miss Marchmont isn't nearly as forbidding as she looks."

"Me, frightened? Not on your life! Kitty Jessup doesn't frighten so easily." To prove her point, she raised her hand to the opaque glass inset in the door and rapped smartly.

"Come in," came a voice from within the office.

"Shall I wait for you?" Emily offered.

"I should say not! I'm not a baby. Thanks, Emily, for doing my hair. Now run along!" And she squared her shoulders, took a deep breath, and marched forward to meet her doom.

chapter two

Lord Birkinshaw did not expect his wife to fall into parox-
ysms of delight when he informed her of his intention to wed
their daughter to Lord Edgerton's younger brother, but neither
did he anticipate an enraged opposition. The violence of her
reaction took him by surprise. Hermione Jessup, Lady Birkinshaw, had already retired for the night when he burst in on her
with the news, and the fact that he'd awakened her just as she
was drifting off into sleep only exacerbated her fury.

"Toby *Wishart?* You intend to shackle our daughter to *Toby
Wishart?*" she all but shrieked, sitting up so abruptly that
wispy tendrils of her hair, which had escaped from beneath
her nightcap, trembled. "How did you ever *come* by such an
addle-brained scheme? Not only is the fellow completely
lacking in prospects, being a younger son, but he's known far
and wide as a ramshackle *scapegrace!*"

His lordship opened his mouth to respond, but his lady
would not be silenced. Now wide awake, she launched on an
impassioned diatribe, her plump cheeks shaking like blanc-
mange and her still-beautiful eyes flashing fire. It was typical
of her husband, she declared vehemently, to come, without
taking a moment for consultation with his wife, to such a
thoughtless, hasty decision. "In our twenty-odd years of marriage you've made more than a thousand impulsive decisions
—most of which, I might point out, proved to be completely
foolish!—but for sheer *idiocy* this one outdoes them all!"

"Oh, is that so?" was his lordship's brilliant response. "So
you say!"

"Of course so I say! What else can I say when my green-
headed husband plans to shackle my only daughter to a penniless loose screw!"

"Penniless?" Lord Birkinshaw demanded gleefully, pouncing upon the cue she'd provided for him to play his trump card. "You consider twenty thousand pounds *penniless?*"

Lady Birkinshaw gaped. "Twenty thousand—? Whatever are you babbling about?"

His lordship chortled triumphantly. "You heard me."

His lady threw off her comforter and rose from the bed, looking awesomely threatening despite the demure innocence of her long-sleeved white nightgown. With arms akimbo and hands on her hips, she peered closely at his leering face and demanded, "Thomas Jessup, are you *soused?*"

"Sober as you, my dear," he answered with a self-satisfied smirk.

"I very much doubt that. Anyone who can claim that a ne'er-do-well like Toby Wishart possesses a fortune must be raddled . . . or at least tiddly."

"I am neither soused, raddled, nor tiddly, ma'am. And I did not say the boy has a fortune now. But he *will* have it on the day he marries our Kitty. Edgerton himself gave me his word on it."

Her ladyship sank down on the bed, silenced. *Twenty thousand pounds!* A sum of that size changed the picture completely. It was perhaps not the most enormous fortune of anyone now on the marriage mart, but it certainly wasn't a sum to be casually tossed aside. Lady Birkinshaw realized at once that the situation was now one she had to reconsider. "Good God," she muttered, "if word gets round that Edgerton means to be so generous to Toby, every matchmaking mama in London will be after the scamp!"

"Won't make no difference," her husband assured her complacently. "Kitty's to have him. Edgerton and I shook hands."

But his wife hardly heard him. Her mind was busily occupied in weighing the advantages of the proposed match against the difficulties. That there were many advantages was now indisputably clear. For one thing, it was unlikely that their Kitty, attractive and spirited though she was, would find very many suitors of better—or even equal—prospects. Among the eligibles, there were only three or four at most whose fortunes were greater; on the other hand, there were dozens of young bachelors circulating among the ton who couldn't lay claim to half such wealth. And Kitty was so contrary that she might, if given a choice, attach herself to one of the latter.

Like her husband, Lady Birkinshaw considered her daughter to be quite unmanageable. She had been dreading for years the troublesome necessity of bringing her daughter out. Although she was a fond mother and was second to none in her admiration of her daughter's looks, coloring, charm, wit, and spirit, she knew in her bones that Kitty would be rebellious and perverse during the come-out season. Kitty was the sort who would resent the rigid propriety that was expected of young ladies during their "presentations." The girl would certainly balk at having to go to fittings, she would want to choose shocking ball gowns in dreadful colors, she would fall into scrapes at just the times when her behavior should be irreproachable, and she was certain to make her poor mother's life a purgatory. It would be a decided advantage to be able to avoid the entire experience.

Her ladyship threw her husband a speculative look. "I've been thinking, my dear," she admitted reluctantly, "that there may be some merit in your plan. The boy is a handsome devil, his family is among the best in England, and with a fortune of that size he must be considered a good catch."

"That is my view exactly." Her husband grinned, sitting down beside her on the bed. "We might go through a whole season without her getting herself a better offer."

"Knowing Kitty's propensity for contrariness, we have to consider the possibility that she might do a great deal worse," Lady Birkinshaw agreed.

His lordship, having won the day, puffed his chest up proudly. "A *great* deal worse," he seconded. Then, taking his wife's hand in his, he added with a mischievous glint, "Do you know what else occurred to me, Hermione, my love?"

"What?" she asked, glancing up at him.

"If we marry her off now, we wouldn't have to bring the girl out! Save ourselves *months* of storm and strife."

Her ladyship giggled guiltily. "Yes, I thought of that, too. If we go through with our plan, we'd avoid months of tension. If we had to bring her out, we'd have quarrels about everything. About gowns, and bonnets, and hairdressings—"

Her husband nodded knowingly. "—about dressmakers and milliners . . ."

"—about what invitations to accept . . ."

"—and whom to refuse . . ."

"—and we'd have to be always making up excuses for Kitty when she forgot appointments . . ."

"—and soothing the ruffled feathers of those she'd offended . . ."

"—and explaining away her excesses . . ."

"—and greeting callers at all hours . . ."

"—and arguing over whom to invite to our own ball . . ."

"—and sending out cards . . ."

"—and making up menus and buying extra linen and plate . . ."

"—and turning the house topsy-turvy . . ."

"—and dealing with all the tradesmen . . ."

"—and paying all the *bills!*" His lordship rubbed his pudgy fingers over his forehead as if wiping away all the imaginary strain. "Won't it be glorious not to have to go through any of that?"

Laughing, her ladyship reached up, pulled down her husband's head, and kissed him. "We're a dreadful pair of parents, Thomas," she muttered into his shoulder.

"I wouldn't say that," he demurred, chuckling. "It's for her own good, after all. If we do some good for ourselves in the process, I see nothing reprehensible in it."

Lady Birkinshaw shook her head in reluctant admiration. "You're quite right," she said, undoing his neckcloth and nuzzling him fondly. "The more I think about it, the more I realize that my rottyheaded husband has, for once, done something sensible."

Thus the matter was settled. They were agreed. In the spring Kitty would be wed to Toby Wishart, will-she or nill-she. Now all they had to do was convince the girl.

That, Lord and Lady Birkinshaw knew, would not be easy. Kitty would fight their decision tooth and nail. They were certain to be met with tears and tantrums, not one bit of which they wanted to face. So Lord Birkinshaw suggested they avoid facing the girl altogether. All they needed to do, he said to his wife next morning, was send Kitty off to Suffolk directly from school. Why put themselves through the agony of dealing with her at home? "Let the chit spend a fortnight or so at the Edgerton estate becoming acquainted with her betrothed. I'll arrange it with Edgerton first thing tomorrow. By the time the fortnight's passed, she'll have grown accustomed to the idea."

Lady Birkinshaw nodded in shamefaced agreement. It was perhaps not the most courageous way of handling their daughter, but it was certainly the most expedient. If they wrote a letter to the school and sent her off to the country with dispatch, the girl would have no opportunity to enact a scene.

The next afternoon, with his wife standing over him, Lord Birkinshaw sat down at his desk to compose two letters—one to his daughter, and one to the headmistress of the school. The letter to Miss Marchmont was businesslike and terse. The instructions within (written in so pedantic and formal a style that a reader might easily have assumed they'd been composed by his solicitor) were quite explicit: his daughter, Miss Katherine Jessup, spinster, at the moment residing at the Marchmont School, was "herewith withdrawn" from that institution for the purpose of preparing herself for a marriage to The Honorable Tobias Wishart, "said marriage to take place six weeks following the first reading of the banns at our parish church this Sunday." In the meantime, the said Miss Jessup, having been graciously invited by Lord Edgerton to spend a fortnight at his estate in Suffolk for the purpose of acquainting the betrothed couple with each other, was to pack up her things at once. On the very next day ("before she'll have time," Lord Birkinshaw explained to his wife, "to concoct a scheme to make mischief") a carriage would arrive to convey her to the Edgerton estate. She was to remain there in Suffolk under the chaperonage of Lord Edgerton himself "until such time as we, her parents, shall arrive to escort her home to embark on the wedding preparations."

Lord Birkinshaw added a *post scriptum* to Miss Marchmont in which he wrote that he would be "eternally obliged" to her if she would take the trouble to provide for his daughter a suitable abigail to accompany her on the journey and to stay with her throughout the visit.

The letter to Kitty conveyed the same basic information and—to ensure that Kitty would take the news seriously— had the same firmness of tone. But Lord and Lady Birkinshaw were at heart quite loving parents (despite the fact that the letter might have seemed to an impartial observer impressive evidence to the contrary), and they couldn't bring themselves to dispatch the letter without enclosing some sign of their affection. Thus his lordship appended a *post scriptum* to Kitty as well, informing her that a large trunk, in which her mother would place many charming new bits of finery for Kitty to wear in the country and in which he would tuck twenty guineas for pocket money, would be strapped atop the carriage he was sending to convey her to Suffolk. With these provisions, he wrote, he hoped he had anticipated all her needs.

"There!" he said to his wife when his labors over the letters had been completed. "That should do the job well enough."

Lady Birkinshaw sighed guiltily. "Poor Kitty. Don't you think she'll find it rather cold?"

His lordship ran his eyes over the sheet in concern. "Perhaps it *is* rather cold," he agreed, taking up his quill again. He chewed the tip thoughtfully for a long moment and then smiled as the solution came to him. Laboriously he added one more sentence: *Your mother and I desire, of course, to express our very best wishes for your happiness.*

chapter three

Kitty inched her head round the door fearfully and peered inside. But there was nothing frightening about the headmistress's study; in fact, the room's atmosphere seemed permeated with a blessed stillness. The afternoon sunlight poured in through the room's huge window in glistening streaks, covering the mahogany desk, the carpet before it, and the very motes in the air with gold. But the chair behind the desk was empty. To the nervous girl in the doorway it seemed like the setting of a scene in a play, the chair in the center of the spotlight awaiting the entrance of the villainess.

But she soon saw that the villainess was already on stage. Miss Marchmont was standing at the window reading a lengthy, closely written letter. The headmistress's appearance was, as always very intimidating, especially to the young and the guilty. She was painfully gaunt; six feet tall, she was appropriately called Betty Beanstalk by the pupils when they spoke of her behind her back. She had hollow cheeks, a high forehead, and a prominent nose, and the corkscrew curls which framed her face did little to soften its hawklike masculinity. The look of a hawk was especially noticeable at this moment, for Miss Marchmont was peering at her letter with a particularly angry frown.

Kitty had made no sound during her examination of the scene, but some instinct told Miss Marchmont she was there. "Well, come in, come in!" the headmistress snapped, not looking up from her letter. But as soon as Kitty closed the door behind her, Miss Marchmont lifted the lorgnette which hung on a chain round her neck and stared at the girl through it. "Ah, Kitty, my dear," she said with the grimace that was her way of smiling but which was often construed by the young and the guilty to be a frown, "do sit down."

Kitty dropped a curtsey, mumbled a greeting, and sank nervously upon the chair facing the desk. "You s-sent for me, ma'am?"

"Yes, I did. Do you have any idea why?"

"No, ma'am."

Miss Marchmont sat down at her place behind the desk and fixed her eyes on Kitty's face. "Are you sure?"

Kitty's eyes fell. "Almost sure." She twisted her hands nervously on her lap. She took a breath and then another. The room was so silent she could hear the ticking of the grandfather clock in the hallway outside the closed door. Time began to stretch so that the space between each tick of the clock became interminable. The silence thickened and made the air oppressive. Kitty suddenly decided she could bear it no longer. "If you've sent for me because of the poor, undernourished little terrier I've been keeping in the tool shed," she blurted out hurriedly, "I hope you understand that if I hadn't found it, it would have starved or been mauled by the wheels of an unheeding carriage."

Miss Marchmont's lips twitched in what an impartial observer might have described as amusement but what appeared to Kitty as annoyance. "So you've been keeping a dog in the tool shed, eh?"

"It's only a puppy," she corrected, automatically defensive. Then she blinked as the import of the headmistress's remark dawned on her. "Oh, *blast!*" she exclaimed. "You didn't know about it, did you?"

"No, I did not."

The girl wanted to kick herself. Why had she permitted her nervousness to make her a blabbermouth? She felt her cheeks redden in embarrassment. "Then why—?"

"Why did I send for you? Try another guess."

Kitty clenched her fingers and swore to herself she would not be tricked again. "I have no idea, ma'am."

Miss Marchmont leaned forward. "No idea at all?"

"No!" She looked at her inquisitor directly in the eye. "None."

Miss Marchmont resorted to her lorgnette again. "You're quite certain?"

"Quite!" Kitty was prepared to outstare the headmistress for as long as she had to. The silence no longer frightened her.

She stared stoically back at Miss Marchmont's impassive face. But after a moment or two, she realized she was no match for the lorgnette. The glasses glinted with reflected light and seemed to the nervous girl to be sending out evil rays that could penetrate her soul. Her eyes fell. "At least I don't think it . . . it could be the . . ."

". . . the—?" Miss Marchmont prodded.

". . . the play?"

"The play?" Miss Marchmont's expression remained unreadable.

"It isn't meant to offend, you know," Kitty assured her hastily. "It's only intended to be a series of gentle gibes—"

"Ah, yes. Gentle gibes, to be sure. Against—?"

"Only twitting the faculty and . . . yourself. If you found anything offensive in it, it can be changed, I promise you. Why, we haven't even begun rehearsals yet. No one's even read it yet, except Clara . . . and she's only read the opening act."

"I'm much relieved to hear it," Miss Marchmont murmured, amusement now quite apparent in her eyes.

Kitty recognized the glint and winced. "Dash it all, I'm *ten ways* a fool! You didn't know about the play either, did you?"

"No, I'm afraid not," Miss Marchmont admitted.

Kitty exploded in self-disgust. "Confound it! I've confessed to two additional crimes—just handed them to you on a platter!—and I still don't know what crime you've called me down to punish me for!"

Miss Marchmont's face seemed to fall. "Heavens, child," she exclaimed in surprise, "I don't only see my pupils to inflict punishment!"

"In my case you do." Kitty sighed.

"Do I?" Miss Marchmont stared at Kitty thoughtfully. "Yes, I suppose that's true. I hadn't realized . . . I wonder if that comment isn't a greater reflection of *my* shortcomings than yours," she said, more to herself than the girl before her.

"I don't mean to imply that I haven't deserved it," Kitty said, suddenly finding herself unwilling to let Miss Marchmont take the blame.

"That also is true. You *have* been a most devilish prankster." The headmistress's tone was, of all things, quite affectionate. "But I haven't sent for you this time to discuss a prank."

Kitty looked up in astonishment. "You haven't? Then why *have* you sent for me, ma'am?"

"Are you sure you have nothing else to confess before I tell you?"

"Yes, ma'am," the girl said, grinning ruefully, "very sure."

"Then please turn your attention to this." Miss Marchmont picked up a sealed letter that had been lying on the desk before her and handed it over to her high-spirited pupil.

It was a letter from her father. Kitty recognized the hand at once, even though he hardly ever wrote to her. "Good Lord!" she exclaimed, staring at the seal with a sudden chill in her bones. "Something must have happened at home!"

"There's no need for alarm," Miss Marchmont said. "I, too, have had a letter from your father, and I am aware of the information your letter contains." She threw her pupil a speculative glance. "It is possible you may even consider the news to be quite exciting."

"Exciting?" A weight seemed to lift itself from her chest. If her interpretation of Miss Marchmont's manner was correct, she was not to be punished. Nor was she to be the recipient of tragic news. She had nothing at all to be worried about. For the first time since she'd been summoned, she felt her usual, lighthearted self. She was absolved of past transgressions and was therefore quite ready for life's next adventure. If this letter promised something exciting, she was quite eager for it, whatever it was. Or so she thought while she broke the seal.

She read the letter twice before the full import broke upon her. Then she read it once more to make sure she had not misunderstood. By this time the color had completely receded from her cheeks. "He cannot *mean* it!" she muttered, aghast.

Miss Marchmont eyed her curiously. "You do not like your father's plan for you, then?"

"*Like* it?" The girl was horror-struck. "How can I like it? Would you?"

"I must admit that I would not. But then, I was not made for wedded life. I've always been more interested in education than in matrimony. You, on the other hand, have surely grown up in the expectation of being wed as soon as you came of age, have you not?"

"Yes, but I'm not of age. Not yet." There was a crack in her voice. "This is . . . too *soon!*"

The headmistress took off her spectacles and looked at the girl with sincere sympathy. "I am very sorry, Kitty. In my view, you should at least have been permitted to finish your schooling here before . . ." She paused, sighed, and lowered her eyes. Lord Birkinshaw's letter had made her furious, but she knew it would do the girl no good to show her feelings. She pulled a handkerchief from her sleeve and polished her glasses vigorously before she was able to go on. ". . . before being launched into wedded life. But your parents seem to have made an irrevocable decision. We have no choice but to abide by it."

Kitty's lips trembled. "I s-suppose so," she said tonelessly.

There was no reason to prolong this torture, Miss Marchmont decided. "We have many things to discuss, my dear," she said, getting up from her chair, "and much to do before your father's carriage comes for you. But perhaps you'd like to be alone for a while first, to pull yourself together."

"Yes, please, Miss Marchmont," the girl said, rising also. She dropped a curtsey like an automaton and went dazedly from the room.

Emily, who had waited for her in the corridor despite Kitty's orders to the contrary, noticed her pallor at once. "Good heavens, Miss Jessup, was it something really dreadful?" she asked in a whisper.

Kitty nodded. "Very dreadful."

"Oh, dear. She hasn't sentenced you to Coventry, has she?"

"I wish it was only that. A week in the solitary bedroom would be bearable. At least I'd know that it would soon *end.*"

Emily's brows rose. "Do you mean it's *worse?* Not . . . ? She couldn't have . . . ! You haven't been *expelled*, have you? Is she sending you home?"

"Even worse than that. I am being sent off to . . . to . . ." She could barely bring herself to utter the word.

"To where?" Emily prodded.

"To . . ." Kitty's tightly held self-control deserted her, and she fell into the maid's arms with a choked cry. "Oh, Emily, how can they have *done* this to me? I'm not . . . *ready!*"

"But what *is* it, miss?" Emily asked, truly alarmed. "*Where* are they sending you?"

"To someplace worse than school, worse than Coventry, worse even than prison!" She lifted her head, stared straight out before her, set her shoulders, and marched off down the hall, her last words echoing back to Emily like the thrums of a muffled drum. "I'm being sent off to . . . to *death!*"

chapter four

When a young woman of not-quite-eighteen is struck a severe blow, she can immediately resort to the one course of action guaranteed to be both appropriate and effective: she can throw herself upon her bed and cry. The act is appropriate because it is instinctive (girls have done it since the beginning of time), and it is effective because it postpones other action (which might be dangerous or ill-considered when the girl is in turmoil) until the weeper's brain has ceased to seethe. Kitty wisely took just such action.

When her bout of tears had ended, it was bedtime. The girls of the upper school, dressed in their nightgowns and supposedly asleep in their beds, had waited patiently for her sobs to subside, and they now gathered round to hear her explanation and to offer their sympathy and advice. The door of their dormitory room was safely shut against all intruders, they'd all perched comfortably upon Kitty's bed, and they'd lit only one candle (shaded by a green glass ginger jar which they kept hidden away under a floor board for just such occasions) so that no telltale light would seep under the door to alert the night guard that a colloquium was in session.

Kitty read her father's letter aloud in a voice that still trembled with despair. When she'd finished, there was a shocked silence, for the enormity of the problem momentarily overwhelmed the white-gowned listeners. "Good God!" Bella breathed in something like awe.

"Yes, exactly so," Kitty muttered glumly. "I couldn't have expressed it better myself."

There was an immediate outpouring of sympathy, but it was not sympathy that Kitty wanted. "I need advice," she told them firmly. "Good, practical advice. How am I to get out of this fix?"

They promptly set their minds to the problem. They were not without imagination, and soon they were able to offer a number of suggestions. The ideas they concocted varied with their personalities. Hannah, the quietest of the group, was the first to get an idea. "A rope ladder," she suggested. "We'll tie our sheets together. Then all you need do is climb down and run away."

Of course this suggestion was immediately vetoed. There was no place to which Kitty could run. Where could she go without funds or resources? If she had a maiden aunt who could be counted on to be sympathetic to her plight and take her in, something might be contrived, but Kitty could think of no such convenient relation.

Dolly suggested falling into a trancelike illness that might frighten her parents into relenting, but everyone else disagreed. Kitty looked much too healthy to feign illness. However, that idea led directly to Bella's notion: the threat of starvation. "If you refuse to eat a morsel of food until they release you from this betrothal, you might get your way. My threats to starve myself work wonders with my father."

"Your father is a pussycat," Kitty pointed out. "Mine is a mule."

Plump little Clara had listened to the discussion with frowning detachment. "I don't know why you're making these suggestions at all. You're all doomsayers without there being a sign of doom! I don't think the situation is the *least bit* tragic."

"Not tragic?" Kitty exclaimed in offense. "I thought you were my best friend!"

"I *am* your best friend. But I, for one, would consider such an event quite fortunate . . . at least until I laid eyes on the man in question. After all, he might very well turn out to be handsome and charming. If one found him so, one could then live happily ever after."

"And if he turned out to be a bag-pudding," Bella demanded, "what then?"

"*Then* one could lower a rope ladder or starve oneself to death," Kitty muttered with hopeless irony.

The girls' colloquy did not prove fruitful. Before a really useful plan could be concocted, Miss Hemming, who had night patrol, came in and discovered them. Her shrill scolding sent the girls scurrying to their beds. But after she left, Clara crept over to Kitty's bed to offer one last bit of hope. "I wouldn't despair, my love," she whispered. "I think you may be pleasantly surprised by your betrothed. Tobias Wishart is a very romantic-sounding name, isn't it? You may very well fall in love with him at first sight. And if you don't, you'll think of some way out of it. If there's anyone in the world who can find a way out of a fix, it's you."

The two girls embraced and, realizing it was for the last time, shed a few tears. Then Kitty buried her head in her pillow, expecting to spend a sleepless, agonizing night. However, her friend's last words echoed in her mind and gave her unexpected comfort. Although Clara was surely mistaken in hoping that she would fall in love with a fellow named Tobias (*Tobias,* ugh!), she was *not* mistaken in her evaluation of Kitty's talent for devising schemes. If Kitty found herself in a fix, she was quite capable of getting herself out of it. With that consoling thought, and with the resiliency of youth, she soon fell asleep.

The next morning proved to be so full of hectic activity that Kitty had no time to think. There were three trunks to pack, dozens of people to take fond leave of, addresses to exchange, and a special assembly of the entire faculty and student body (arranged by Miss Marchmont to honor her departing pupil) to attend. By the time the assemblage had been dismissed, the carriage was in the drive, the gatekeeper was loading Kitty's trunks upon it, and Emily was waiting at the door with Kitty's bonnet and pelisse. Only then did Miss Marchmont remember that she'd done nothing about Lord Birkinshaw's request to find an abigail for Kitty. "Oh, dear!" she gasped, stricken. "Where on earth shall I find someone for you *now?*"

Kitty was so depressed at having to make this untimely departure that the subject didn't even interest her. "I'll manage without one," she told the headmistress, taking her bonnet from Emily's hand and thrusting it carelessly on her head.

"But I can't allow you to travel all the way to Suffolk unchaperoned," Miss Marchmont stated flatly. "We must think of *someone* . . ."

"Father's coachman will provide all the chaperonage I need. Besides, in my present mood I don't want to endure the company of some insipid biddy. If I had to listen to hours of nonsensical babble, I'd have the vapors."

Miss Marchmont snorted. "*Vapors*, indeed! I don't believe you even know what they are."

But Kitty didn't hear. Her attention had been caught by Emily, who was waiting to help her on with her pelisse. Kitty's eyes lit up. If any of her friends had been watching, they would have recognized at once the dawn of a mischievous idea. *Emily*, she thought, *Emily! Why didn't I think of her before? She'd be perfect!*

Kitty turned to Miss Marchmont slowly. "Of course," she murmured softly, "if I had someone like Emily for my abigail . . ."

Emily gaped. "Me?"

The headmistress frowned. "Are you speaking of *our* Emily? No, no, my dear, Emily is quite out of the question."

"Really, Miss Marchmont?" Kitty looked curiously from one to the other. "Why is that? I'm sure my father would pay her well. And she and I have become very good friends. I know we'd suit—"

"Emily is not a servant!" the headmistress said firmly. "Her position here is something quite special—"

"I think I'd *like* to go with Miss Jessup, ma'am," Emily put in quietly.

Miss Marchmont's brows knit. "Are you serious, girl? You cannot wish to spend your life as a mere lady's maid—"

"But it wouldn't be for life, ma'am," Emily pointed out. "Only for a fortnight, isn't that so?"

"That's true, Miss Marchmont," Kitty said in eager support. "Only until my parents come to Suffolk for me."

The headmistress was not convinced. Taking Emily's arm, she led the girl aside. "Emily, my dear," she said in a low voice, "I don't wish to question your judgment, but I think you are making a hasty, impulsive leap. You know that I've been grooming you for a better life than you would have as a maidservant. I believe you capable of becoming a teacher . . . to join the faculty here, if you wish, or elsewhere, when you are ready. You will be able to earn a respectable competence and live the life of a gentlewoman. Do not throw that prospect aside on a sudden whim!"

"I know this is very sudden, ma'am. But surely a short

time away from the academy would not ruin my prospects here, would it?" Emily asked.

"No, of course not. You would be most welcome to return at any time. But why do you wish to waste even a fortnight as Kitty Jessup's maid?"

Emily lowered her head. "It is difficult to explain. Please don't be cross with me, ma'am, for I don't mean to sound ungrateful for all you've done for me. But . . ." She hesitated.

"Go on, girl, I'm listening," Miss Marchmont said impatiently.

"I've never spent a night away from here since I was nine." She raised her head and looked her mentor squarely in the eye. "Going away with Miss Jessup will be like a . . . a holiday, don't you see?"

"A holiday? No, I'm afraid I don't see. Kitty Jessup is a clever, taking little minx, I admit, but how can doing her hair and pressing her skirts and running about at her beck and call be considered a holiday?"

"Because it would be a *change*, you see. I shall be able to look out of a window onto something new. And it *is* Miss Jessup, you know. She's so completely—how shall I say?— unpredictable. I have a feeling in my very bones that going off with her will be an *adventure!*"

Miss Marchmont studied her protégé for a long moment. Then she merely nodded, turned, and strode back to Kitty. "Very well, Miss Jessup, you win. You may have Emily as your abigail for a fortnight's adventure."

Kitty squealed in delight and threw her arms around her new maid. "Oh, splendid!" she cried. "That's absolutely splendid!"

Emily smiled one of her rare smiles. "Yes, miss. Splendid."

"Then let's not stand here gaping at one another," Kitty said, bouncing about in impatience. "Run and get your wrap at once!"

"But I have to pack my things—"

"Never mind that. I have more than enough for both of us." And without giving her time for more than snatching up her shawl and giving Miss Marchmont a quick embrace, Kitty took the girl's hand and pulled her to the carriage.

"Oh, dear...this is all happening so quickly!" Emily gasped, pausing at the foot of the carriage steps.

Kitty grinned. "That's how adventures usually start."

"Adventures?" Emily gaped at her aghast. "How did you—?"

"Miss Marchmont said the word, and I understood at once." She turned the bewildered Emily about and propelled her up the steps. "If it's adventure you want, my girl," she said in her ear, "adventure you shall have."

chapter five

Kitty waited until they'd left London far behind before she told Emily her plan. By this time Emily (who'd kept her nose pressed to the window, utterly fascinated with the passing scene) had become so enchanted with this glimpse of the world beyond the gates of Marchmont Academy that any lingering doubts about the wisdom of her decision to leave the school were completely dispelled. But when Kitty unfolded the details of what seemed to Emily an insane scheme, those doubts came back at once. *"Change places,* miss? Pretend to be *you?* You're cozening me, aren't you? I *couldn't!* Not in a million *years!"*

"Don't be a goosecap! Of *course* you could."

"Miss Jessup, stop bamming me! You can't seriously wish me to take your identity! To wear your clothes? To eat at the table with his lordship? To sit and *chat* with him? If you think me capable of doing all that, you've taken leave of your *senses."*

Kitty took no offense. She was accustomed to this sort of reaction. Every one of her wild proposals to her schoolmates had met with a negative reception at first. She'd always found it necessary to overcome a barrage of opposition, but her enthusiasm and her powers of persuasion had always won the day. She would win this struggle as she'd won all the others. "Believe me, Emily," she said, her eyes shining with excitement as she launched into an argument, "it won't be nearly as difficult as you imagine. You wanted an adventure, didn't you? This will be the greatest adventure of your life."

"I didn't bargain for *this* sort of adventure, miss. It could never work! I've been a maid-of-all-work all my days. I've never even set *foot* in a great house, much less sat down to dinner with a nobleman. I wouldn't know what to do . . . or say! I would *die!*"

"You underestimate yourself, my dear. You'd be much better at it than I, I assure you. Miss Hemming says I'm the greatest gawk alive. You, on the other hand, are graceful and pretty and speak in a lovely, low voice. You've been at the school for longer than I—why, you're going to *teach* deportment to clods like me! You're much more a lady than I could ever be. Really!"

Emily eyed her employer suspiciously. "You needn't flummery me, Miss Jessup. I know butter sauce when I smell it."

"It's not butter sauce, Emily, I swear. You'll find the whole thing much easier than you expect. All you need do is be yourself. Just act a bit proud, don't pick up anything anyone drops, don't call me miss, and don't curtsey to any of the servants, even the most hoity-toity of them."

"I just *couldn't,* Miss Jessup, I know it!" Emily insisted, feeling a rising panic. "And I'm not sure you could do it, either. You don't know what it's like to be a maidservant. I can assure you, you'd not find it pleasant."

"I'm not afraid of hard work. I think I should like it, rather. It will be like . . . well, like an actress playing a role. I think I could make a rather good actress if I set my mind to it."

"But I don't think *I* would make a good actress, miss. Not at all! Besides, I don't know what you hope to gain by such a deception."

"I'll gain *time,* if nothing else." Kitty's voice quivered with earnest conviction. "I'll be able to observe Tobias Wishart without his knowing. I'll take note of all his faults. By the time my parents arrive, I'll have gained sufficient information to plead my case to my father. And even if I can't convince him that the match would be unsuitable, the Wisharts, when they learn what I've done, will be so disgusted with me that they won't wish me to wed into their family."

"But what if you find that you *like* Mr. Wishart? It will be too late then to make amends, won't it?"

"Yes, but it's extremely unlikely that I'd like him well enough to wish to *wed* him. That's the whole point, don't you see?" All the excitement of game-playing seemed suddenly to fade from her eyes as a shadow of sincere distress suffused her face. "I'm too young for marriage, Emily," she said quietly. "I haven't even lived yet. I want to be *free* for a while. I want to meet *hundreds* of eligibles before I'm shackled. To be thrust right from the schoolroom into wedlock seems to me to be vastly unfair. I shan't have had a chance to have *fun!* I want to go to parties, to flirt, to dance, to break a hundred hearts before I'm saddled with a husband. Do you understand?"

Emily shook her head. "No, I don't think I do. If a nobleman wanted *me* for a bride—to take me to live in his great estate, to provide me with servants and lovely clothes and jewels, to give me the freedom to spend my days with books and a pianoforte of my own—why, I'd think I was the most fortunate girl in the world."

"That's what you think now. But if you had to spend weeks, months, *years* with a stuffy old bore of a husband who would be forever giving you orders and scolding you for buying too many hats and keeping you from going to parties with your friends and expecting you to sit on his knee whenever he liked . . . well, you might not think yourself so fortunate. Meanwhile, I'm offering you the chance to *live* your dream, if only for a fortnight. You'll live on a great estate, with servants and lovely clothes and all my jewels (which are not worth a queen's ransom, I admit, but my grandmother's pearls are quite lovely, and I have with me a garnet brooch that was given to the third Lord Birkinshaw by Charles the First), and you'll be quite free to read and play the piano to your heart's content."

Emily was not convinced. "And when the deception is discovered, and I am being marched off to the gallows, I can console myself with my memories of my magnificent masquerade, is that it?"

"Nothing dreadful will happen to you, Emily, I promise! I shall take all the blame. I shall declare that I forced you into this deception and that, since you are in my employ, you had no choice but to obey. Please, my dear, say you'll do it. It is the only way I can think of to save my life."

Emily wrung her hands nervously. "I don't wish to disoblige you, miss, I truly don't. But my innards are shaking already. I'm bound to make a botch of it."

"No, you won't, Emily. I'll be your abigail, at your side whenever you need me. It's only for a fortnight, after all."

Emily had to succumb. She would be given no peace until

she did, she knew. When Kitty Jessup made up her mind, there was no stopping her.

When Kitty realized she'd won, she embraced the maid with a glad cry and immediately set about implementing her plan. She undressed herself down to her under-petticoat and made Emily do the same. The two changed clothing, Kitty giggling with pleasure at her transformation into shabbiness and Emily moaning with trepidation despite the unaccustomed but pleasant sensation of silk and lustring against her skin.

Kitty's clothes were a bit too large for Emily, but the girls managed to make do with the help of a few pins from Emily's (now Kitty's) well-stocked pocket. When the clothes had been exchanged, Kitty turned her attention to their hair. She undid Emily's braid and recombed her hair into a more stylish knot at the nape of her neck, making sure that a few soft tendrils were permitted to escape at the sides of her face. Then Emily loosened Kitty's fashionable bun and let the red tresses hang loose in their natural disarray. This would do for a housemaid during travel, she warned, but Kitty would have to pin it up or braid it during her "working hours." For the time being, however, Emily provided her with a shabby mobcap which partially covered her unruly locks. The cap was an unmistakable symbol of her new station in life, and it would suffice to make her hair presentable.

The only real difficulty the girls encountered occurred when they tried to exchange footwear. Kitty's foot was larger than Emily's; she couldn't squeeze her foot into Emily's worn boots without giving herself a great deal of discomfort. In the end each girl had to wear her own. "No one will notice," Kitty said reassuringly. "During the bustle of arrival, everyone will be too busy to notice our shoes. And once we've unpacked, we can stuff the toes of all my slippers with paper. You'll do very well that way. As for me, I'll scuff up the tips of these half-boots in a coal scuttle at the first opportunity. We shall brush through, I promise you. Well, how do I look?"

Emily had to admit that Kitty looked every inch a dowdy little Irish housemaid. But she would *not* agree that she, Emily, could ever pass for a great lady. It was not until Kitty placed her feathered bonnet upon Emily's head and made her look into a hand mirror that Emily was convinced. Seeing herself so splendidly arrayed left her speechless for a moment.

Then she whispered, awe-struck, "Good heavens, Miss Jessup, is that *me?*"

They exchanged seats (with Kitty riding backward this time) and tried to adjust their minds to their new roles. Emily's hand caressed the soft lustring of her new skirt while she tried to drill herself in the proper (for a lady) use of names and titles. She must not, she warned herself, let herself slip and call Miss Jessup *miss*. Miss Jessup must, from now on, be called *Emily*.

"And say it arrogantly," Kitty reminded her. "You're the mistress, and if I don't come at your beck, you must be *very severe* with me."

The maid cast her employer a look that combined doubt with reproach. "Easy for *you* to say," she muttered.

They arrived at Edgerton Park in the late afternoon. Both young ladies had their noses pressed to the carriage windows to see the manor house. Once inside the estate's massive gate, they drove down a long avenue lined with old rhododendrons and thick, dark yews that hid the view. When the carriage made a final turn and the mansion burst into view, they both gasped. The house was enormous, with a wide, three-storied facade and two lower wings. It was built in the grand Palladian manner, with window arches and a beautiful Corinthian portico topped by the most impressive pediment Kitty had ever seen. The whole structure seemed to be set upon three massive stone platforms that formed a multileveled terrace extending several feet beyond the front doorway.

While they gaped, the front door opened and the butler emerged, followed by two footmen. The butler made his way across the terrace with measured dignity. He bowed to the faces in the coach window without the flicker of a smile, although anyone else would have found the girls' ingenuous awe amusing. The Edgerton butler was famous among his peers for his lack of facial expression; he'd long ago trained his face in impassivity. The butler was proud of the fact that he'd never been caught in a smile.

While the footmen let down the carriage steps, the butler himself opened the carriage door and helped Emily to climb down. Kitty waited for him to do the same for her, but he quite ignored her. For a moment, Kitty was nonplussed by the seeming rudeness, but a nervous glance from Emily reminded her that there were some niceties she would have to learn to do without.

The butler bowed again to Emily. "Welcome to Edgerton, Miss Jessup," he said. "I'm Naismith, his lordship's butler."

"How do you do, N-Naismith?" Emily managed.

Kitty jumped down from the carriage just in time to see a tall gentleman emerge from the doorway. They all watched in silence as he approached. He wore a casual coat of gray corduroy and a pair of country boots, but he seemed to the two goggle-eyed girls to be the most elegant creature they'd ever set eyes upon. Kitty realized at once that this gentleman could not be her betrothed. She had the distinct impression from her father's letter that Tobias Wishart was still a youth; this gentleman was quite old—thirty at least. He must be Lord Edgerton, Wishart's older brother. But a fleeting thought crossed her mind that if the younger Wishart resembled his brother it would be no bad thing.

"Miss Jessup!" Lord Edgerton said, striding up to Emily and taking her hand. "What a delightful surprise! We didn't expect you 'til nightfall. Your coachman has made good time."

Kitty felt her heart jump. She'd forgotten about the *coachman!* Her father had sent Gowan, who'd known her since childhood. He was now occupied with untying the luggage, but at any moment he could notice what was going on and give the game away!

"Yes, your lordship," Emily was murmuring shyly. "I am . . . very p-pleased to meet you."

Kitty noted with relief that Gowan had gone to the back of the coach to help the two footmen unload the trunks and thus would be unable to see whom his lordship was greeting. Edgerton, meanwhile, was offering Emily his arm. "May I show you inside?" he was asking her, looking at her face with a slightly upraised brow. "I believe Naismith has a tea table ready."

"Well, I . . . er . . ." Emily threw Kitty a look of terrified desperation. ". . . the luggage, you know . . ."

Kitty glared at her. "I'll see to the luggage, miss," she said pointedly, while at the same time playing with her role by giving herself a tinge of Irish in her speech. "Sure you've no need t' worry yerself. Go along with his lordship." She gave Emily a little nudge and grinned widely. "You don't want the nice tea gettin' cold, now do ye?"

"Your abigail is quite right," Lord Edgerton said, firmly drawing Emily's arm through his. "We can't have you drinking cold tea. Besides, my mother is awaiting us. She's most eager to make your acquaintance."

"Th-thank you, your lordship," Emily murmured, taking a deep breath and proceeding across the terrace on his arm.

"You know, Miss Jessup," Kitty heard him say just as they moved out of earshot, "you're not quite as I expected."

But Emily's response could not be heard. The pair, followed by the impassive butler and both the footmen, soon disappeared from sight. Kitty frowned, not at all certain about Emily's ability to carry this off. To make matters worse, she was equally uncertain about her own role in this affair. For instance, what she was supposed to do next?

She looked about her uneasily and found Gowan, with a trunk hoisted on his shoulder, staring at her curiously. "What're you up to, Miss Kitty?" he asked disapprovingly.

"Up to?" she responded with pure innocence, her brain bubbling with the joy of challenge and adventure. "Whatever do you mean?"

"Y're up to somethin', I kin tell. Those ain't yer clothes."

Kitty put out her chin. "They are now. I made a wager with my abigail and I *won*. Not," she added, tossing her head coolly, "that it's any of your business."

The wizened coachman, with the familiarity that comes from years of association, sneered at her. "It's a queer winnin' that trades gold fer dross. Somethin's brummish about this. An' I might make it my business to tell yer da' that ye went to meet yer betrothed wearin' muslin an' a mobcap."

"Do what you like," Kitty retorted, striding away across the terrace, "but you'll only be making a fool of yourself. Muslin and mobcaps are all the rage in Paris this season."

"All the rage?" The coachman stared after her for a moment and scratched his forehead with his free hand. The girl was probably trying to tip him a rise, he thought. It was very like her to try to pitch him some gammon. But on the other hand, it was just possible that housemaids' garb *had* become stylish for the nobs. After all, weren't the sprags who liked to drive coaches for sport always trying to buy his overcoat from him?

The bemused fellow shook his head. The ways of the gentry were beyond him. His best course of action, he decided, was to put the matter out of his mind. This he did with a sigh and a shrug, and, without troubling his head about it further, he trudged off to deliver his load.

chapter six

Lord Edgerton led the way to the Blue Saloon, a room of relatively modest proportions that his mother preferred at tea-time to the much larger East Drawing Room which, his lordship explained as they entered the house, was the more suitable room for tea parties. Emily, scurrying to keep up with his lordship's long stride, was awestruck at the magnificence surrounding her. They'd entered the mansion through a double door at least fifteen feet high, passed without a pause through a domed, round entrance hall called the Rotunda, whose marble floors gleamed richly in the light of six windows cut into the base of the dome, and then proceeded down a wide corridor which was wainscoted in gilded oak and boasted a ceiling gorgeously decorated with painted cherubs disporting themselves on painted clouds. Wide-eyed Emily had never seen the like.

The Blue Saloon was not, in Emily's view, the least bit modest. It was at least thirty feet long and contained three blue velvet sofas, a dozen chairs of all sorts, a tea table elegantly set with silver service and platters of sandwiches and scones, several lamp tables, and, in the far corners of the room, two magnificent Chinese vases atop matched pedestals of sculpted marble. The room's four recessed windows reached from floor to ceiling, each recess containing a jardiniere covered with plants and topped with swags of ecru satin with a blue floral print. The blue flowers were also visible in the design of a Persian carpet that almost completely covered the floor. If this room was modest, Emily couldn't imagine what the Drawing Room would be like.

They found Lady Edith seated behind the tea table, her attention not on the approaching guest but on a brooch she was attempting without success to pin to the left shoulder of her gown. "Here's Miss Jessup, Mama," Edgerton announced informally. "Miss Jessup, this is our mother, Lady Edith Wishart."

Emily dropped a curtsey. "How do you do, your ladyship?"

Lady Edith glanced up at her guest with a nervous little smile. "How do you do, my dear? Excuse me for a moment from further conversation. I seem to be having difficulty with this catch."

Lord Edgerton gave an imperceptible sigh before leading his guest to a chair beside the tea table. "You must forgive Mama, Miss Jessup. I'm afraid she's often abstracted. She always has difficulty with anything the least bit mechanical. Although why she is struggling with that bauble herself, when she has a perfectly competent dresser to help her out of just such difficulties, is quite beyond my comprehension."

"That's because you know nothing of the difficulties we women face," his mother responded, a tinge of querulousness in her voice. "The brooch was perfectly in place when I left my room. But a moment before you entered, I reached for a scone—which of course I shouldn't have done until you'd come in and I'd served the tea, but I hadn't had a bite since breakfast and I was famished—and just as I reached out I felt a prick in my shoulder. When I looked down, I saw the pin had come undone. How it managed to undo itself in the short time since I came downstairs I just can't explain."

"I'd be happy to do it up for you, ma'am," Emily volunteered without thinking. "I'm quite handy with pins and catches and—Oh!" She looked up at his lordship in horror. "I'm sorry," she whispered, wide-eyed. "I suppose that was not...I mean I shouldn't have said..." Her voice faded away in hideous embarrassment.

"On the contrary, my dear," Edgerton assured her, hiding his puzzlement at her strangely diffident behavior with a smile, "I'd be most grateful to you if you *could* help Mama. If you don't, she'll be fussing with that brooch forever, and we shall never get our tea."

Relief flooded Emily's chest. She jumped up from her seat and ran eagerly to Lady Edith's side. Kneeling down beside the dowager, she managed, despite the fact that her fingers were still shaking, to lock the pin in the catch.

Lady Edith tested the brooch, found it secure, and beamed.

"Oh, my dear child," she cooed, "I most sincerely thank you. You do seem to be a treasure." She turned to her son and pointed an accusing finger at him. "I thought you said, Greg, that the girl was a hoyden. She doesn't appear the least bit hoydenish to me."

"Nor to me, Mama, nor to me," his lordship said, shutting his eyes and shaking his head in mock despair. Leading Emily back to her chair, he explained calmly that his mother's lack of tact was more than made up for by her charming ingenuousness. "I did describe you in those terms," he admitted, "but only because that's how your father described you to me."

"Yes, I suppose he would. I . . . I am often described in that way," Emily responded, realizing how well the word did describe Kitty.

"Are you indeed?" He pulled up a chair beside her. "Judging from the impression you've made on us thus far, Miss Jessup, I would have chosen *hoyden* as the *least* appropriate word for you in the entire dictionary."

"I quite agree," said his mother, still beaming as she poured the tea. "You don't seem to have a hoydenish bone in your body. Though I don't suppose bones *can* be hoydenish, can they? Do you take two lumps, my dear? No, I suppose only one. You could not have kept such a tiny waist if you were in the habit of taking two. Oh, dear, the tea is quite strong. What is keeping Naismith, I wonder? I sent him for some more hot water and a plate of those raisin biscuits everyone likes. Well, never mind. Here, Greg, give the child her tea. The tedious journey from London is dreadfully exhausting, and even if the tea is strong it's bound to give the child a lift. There's nothing like tea to bring one's spirit back, I always say."

"Yes, Mama," his lordship said obediently, throwing Emily a conspiratorial wink as he handed her the cup.

Lady Edith, having decided that the girl her eldest son had so abruptly thrust upon the household was not going to be at all troublesome, leaned back in her chair, sighed contentedly, and stirred her tea. She was an artless woman who often found life intimidating. Anyone whose motives she didn't understand frightened her, so early in her life she developed a simple method by which to protect herself. She evaluated everyone she encountered by holding them up to a shallow-witted yardstick which measured only one characteristic: kindness. People, she decided, were either kind or unkind. She kept a safe distance from those she judged unkind, but to those who seemed kind she gave instant affection and intimacy. This intimacy she was eager to offer to Emily at once, without requiring any further evidence of the girl's character than she'd already seen. And what better way could she find to show her warm feeling to this lovely child who was to become part of the family than to disclose a confidence that her son had warned her not to reveal? "Dear child," she began, leaning forward in her chair and smiling at Emily fondly, "has Greg explained to you why Toby will be a bit late?"

Greg lifted his head and glared at her. "No, Mama, I did not, I was trying to spare her feelings."

"Nonsense," his mother said, waving away his annoyance with a flick of her wrist. "There's nothing in it to hurt the child's feelings. You see, my dear, Toby promised to be here early to greet you, but his man arrived about an hour ago and told us that Toby stopped off at Manningtree to call on a friend. He should not have done so, I admit, but our Toby is notoriously unreliable."

"Is unreliability supposed to be an excuse?" Edgerton asked irritably. But he bit back the other angry words that rose to his throat. His brother was behaving like a damnable loose screw, but his own good manners prevented him from showing his annoyance. It was inexcusable of Toby to have delayed his arrival, especially when he'd been clearly informed that his presence was necessary. Edgerton would certainly give his brother a dressing down as soon as the fellow showed his face.

And to make matters worse, his sister, too, had failed to make an appearance to greet their guest. What a harum-scarum family they must seem to poor Miss Jessup! "I must apologize for both my siblings, Miss Jessup. My sister, too, seems to be missing. Where is Alicia, Mama? Why hasn't she joined us for tea?"

Her ladyship's face fell. "She was taken with a migraine again, I fear. It came on her quite suddenly, just before luncheon. The pain was so severe that she took immediately to her bed. My poor little Alicia is very delicate, Miss Jessup. Her health has always been precariously balanced." She took a handkerchief from her bosom and sniffed into it. "I sometimes think she will not long be with us. I don't know how I sh-shall *bear* it if she is taken from us."

"She will *not* be taken from us, Mama," Edgerton said, gritting his teeth. He usually listened to his mother's babblings with patient endurance, but today he was feeling on edge. "Please don't indulge in these waterworks in front of our guest. Besides, Dr. Randolph assured you only last week that your daughter is likely to outlive us all."

Emily, not having shared Edgerton's long experience with his sister's hypochondria, couldn't help being touched by Lady Edith's tears. "Have you tried a licorice tisane?" she offered shyly. "Miss Marchmont uses it at the school whenever one of the girls complains of the headache. It seems to work wonders."

"Licorice?" The damp handkerchief fluttered from her ladyship's fingers to her lap. "You can't mean it! Why, we've tried all sorts of tisanes—fennel in the barley water, and prunes, and sometimes even the rind of lemons, boiled and pushed through a sieve. But I've never even *heard* of using licorice."

Lord Edgerton stared at Emily in surprise. It had been astounding enough to find that the girl—whom her father described as wild, unpredictable, and given to scandalous behavior—looked and behaved like a frightened little wren, but to observe her sitting there opposite him with her hands nervously clasping her saucer and her elbows primly pressed against her sides while she exchanged recipes for medicinal draughts with his mother . . . well, that was completely beyond his expectations. The only explanation he could think of was that she was teasing them. "I think, Mama, that Miss Jessup is cutting a wheedle. Licorice sounds very much like a hum to me. You are shamming it, aren't you, my dear?"

"*Shamming* it?" The girl appeared to be sincerely shocked. "Oh, *no,* my lord, of course not! I would never joke on matters of health."

"Really, Greg," his mother chided, "that was most unkind of you. Anyone can see that Miss Jessup is nothing if not sincere. Do you think, Miss Jessup, that you might concoct one of your tisanes now? I could have Naismith bring the ingredients to Alicia's room, if you'd be so obliging as to mix them for us."

"I'd be most happy to be of service," Emily said eagerly. "We shall only need a bit of dried licorice root—or a teaspoon of extract, if you have some—and the juice of two lemons. And the barley water should be quite hot, of course . . ."

"Licorice extract, lemon juice, hot barley water," Lady Edith echoed, rising from her chair. This caused her forgotten handkerchief to flutter to the floor. "I shall tell Naismith to bring them to us in Alicia's room. There's no need for you to hurry your tea, my dear, but as soon as you're ready we can go upstairs."

"Oh, I'm quite finished," Emily said, jumping up. She placed her cup and saucer on the table and automatically knelt down to pick up her ladyship's handkerchief. Just as she reached for it, she remembered Kitty's warning: *Don't pick up anything anyone drops.* Quickly, she withdrew her hand. But she was too late. Lord Edgerton, who had risen when she did, had already bent down and was picking it up himself. When they both stood erect, she couldn't fail to notice that he was looking at her with an intent stare, as if she were a puzzle he couldn't quite unravel. Her face reddened painfully. "I'm . . . sorry . . ." she mumbled.

"Whatever for?" he asked, holding out the lacy kerchief.

"Oh, no, it's not mine. It's . . . it's your m-mama's," she explained, feeling breathless and very stupid. "I only meant to g-get it for her. Have I . . . committed another faux pas?"

"Faux pas?" Lady Edith asked, looking round. "Whatever can you mean? I am not aware of your committing *any*."

"Neither am I," his lordship agreed. He handed the handkerchief to his mother but continued to address his visitor. "You are, I venture to say, the most *proper* guest ever to have graced this room."

"My son is quite right, my dear. You mustn't feel ill at ease among us, you know. We're a very ordinary, unaffected family. And you've done nothing at all out of the way, I promise you. You aren't discomfitted by having to take leave of my son so abruptly, are you?"

Emily hadn't even been aware of *that* solecism. "Oh, dear," she muttered miserably, "I didn't think . . . that is, I suppose I should have . . . I mean, perhaps his lordship would prefer me to remain . . . ?"

"Not at all, Miss Jessup, not at all," Edgerton reassured her. "You must make yourself completely at home. By all means go along with Mama, if that's what you wish to do. Don't give me another thought."

"No, indeed," his mother agreed, "don't worry about Greg. He's only too happy when we females leave him to his own resources. Whenever we're fixed here at Edgerton, he involves himself in estate business to the exclusion of almost everything else. He keeps himself busy from morn 'til night, unless we order him to cease and desist. If he had his way, he'd never join the ladies at all."

"That is an outright calumny, Mama," the maligned son said as he opened the door for them. "I'm always pleased to join you at dinner."

"Perhaps so," his mother retorted as she passed him by, "but whether it is for the pleasure of our company or the taste of the roast I couldn't say."

Emily, hurrying after her hostess, dropped him an awkward curtsey. "Pray excuse me, my lord," she mumbled.

"Until dinner," he answered with a smile and a bow. "When you've finished with your tisane, Miss Jessup, Naismith will show you to your room. Please ask him for anything you might need. You'll have plenty of time to rest, for I've put off dinner for two hours. We dine at seven tonight, if that is satisfactory to you. Toby's bound to have arrived by then."

"Oh, yes, my lord, quite satisfactory. Thank you, my lord." And with another quick bob, she scurried after Lady Edith.

Edgerton watched after her until she rounded the stairway landing, his brow knit in confusion. Could this be the same girl that Lord Birkinshaw had described—the one who made her schoolmates drunk, who flirted with a footman, who ran up enormous bills at her shoemaker's, and who pawned her mother's emerald? In appearance and manner, she certainly did not seem the sort. She seemed too timid to have even *thought* of such deviltry.

It was possible, of course, that she'd been sternly warned to be on her best behavior. If so, the girl was making a valiant effort. She'd given no sign, thus far, that there was now or had ever been a mischievous thought in her head. She'd been polite to a fault. In fact, she seemed always to be begging pardon for behavior that needed no apology. Edgerton couldn't understand it.

But there was no cause for concern, he told himself. After all, the girl was to spend a fortnight under this roof. If she truly *was* wild, could she possibly hide her natural roguishness for fourteen days and nights? Could the notorious Kitty Jessup spend an entire fortnight concocting tisanes, blushing shyly at compliments, making sick calls on his sister, and generally being obliging and obedient? He doubted it. No one, not even Kitty Jessup, could dissemble for so long. It was not possible. In that length of time, her true colors were bound to show themselves.

Thrusting his hands comfortably into his pockets and whistling softly, he strolled down the hallway to his office. There was something amiss here, but he felt surprisingly exhilarated by the challenge of the mystery. He smiled to himself at the prospect of solving it. The next couple of weeks might prove to be more amusing than he'd expected.

chapter seven

"And what, may I ask, are you doing hanging about the Rotunda as if you had nothing in the world to do but stand there and gape?" the butler demanded, having been distracted from his mission (carrying a covered china teapot of hot water and a plate of freshly baked raisin biscuits to the Blue Saloon) by the sight of Kitty, who'd just come into the house and was interestedly studying her surroundings.

Kitty, unaccustomed to hearing that tone of voice from a servant, reflexively put up her chin. "I'm not hanging about," she said coldly, "and I wasn't gaping. I was merely admiring the way the light slants in from those windows. Do you always greet guests in this rude fashion?"

"Guests? Since when does an abigail consider herself a guest?" Naismith looked her up and down, frowning in disapproval. Although he never smiled in any circumstances, he found frowning to be an efficacious expression in dealing with underlings. Thus, though his lips would never turn up, they quite often turned down. "Lord Birkinshaw must run a ramshackle household, I must say."

Kitty, reminding herself that she was now a servant and had to watch her tongue, nevertheless couldn't help taking offense. "Oh?" she asked, trying not to show her anger. "Why do you say that?"

"Judging from *your* deportment and appearance, my girl, I would guess that the Birkinshaws have a shockingly careless staff."

"I don't see what's wrong with my deportment. And as for my appearance,"—she looked down at herself uneasily—"this is only my traveling dress, after all."

"You've a very free and easy way of speaking, my girl. Too free and easy for this establishment, I can tell you. I'll cure you of that soon enough. You mayn't have learned anything in the Birkinshaw household, but you'll learn something here. Howsomever, I haven't time to deal with you now. Go upstairs and unpack your mistress's things. And report to me downstairs in one hour." Having delivered these orders in what he considered a sufficiently threatening manner, the butler turned his back on the girl and proceeded on his way.

"But wait!" Kitty cried, following him. "I don't know where—"

Naismith turned round as furiously as his butlerish self-control allowed—that is, angrily enough to jiggle the cover of the china pot he carried but not so precipitously as to dislodge it. "You will address me properly, if you please. I am *Mr. Naismith* to you." He glared down at her, imperious as a lord. "You will say 'Please, Mr. Naismith,' and wait to be acknowledged before you say anything further." Then, rolling his eyes heavenward (for he often felt that the gods above took particular delight in making his life troublesome), he added, "Didn't they teach you *anything* where you come from?"

"But . . ."

"Please, Mr. Naismith," he prompted in disgust.

"Please, Mr. Naismith, I don't know where—"

The butler reddened in frustration. "Didn't you understand me? You were not acknowledged! Don't you know how to wait?" His eyes turned heavenward again. "Why am I *always* afflicted with gowks like this to deal with?" The volume of his voice rose to an unaccustomed level and reverberated in the cavity of the dome above him. The echo, like a heavenly reprimand, reminded him of the inappropriateness of scolding a maid in a public room. He winced and forced himself into calmness by taking two deep breaths. "What is your name, girl?" he asked, still disdainful but much more subdued.

"K—Emily, Mr. Naismith. Emily Pratt."

"Well, Emily Pratt, I can see we shall have our hands full with you. But I have more important tasks at the moment." He turned again to go.

"Please, Mr. Naismith . . . ?"

He stopped in his tracks but did not turn. "Yes?"

She hesitated. "Is that an acknowledgment?"

He glared at her over his shoulder. "Of course it's an acknowledgement. What did you expect, a bow from the waist? Well, girl, speak up. I haven't all day."

"I don't know where Miss Jessup's room is."

"Then ask, for heaven's sake, *ask!*"

"I've been *trying* to ask ever since I came in," she retorted.

"Saucy puss!" he muttered, shaking his head in exaggerated hopelessness. "I shall have a great deal to say to you later, you can be sure of that. Meanwhile, ask one of the footmen at the bottom of the main staircase to show you up. What do you think they're stationed there *for?*" And he disappeared down the hall, shaking his head and muttering to himself about the shocking decline in the quality of servants in these godforsaken times.

The footman who escorted Kitty to "Miss Jessup's room" did not seem to her to be of particularly high quality either. He leered at her in outspoken admiration of her face and form and made lewd insinuations regarding future encounters. His name was Gerald, but he insisted she call him Jemmy, "since we're bound t' be good friends." Then he licked his lips suggestively and added, *"Really* good friends!"

By this time they were at the door. Kitty, weary from the trip and full of misgivings about what she'd done, merely turned in the doorway, glared at the footman, and shut the door in his face.

Emily was not in the room. A housemaid, who was just completing the chore of dusting and airing the room, told her that Miss Jessup was visiting the sickly Miss Alicia. "Jemmy tol' Lily, an' Lily tol' me that Miss Jessup was fixin' Miss Alicia a tisane."

"Fixing a *tisane?*" Kitty echoed in horror. "Good God! Whatever for?"

The housemaid shrugged. "Sounds a queer start t' me," she confided, gathering up her dustmop and broom. "We'd 'eard, downstairs, that Miss Jessup was a real high flyer. But someone who likes t' spend 'er time makin' tisanes don't sound like a high flyer t' me."

"Nor to me," Kitty muttered under her breath. She'd have to give Emily a good talking-to.

But Emily did not return to her room in time to receive Kitty's scold. Kitty emptied the large portmanteau, the boxes, and all the packages her parents had sent and stowed away all the contents, but still Emily did not appear. The hour the butler had given her was almost gone. There was nothing Kitty could do but lay out a gown for Emily to wear to dinner and go down and face Mr. Naismith. She only hoped he would finish with her in time to permit her to return and assist Emily to dress for dinner. She had a strong feeling that Emily would be in dire need of her assistance and advice.

She was halfway down the main staircase when she realized she should have taken the back way down. Fortunately, no one was about. She scrambled back upstairs and searched for the servants' staircase, nervously opening the doors of two unoccupied bedrooms before finally coming upon the passageway that contained the stairs. With a sigh of relief, she ran quickly down.

The stairs led directly to the servants' hall. It was a huge, dark room with a high vaulted ceiling on which the smoke of hundreds of years of cooking had accumulated. The room was gloomily lit by several windows placed high on the walls, but Kitty had to admit that, except for the ceiling which was unreachable, the entire place was scrupulously clean. It was evidently used both as a kitchen and a dining room for the servants, for in the wall directly opposite the door in which she stood was an enormous fireplace that Kitty could see was used for cooking; it contained a number of frying pans, griddles, pots, and kettles which hung from chains over the fire. But there was also a large Rumford stove (similar to the one her mother had bought for the Birkinshaw kitchen) on which something was boiling. Whatever it was emitted a deliciously aromatic smell of sage and onions, reminding Kitty that she hadn't eaten since morning and was now painfully hungry. But if she was to spend time being scolded by the butler, and if then she had to help Emily dress for dinner, and if the staff then would be busy serving that dinner, it might be very late before anyone would think of offering her something to eat. She wondered for the first time in her life when the servants had time to take their meals.

The only persons she could see from her vantage point in the doorway were the cook—a tall, muscular, red-faced female who was so busily kneading dough at a worktable near the stove that she took no notice of Kitty at all—and three scullery maids who were assisting her. One was hovering over the cook's shoulder, adding flour to the dough whenever the cook nodded her head. The second was sitting on a stool on the opposite side of the worktable, scraping carrots. The third was setting mugs at each place of an ancient and very long dining table in the center of the room. This was evidently where the servants took their meals. The sight of the servants' table being set gave Kitty a glimmer of hope—perhaps she'd be permitted to eat soon.

She was about to ask the scullery maid when the servants' dinner was served when a rebuking cough, coming from somewhere above her, reminded her of why she was there. "Well, girl, how long do you intend to linger down there?" came the butler's voice. She stepped into the room and turned in the direction of the voice. She discovered Naismith standing above her on a balcony which bridged the corner at her right and which therefore couldn't be seen from the doorway. As soon as their eyes met, the butler lifted his hand and beckoned her—with the imperious gesture of a monarch summoning a slave—to mount the curved stone steps in the corner which led up to his perch.

"Here I am, Mr. Naismith," Kitty said cheerfully when she came up to him.

"So you are." He studied her with displeasure for a moment, while she, in turn, looked about her. The balcony was larger than it seemed from below and led, through a doorway behind them, to what Kitty realized must be the butler's office and his living quarters. But the balcony itself was furnished with a pair of comfortable armchairs and a table on which were set some crystal goblets and several decanters of liquor. But until Naismith said, "Well, Mrs. Prowne, what do you think of her?" Kitty hadn't realized that someone else was there.

Kitty turned round to find that a tiny woman with black eyebrows and the whitest of white hair was seated in one of the armchairs, her fingers nimbly stitching a strip of lace onto a white muslin cap. "Wild little thing she looks t' be," the woman said, barely glancing up from her work. "Just as you said."

"It's only my hair," Kitty protested in self-defense. "I haven't had time to braid it."

"Mrs. Prowne was not speaking to you, girl," the butler said with a glare. "Were you not taught never to speak until spoken to? You see, Mrs. Prowne? Not only has the girl no manners, but she has something to say about everything."

Mrs. Prowne nodded. "Very free with 'er mouth, just as you told me, Mr. Naismith. I see just what you mean." Taking a momentary pause in her needlework, she peered up at Kitty and wrinkled her nose in distaste. "Goodness me, child, take off that 'orrid cap. And is that shabby frock your *service* dress?"

"She told me it's her traveling dress," Naismith said, his voice tinged with revulsion.

"Then she should've changed into 'er service garb before presentin' herself to us," the woman said, equally revolted.

Kitty, removing her offending headdress, remembered that Emily had brought no clothes with her and that nothing in any of the boxes she'd just unpacked was at all suitable for a servant to wear. She looked from one to the other in alarm. "But I . . . I have no other dress," she admitted.

"No other dress? Didn't Lady Birkinshaw give you a maid's black t' wear at Birkinshaw House?"

"No, ma'am."

"What sort o' housekeeper does Lady Birkinshaw employ?" Mrs. Prowne asked in rhetorical disapproval. "I'm housekeeper here, and though we're miles from London and her ladyship permits a bit o' informality here in the country, I wouldn't dream of lettin' the lowest o' the sculleries run about without a proper black on 'er back."

Naismith shook his head. "I told you, Mrs. Prowne, that Lord Birkinshaw must be a ramshackle sort—"

"He is not!" Kitty declared. "I don't have a 'black' because I don't come from Birkinshaw House. I come from the Marchmont Academy where Em—I mean where I was . . . er . . . maid-of-all-work. When Lord Birkinshaw wrote that he wanted an abigail to accompany his daughter, Miss Marchmont let me come."

Naismith's eyebrows rose. "A maid-of-all-work? You mean you're not Miss Jessup's true abigail?"

"Miss Jessup doesn't have a true abigail. She's been away at school since she was thirteen."

The butler gave the housekeeper a knowing glance. "Maid-of-all-work, eh? That explains it, then. This creature is . . . well, almost an impostor."

"Or at best a waif without a bit o' proper trainin'," Mrs. Prowne said, sewing away placidly. "No wonder she's a wild one."

"And makes so free with her tongue." Naismith rubbed his chin thoughtfully. "I suppose I'd best recommend to his lordship that we engage someone else to wait on Miss Jessup."

"Engage someone *else?*" Kitty felt the blood drain from her face. "Do you mean you'll . . . *sack me?*"

Naismith didn't deign to respond, but the housekeeper shrugged. "Well, after all, child, you 'aven't been schooled proper—"

"I've been in school since I was *nine!*" Kitty cried.

"This is *Edgerton Park,* girl," the butler stated magisterially. "Edgerton isn't to be compared with your piddling *school!* We can't have someone on our staff who's never served in a noble house."

"But you *can't* sack me!" Kitty declared in desperation. "You don't know what that would—" She stopped her tongue abruptly. She knew she had to be very careful in what she said. If her plan was not to collapse here and now, she had to find the right words to convince these two to keep her on, not only as a member of their staff but in the position of abigail to "Miss Jessup." The situation was indeed desperate, but desperation made her mind race double time. Her powers of invention, stimulated as always by danger, began to go to work. "You have no right to sack me," she pointed out with blithe confidence. "It was Miss Jessup who engaged me, and she wouldn't permit it."

"Oh, pish-tush," the housekeeper said. "Miss Jessup'd probably *enjoy* havin' a more experienced maidserv—"

"She *wouldn't!* I'd wager a guinea she'd have a tantrum! After all, she chose me herself. Do you think she'd be pleased to have you override her choice?"

The housekeeper cocked her head thoughtfully, looking like a black-eyed, white-crested bird. "The chit may 'ave a point in that, Mr. Naismith. She just might 'ave a point there."

The butler's brow knit. "Yes, she might at that. If Miss

Jessup engaged the girl herself, I can see that she might very well object."

Kitty leaped at her advantage. "Of *course* she'd object. Very fond of me, she is. Very fond. I do her hair for her every day at school, you know."

"Do you indeed?" Naismith muttered dryly. "I hope you do it better than you do your own. Well, this *is* a situation, is it not, Mrs. Prowne?"

"Aye, indeed, Mr. Naismith. It seems we do 'ave a situation 'ere."

Kitty looked from one to the other in confusion. "What situation?"

"It isn't as if a lady's personal abigail is like an ordinary housemaid, you know," the butler muttered, half to himself.

"No, indeed not, Mr. Naismith," the housekeeper agreed. "No indeed. An abigail's quite a bit superior, especially to a maid-of-all-work."

"I don't see how we're to manage it." He rubbed his chin speculatively. "This creature would have to sit above the housemaids at the table. She'd have to be the equal of our Miss Leacock."

"Miss Leacock?" Kitty asked, puzzled.

"She's dresser to 'er ladyship. And to Miss Alicia, when she's feelin' up to gettin' dressed. Comes from London, Miss Leacock does. She used t' dress the Countess Trevelyan before that poor lady passed on. Very genteel, Miss Leacock. You never could pass as an equal to 'er."

"I could try," Kitty murmured, feeling more chastened than ever before in her life. She didn't dream, when she'd plunged into this adventure, that she'd find herself deficient in—of all things!—the proper qualifications for the post of *abigail*.

The butler circled round the stricken girl, observing her from all angles. "She wouldn't be bad-looking if she tied back that hair."

"And a proper black bombazine would do wonders. Here, girl, try on this cap." The housekeeper made a few last stitches, snapped the thread neatly with her teeth, and handed the lace-trimmed mobcap to Kitty.

"Thank you," Kitty said humbly, hastily tucking as much of her hair into the cap as she could. "There! Will I do?"

Both the butler and the housekeeper circled her this time.

"With the bombazine, she'll look a bit more suitable," Naismith said somewhat dubiously.

"And with 'er hair in a proper braid," Mrs. Prowne agreed.

"After all, she'll be with us only for a fortnight," he added, consoling himself.

"And if any of the maids object to 'er place at table, we can always say she's guest-staff—not really one of us a-tall."

The butler nodded. "Very well. Take her away and get her dressed. And do it as quickly as you can, Mrs. Prowne, for she should be seeing to Miss Jessup's *toilette* by this time."

"Aye, Mr. Naismith, it won't take long. Come along, girl, follow me."

As the housekeeper (so tiny in stature that she made Kitty feel tall) hurried down the stone steps with Kitty close behind, the butler turned to his table and poured himself a brandy. He took a large swig, rolled the liquor round his mouth, swallowed, and sighed deeply. Then he leaned over the railing. "You, girl," he barked down at Kitty who was just disappearing from his view, "remember that you're employed here through my graciousness. So *try* not to do anything—or *say* anything—to make me sorry!"

Kitty merely nodded and continued on her way. The butler looked up at the vaulted ceiling in disgust. "I'll be sorry," he muttered to the gods above who were forever trying to do him in. "I can wager his lordship's best brandy on it. That girl'll make me sorry."

chapter eight

Kitty appeared at Emily's door twenty minutes later in full housemaid regalia. Her hair was pulled tightly back and braided in one firm plait, her head was topped with the frilled cap, and all the rest of her was clothed in a black bombazine dress trimmed with the primmest white collar and cuffs and covered by the most stiffly starched apron either of them had ever seen. Emily gaped at her for a moment and then burst into laughter. "Oh, it's you, Miss Jessup," she managed to say between giggles. "I almost didn't recognize you!"

"Hush! Do you want someone to hear?" Kitty hissed, closing the door quickly. "I told you never to call me that! I'm *Emily*, remember!"

"I'm sorry, miss. It's not easy to change the habits of one's lifetime."

"I know," Kitty agreed ruefully. "I almost found myself dressing down the butler."

"Really?" Emily's dimpled smile appeared again. "What did you say to him?"

"I started out by asking him—in my best lady-of-the-manor voice, mind you!—if he was always so rude to guests, but he quickly put me in my place, saying in the most pompous way imaginable, 'Since when, young woman, is an abigail to be considered a guest?'" Kitty imitated his nasal intonations to perfection and even aped his manner of turning up his doleful eyes to the heavens.

Emily collapsed in laughter on the bed, and Kitty joined in, perching on the edge. But she recovered herself quickly, realizing that they didn't have much time. "Really, Emily," she said, turning serious, "whatever possessed you to spend the afternoon making tisanes? You've got to learn to stop *doing* for people."

"Was it wrong of me to do so?" Emily asked, her elongated dimples disappearing with her smile. "It took only a few moments, and when Alicia began to feel better, Lady Edith was so grateful."

"Was she? Then you must be playing your part very well." Kitty eyed her with a touch of envy. "And a great deal better than I am."

Emily shook her head. "I don't know, Miss Jessup. Lady Edith seems pleased with me, and her daughter, too, but his lordship has several times stared at me with a puzzled expression, and he's remarked more than once that I am not quite what he expected."

"Oh, no, has he really?" Kitty got up and began to pace about worriedly. "Did he say in what way?"

"Not exactly. Though he did tell his mother before we arrived that he expected you . . . me . . . you to be hoydenish."

"Hoydenish?" Kitty stopped in her tracks. "He called me *hoydenish?*" Her cheeks reddened angrily. "What effrontery! Whatever gave him *that* idea?"

A bit of dimple showed itself in Emily's cheeks. "I can't imagine," she said almost seriously.

Kitty caught the glint in the other girl's brown eyes and instantly realized how foolish she'd sounded. Her anger subsided at once. "Very well, I *am* hoydenish," she admitted with a sheepish grin. "I admit it. But I don't see how it's become known to the world at large. I suppose my father told him so."

"Probably so," Emily agreed.

"Well, never mind. *You'll* show him that Kitty Jessup can behave like the most ladylike creature in the world. Come, let's get you dressed for dinner."

Emily obligingly shed herself of her traveling dress while Kitty, in proper abigail manner, undid the buttons of the gown she'd laid out and helped Emily into it. However, when Emily remarked that Toby Wishart was expected to arrive for dinner, Kitty promptly raised it up again and pulled it over Emily's head. "In that case, you must wear something more enticing. Here. Let's try the lavender crepe with the silver threads. That should catch his eye."

Emily complied, but she didn't understand Kitty's motives. "Why should I be enticing?" she asked. "You don't want him to *like* me, do you?"

"Why not?" She led Emily to the dressing table and began to brush her hair. "The more he likes *you,* the less likely he is to like *me* when the truth of my identity is finally revealed. Oh, dear, I'm all thumbs at this. You'd better do your own hair. You're so much handier than I."

Emily took the brush. "You did your braid very well. I don't think I could have done it better."

Kitty shrugged. "Mrs. Prowne plaited it. She's the housekeeper, you see, and she was given the task of turning me out. But I'm sure she'll expect me to braid it myself tomorrow, and you know what a botch I'll make of it then. However, we can't concern ourselves with that now. Here, I'll pin the bun for you. There, that's lovely. Just let the curl hang over your shoulder, so. Good. Now stand up and let me adjust the neckline of your gown. I think you should show a great deal of decolletage, don't you?" And she proceeded to pull the neckline down so that the upper curves of Emily's breasts were visible. Then she carefully pinned the decolletage in place with pins that Emily supplied.

By the time all was done, the hour was quite advanced. Emily nervously remarked that the entire household might already be awaiting her arrival downstairs. "I'd better go. Do I look presentable?"

Kitty studied her carefully. "Yes, I think you look—oh, no!"

Emily blanched. "What is it?"

"Your boots! You can't wear those dreadful boots with an evening dress. Quickly, take them off. Where are my black slippers? Did I put them in the cupboard there?" She rummaged through the shelves wildly, tossing things about in careless haste. "If I can only find them, we can stuff the toes with a couple of handkerchiefs and they'll do well enough. Now, where—?"

But it was Emily who found them, and it was Emily who found the handkerchiefs, too. At last she was ready. But she couldn't bring herself to go. The room was terribly untidy, and she'd been trained not to ignore dishevelment. "I'd better do something about this jumble," she said, looking about her uneasily.

"Don't be silly. Get along with you," Kitty urged.

"I suppose I'd better. I'll put things back in place when I return."

"You'll do nothing of the kind, *Miss Jessup*," Kitty declared. "Who's the abigail here?"

Emily didn't argue. If she had to play *her* role, it was only fair that Kitty play hers. And keeping the room neat was part of Kitty's role. "Very well," Emily said, "I'll go. There's only one thing more I'd like to do." And she turned to the tall mirror that stood in the corner. She hadn't had time before, but surely she could take a moment now, she decided, to take one quick glimpse.

She looked into the mirror and gasped. Surely, she thought, the creature in the glass was someone else entirely. The silky dress with its silvery threads sparkling amid the lavender clung to a form that appeared to her to be more mature and shapely than her own. Her hair glowed with auburn highlights that she'd never noticed before. And her cheeks, which had always seemed to her to be too full and pasty-pale to be pretty, now glowed pink with excitement. But what really reddened them was the sight of her half-exposed bosom. "Goodness, Miss Jessup, you can't mean me to appear so . . . so naked!" she exclaimed.

"You look breathtaking," Kitty insisted. "And dash it all, stop calling me Miss Jessup!"

"But I thought you wanted me to be ladylike," Emily objected, tugging embarrassedly at the neckline.

Kitty thrust her hands away. "I *do* want you to be ladylike. *Ladylike*, not *prudish*." She surveyed her handiwork one last time. "You look absolutely splendid. Don't be goosish, just go." And she took Emily by the shoulders and thrust her out the door.

Emily hurried down the staircase, fearing with every step that she'd trip over the extended toes of the ill-fitting slippers. But no such accident occurred. She made the last turn of the stairs with a sigh of relief.

At the bottom of the stairway she found two footmen awaiting her. "This way, miss," one of them said and led her toward the drawing room.

"Has everyone come down already?" she asked as she hurried after him.

"I believe so, miss," was the impassive answer.

They arrived at the drawing room door. She could hear voices within, and as the footman was about to throw open the doors, she heard a burst of masculine laughter. For some unfathomable reason, that sound caused her courage to fail her. "Wait!" she ordered the footman. "Wait just a moment."

"Wait, miss?" He eyed her with a tinge of surprise.

"Yes. Just a moment." She turned her back on him, looked down at her exposed chest, and flinched. Quickly, and as surreptitiously as the situation allowed, she removed the pins from the decolletage. She returned the neckline to its normal, modest position, tugged the shoulders of the gown in place, and turned back. "Here," she said to the footman in as imperious a tone as she could muster (hoping that her toplofty manner would mask her discomfiture), "get rid of these pins for me."

The footman blinked. "Pins, miss?"

"Yes, pins. Have you never seen pins before?" And with a toss of her head, she grasped his hand, opened his gloved fingers, and dropped the pins into his palm. Then she gave a last pat to her hair. "There, now," she announced, turning to face the doors, "I'm ready."

chapter nine

"Ah, there you are," Lady Edith clarioned, crossing the room and kissing Emily's cheek. "You've only just enough time before dinner to meet Toby and drink your sherry."

"What Mama means," laughed a good-looking young man, rising from a chair at Emily's left, "is that you're tardy but not so late as to need to beg forgiveness."

"Oh, dear," murmured Emily, looking about her in confusion, "*am* I late?"

"Not at all," said Lord Edgerton, also rising to greet her. "You are as punctual as a lovely young woman can be expected to be. My brother, who has just arrived *six hours* later than he should have, is a fine one to be lecturing on punctuality." He struck the boy lightly on the shoulder. "Come and make a leg to Miss Jessup, you mooncalf. Miss Jessup, may I present my brother, Toby Wishart?"

The young man made a deep, wide-armed bow and grinned up at her. "Your servant, miss."

Emily felt herself flush without understanding why. The young man's extravagant bow was obviously a teasing response to his brother's formality, but there was no reason for *her* to feel embarrassed by it. As she bent her knees in a responding curtsey, she studied the young man carefully. He was certainly attractive. Shorter than his brother, he was nevertheless quite broad-shouldered and manly. His dark eyes glinted with humor, his large mouth seemed to twist naturally in a warm smile, and his head was covered with a richness of tight, dark curls. Emily couldn't help thinking that Kitty Jessup—as soon as she set eyes on him—would regret what she'd done. But, for now at least, there was nothing Emily could do but continue to play the game. "How d-do you do, my lord," she said shyly.

"I shall do better with one more sherry," the young man said, turning to the footman who was hovering about behind him, plucking two glasses from the tray and offering one to her.

"That, at least, was nicely done," his brother muttered in his ear. Then, taking Emily by the arm, Edgerton led her across the room. "I hope you noticed, my dear," he said to her admiringly, "that your medicinal talents have had a beneficial effect on my sister. Here she is, fully dressed and with an appetite for dinner."

He led her to the armchair where Alicia, a pale, very thin woman of thirty years, sat huddled in a shawl. Though Emily had met her earlier, she hadn't been able to see her properly, for at that time Alicia had been covered to the neck by blankets. Now that she was able to take a good look at her, Emily couldn't help thinking that the little girls of Miss Marchmont's lower school would find Alicia the embodiment of their image of a spinster. Her posture was hunched, her fingers long and bony, her lips thin, and her hair (a nondescript brown) was tied back in so tight a bun that not a curl or tendril was permitted to escape to soften the gray planes of her face. In addition, she'd chosen a dress of so drab a puce that it emphasized her colorlessness. Nevertheless, as soon as Emily came up to her, Alicia managed a smile. "I must thank you again, Miss Jessup, for what you did for me this afternoon. Dr. Randolph stopped in to see me earlier this evening and was quite astonished at my improvement."

It amazed Emily to see how much that smile warmed Alicia's expression. "I'm so glad," she responded, sitting down on a hassock beside Alicia's armchair. "I'll tell Miss Marchmont, when I get back to the academy . . . that is, I mean, when I next pay her a visit . . . that her licorice tisane is every bit as efficacious as she believes."

"Good God, we're not going to sit about here in the drawing room talking about tisanes, are we?" Toby asked, downing his drink.

"No, we're not," Edgerton said, throwing his brother a look that warned him he was verging on rudeness. "Here's Naismith to announce dinner. Mama, let me have your arm. Toby, I shall give to you the honor of escorting both your sister and our lovely guest to the table. Now, shall we go?"

The dinner was served at a table long enough for at least a dozen diners. With Edgerton at the head and Lady Edith at the foot, Emily, Toby, and Alicia were seated quite far apart. Thus it was almost impossible for conversation to be intimate. For a while, nothing was said except about the food. Lady Edith admired the fish soup, explaining to her guest that it had been "prepared *à la Russe,* you see, Miss Jessup, to give it that distinctive flavor."

Alicia complained that the creamed soup was too rich for her delicate stomach. Lord Edgerton put in a good word about the veal filets. Emily said flattering things about everything that was put before her but was too nervous to eat very much of anything.

It was all very dull until Toby asked for a second helping of the little meat cakes Naismith had served. "Absolutely delicious," he declared, licking his lips. "What are they, anyway?"

"Mutton pâtés, my lord," Naismith informed him.

"Prepared *à l'Englaise,* I presume," Lord Edgerton quipped. But only one person in the room laughed at his joke —a serving maid standing in the corner holding a sauceboat. Everyone turned to see who the servant was who'd had the temerity to laugh, and Emily, noting with shock the maid was none other than Kitty Jessup, choked. Evidently the butler had commandeered Kitty to help serve the dinner.

While Naismith glared at the maid for daring to listen to— and laugh at—the table conversation, Emily's choking sound diverted the attention of the others. "Did you start to laugh at my brother's puerile joke?" Toby asked her. "I don't blame you for stopping yourself. It wasn't worth a laugh."

Emily colored. "No, I wasn't laughing at . . . I didn't understand—"

"Nor did I," said Alicia, coming to Emily's rescue. "What was so funny, Greg?"

"Well, the maid there laughed at it," his lordship said with a grin. "Let *her* explain it to you." He turned to Kitty, cowering in the corner. "Go ahead, girl, tell my sister what was funny."

Kitty threw a questioning glance at Naismith, who merely rolled his eyes heavenward. Then she stepped forward. "It was funny because only the English ever cook mutton," she explained, "so of course it *had* to be *à l'Englaise.*" She glanced round the table at the five pair of eyes staring at her enigmatically. "The French would rather die than serve mutton, you see." There was still no response in those eyes. She threw another look at Naismith and then plunged on. "And what really made it witty, you see, was that her ladyship had said the soup was *à la Russe* ..." There was still nothing but the stunned response, so Kitty looked at Lord Edgerton and shrugged. "Well, my lord, perhaps it wasn't so funny after all."

This was too much for Edgerton. He guffawed. "The girl is quite right," he said when his laugh had subsided. "No quip is funny that has to have so much explanation." Then, turning serious, he studied the maid with interest. "Tell me, girl, how is it you know French?"

Kitty was stricken with terror. Had she given herself away? She stepped back into her corner as if to escape the scrutiny of those five pair of eyes. "French? I don't kn-know French, m'lord," she said hastily, trying to copy Mrs. Prowne's manner of speaking. "I mean ... knowing what *l'Englaise* means isn't ... ain't knowin' French."

"No, of course it isn't," Edgerton said, turning back to the table. "In any case, thank you for finding my quip amusing. I'm glad *somebody* did."

Behind his back, Naismith, glaring at Kitty with fury, jerked his head in the direction of the door. The meaning of the gesture was unmistakable. Kitty slipped quietly out of the room and was not seen again in the dining room.

Meanwhile, Toby returned to his mutton pâtés. "One may say what one likes about mutton," he remarked, "but it's a great deal better for the digestion than the walrus meat the rest of you are eating."

"*Walrus* meat?" Emily squealed, dropping down her fork.

"Now, Toby, must you?" his mother sighed. "Give the child a chance to get to know you before you start on your outrageous stories."

"It really is veal," Alicia assured the blushing girl. "You mustn't mind Toby. He loves to say shocking things and frighten people out of their skins. Just ignore him."

"No, no, keep it up, Toby," said his brother calmly. "By playing tricks on this girl, you're only digging a hole for yourself. I think Miss Jessup is just playing a deep game. Biding her time, as it were. If the things I've heard of her are even half true, she'll give you better than she gets, as soon as she's taken your measure. Am I right, Miss Jessup?"

Emily knew that the real Miss Jessup would certainly have proved him right had she been sitting here herself, but she, Emily, felt quite helpless. All she could do was to play the game as best she could. She picked up her fork and, attacking her veal with renewed energy, tried to respond as she thought Kitty might. "Perhaps, my lord," she said, keeping her eyes lowered with what she hoped was an air of mystery. "Let's wait and see."

The ladies left the table after the pastries had been served, but the gentlemen did not sit long at their brandies. Edgerton was eager to rejoin the ladies so that Toby and Miss Jessup could become better acquainted. When they entered the drawing room, they found Alicia holding forth on her favorite subject, the delicacy of her constitution. Toby felt no compunction in interrupting her. "Are we to spend the evening listening to your symptoms?" he asked rudely. "Why don't we all sit down to a really savage game of silver-loo?"

"Not I," his sister said sourly. "Playing with you gives me the megrims. You are always so set on winning."

"I don't wish to play with you, either," his mother declared. "You always insist on making the stakes too high. I would much prefer an evening of music to one of gambling. Perhaps Miss Jessup would be willing to entertain us. Do you sing, Miss Jessup?"

"Not very well, I'm afraid. But I would be happy to accompany anyone else who would like to sing."

"Ah, you play, then," Edgerton said with a smile, strolling over to her chair. "Will you favor us with a few selections?"

All evening Emily had been eyeing the magnificent pianoforte set between the two tall windows in the room's west wall. She'd longed to run her fingers over the keyboard but had not dared to do it. Now here was her chance. "I'd be happy to, your lordship," she said shyly, standing up and taking the arm he offered.

Edgerton escorted her to the piano bench. She settled her hands on the keyboard, her heart pounding with excitement.

What would Kitty play if it were she at the piano? she wondered. Most likely it would be something easy yet bravura. Emily didn't take long to decide. She began with Haydn's "Gypsy Rondo," a safe and conventional choice. Every "accomplished" young lady was required to memorize the rondo, for it was lively, familiar, and intricate enough in fingering to persuade the listener that the performer had some technical skill. Emily executed it without a flaw.

But as she played, her delight in the tone of the instrument grew, causing her to make her second selection from her own heart—a Bach theme and variations. In her joy at the response of the sensitive instrument under her fingers, she almost forgot where she was.

By the time the Bach was over, Edgerton knew the girl possessed an extraordinary talent. "Your father never told me," he said in amazement, "that his daughter was so musically gifted."

"Thank you, my lord," Emily said, at once very pleased with the compliment and very uneasy, too. She'd never played for an audience before (except for the pupils of the school), so it was good to hear such sincere approval from so worldly a man as his lordship. But she was accepting the praise under false pretenses—in the name of Kitty Jessup, and Kitty, not having been very diligent at her music studies, was no better than average at the keyboard. The dishonesty of the situation made her feel unworthy of the compliment. "I am not so very gifted," she murmured in discomfort.

"Come now, Miss Jessup, I don't appreciate false modesty," his lordship declared. "You must know that your playing is quite beyond the ordinary."

"Oh, yes, Greg is absolutely right," Alicia put in. "I'm not especially musical myself, having always been too delicate to spend the hours needed to practice, but even I could tell that your playing is decidedly superior."

"Such beautiful playing, my dear! So lovely! It brought me to tears," Lady Edith said, sniffing into her handkerchief. "Do play some more for us."

Emily complied, choosing a Mozart sonata that began rather modestly and could be played with cheerful, tuneful ease. This choice, she hoped, would bring more attention to the sonata's own melodic line than the player. But by the time she'd reached the *andante*, she'd again lost herself in the music and was playing with her full vigor. Never before had she played on so superb an instrument. Without realizing it, she let herself go. The chords, the runs, the trills were executed with true musical artistry. Her playing revealed her mastery of the two primary facets of good musicianship: technical precision and deep emotional understanding. The pleasure she took in the playing was magically transmitted to the listeners. They were entranced. The applause at the conclusion was so enthusiastic that it was several moments before the assemblage became aware of the sound of gentle snoring. Toby Wishart had fallen fast asleep.

Lord Edgerton sat through the rest of the evening gritting his teeth. It was a decided relief to him when his mother rose and announced that it was time to retire. The others rose with her, all of them quite willing to bring the evening to an end, but Edgerton insisted that his brother remain downstairs with him. He'd reined in his irritation long enough; he didn't intend to go to bed before making his brother aware of the extent of his displeasure.

"*Damnation,* Toby," he barked as soon as they were alone, "how could you let yourself fall asleep? That is the girl to whom you're expected to make an *offer!* Couldn't you behave in a gentlemanly manner on your first evening in her company?"

Toby threw himself into a chair and ran a hand through his thick curls. "It's been a deucedly long day, Greg, and I'm tired. You know I ain't the sort who likes music. I can bear it all well enough if someone's singing words that I can understand and laugh at, but just to sit still and force myself to listen to an endless evening of piano playing . . . well, that just ain't in my line."

Edgerton sighed in disgust. "You could have *tried,* confound it! Just this once you could have made an effort to attend. You could have concentrated on her hands on the keys, or on the intricacy of the harmonies, or even on the charming way she bit her underlip when she was absorbed—"

"Those things might keep *you* awake, Greg, but they ain't interesting to me. In fact, there's nothing about this girl you've picked for me that I find interesting."

"How can you say that?" his brother demanded angrily. "She's as pretty a creature as any I've ever seen you with, her demeanor is much calmer and gentler than I expected, she is sweet and talented, and is evidently trying very hard to create a good impression. What more can you ask?"

"I can ask for someone a little less *insipid,*" Toby muttered sullenly.

Now it was Greg's turn to run his fingers through his hair. "I wouldn't call the girl insipid, exactly," he said, his brow puckering as he dropped into a chair opposite his brother. "She seems, rather, to be timid. As if she were dreadfully afraid of saying the wrong thing. Her father led me to believe that she's an incorrigible mischief-maker, but—"

"Mischief-maker? *That* one?"

Greg shook his head in puzzled agreement. "I know. When one looks into those innocent eyes it hardly seems possible. The only explanation I can make is that the poor chit was bullied into submission by her father. Perhaps he threatened some dire punishment if she didn't behave herself while she was here. It's too bad, really. I'd have liked to see what she's like when she's being impish."

"That girl hasn't an *impish* bone in her body," Toby stated decisively. "I'd wager a monkey her father's put one over on you."

"You haven't a *farthing* to wager, old boy, much less a monkey. So whether her father put anything over on me or not shouldn't concern you. What *should* concern you is the twenty thousand pounds I plan to settle on you the day you marry the girl."

Toby's mouth dropped open. "Twenty thousand? Do you *mean* it, Greg?"

Greg shrugged. "I don't see why you're so surprised. You heard me promise Father I would deal fairly with you."

"Yes, but twenty thousand is more than fair. It's positively *magnanimous!*"

"Even though Miss Jessup goes along with it?"

Toby groaned. "She certainly sours the brew."

"You'll have to take the brew just the way it is, for I've given my word you'll wed her. It's up to you to find a way to sweeten it, when you're married."

"I don't see why you gave your word without letting me even *see* the girl. It ain't like you, Greg."

Greg felt a twinge of guilt. "It seemed a good idea at the time," he mumbled.

"Perhaps we can get ourselves out of this coil," Toby suggested, his expression brightening. "We can say Birkinshaw misrepresented the merchandise, or some such thing, can't we?"

"Dash it all, you make-bait, Miss Jessup is not *merchandise!*" Greg said furiously, slamming his hand down on the arm of his chair, his momentary feeling of guilt completely dissipated. "She's as fine a young woman as I can imagine, and much too good for the likes of you!"

"That may be," his brother muttered, sullen again, "but I think I deserve the right to choose my own bride."

"Oh you do, do you? On what basis do you believe you 'deserve' it? By your wise, thoughtful, responsible behavior in the past?"

"I say, Greg," Toby objected, rising in offense, "if you're going to throw all my youthful indiscretions in my face every time the subject of my future comes up, I'll never be considered deserving of *anything*."

"Ah, you admit to youthful indiscretions, eh? Does that mean that these 'youthful indiscretions' are now a thing of the past?" Greg smiled up at his brother sardonically. "I believe it has been a week since you were sent down from Cambridge. Am I to view you as 'deserving' because you've been a model of propriety for all of seven days?"

Toby shrugged. "I don't see what being sent down from school has to do with choosing a bride."

"Don't you? Are you truly surprised that I don't find you deserving of that right? If I gave it to you, I can just imagine what sort of bride you'd choose. Describe your choice to me, Toby. Go on, describe her. Would she be someone like that lightskirt in Chelsea who bled us for a thousand before she released you from her clutch? Or would you prefer one like your so-delectable little opera dancer whom you found astride your friend Nelson the moment they believed your back was turned."

Toby's eyes fell. "I admit my taste in women was not quite mature in the past, but—"

"But it has matured since, is that what you're going to say? Is that why you've—since only last month—undertaken the care and feeding of a certain Miss Lolly Matchin of Castle Tavern?"

Toby reddened to the ears. "How did you . . . ?"

"How did I learn of her existence? I didn't spy on you, if that's what you're thinking. I received a letter from the lady, complaining that you promised her some funds that you never delivered. She thought I might be persuaded to make good on your promises. She was, of course, mistaken. I have the missive in my desk, if you'd like to take a look at it yourself."

"No, I . . ." Toby sank down on his chair again. "I don't doubt your word."

"Thank you. But I think you must agree that my doubts concerning the maturity of your judgment are somewhat justified."

"What I do for amusement," Toby growled, "has nothing to do with the matter. I would not choose Lolly for my bride, and you know it."

"That you choose to use her for your amusement is fault enough." Edgerton stood up and looked down at his brother threateningly. "I chose a bride for you, yes. It was a high-handed act, perhaps, but the tradition has been followed by generations of parents and guardians past and present, and with good reason. I make no apologies for it. I did it because I want you to settle down. It is my hope that the responsibilities of marriage will steady you, mature you, and fulfill you. I chose Miss Jessup on a whim, I admit, but I see no reason to regret what I've done. She has everything to recommend her: she comes of excellent stock—the Birkinshaws have an old and honored name; she is healthy of mind and body; and she's been reared with standards and values that are the same as ours. Now that I've seen her I feel even more justified in my decision. She differs from what I was led to expect, but that may be all to the good. Any man worth his salt would be proud to have such a woman bear his name. If you're willing to pledge to her your loyalty, affection, and protection, I shall give you the house in Surrey, twenty thousand pounds, and my blessing."

He turned and strode to the door, but before departing he looked back at the brother who'd slumped deep in his chair and was morosely studying his boots. "But if you're *not* willing, then as far as I'm concerned you may just as well go to the devil!"

chapter ten

Kitty ran straight from the dining salon to the servants' hall, but by the time she got there the story of her indiscretion at his lordship's table was already circulating among the staff. Several of the housemaids, gathering round the hall awaiting their supper call, were whispering in small groups but stopped their chatter as soon as Kitty appeared in the doorway. A couple of footmen eyed her with interest, and the one called Jemmy hooted at her gleefully. The three sculleries began to giggle at the sight of her, and the cook snorted in disdain as Kitty crossed the threshold. "Shame on ye," she said, shaking her head in disapproval. "Makin' yerself a bad name, and ye ain't been 'ere one day."

"It ain't her fault," one of the upstairs maids piped up. Kitty recognized her as the maid who'd been airing Emily's room earlier that afternoon. "Mr. Naismith 'ad no right to use 'er at table. She's an abigail, ain't she? Not a servin' girl."

"No one's askin' you, Peg Craigle," the cook declared, turning to the fire and rotating a roasting chicken on a spit. "If Mr. Naismith says she's t' serve, then she's t' serve. That's all there is to it."

"And let that be a lesson to ye," Jemmy said, crossing over to Kitty and tweaking her cheek.

Kitty slapped his hand in irritation. "Is this matter *everyone's* business?"

"No, o' course it ain't," Peg said, coming to her side. "What a way for you to start 'ere. Tish-tush, Emily, don't be lookin' so grim. Makin' a fool o' yersel' upstairs ain't the end o' the world."

Kitty met the other girl's eyes and gave a reluctant laugh. The girl was quite right; the scene in the dining room would be forgotten by everyone in a short while; there was no need to stew over it. She looked at Peg's laughing Irish eyes and felt a surge of gratitude. This girl might turn out to be a veritable friend in need. "Thank you, Peg," she murmured quietly.

Peg shrugged. "Come an' let me make everyone known t' ye. Over there is Mrs. Duffy, but everyone calls her Cook. The gennleman readin' the *Times* is Mr. Dampler, 'is lordship's valet. An' this 'ere's Lily, who always knows everything what goes on. An' here's Bess, who does all the sewin', an'—"

At that moment, Mrs. Prowne bustled in. "Come on, everyone, let's sit down," she announced. "They're still lingerin' over the pastries upstairs, so Mr. Naismith said to start without 'im."

As if a bell had rung, people seemed to materialize from all directions and the table places filled at once. It seemed to Kitty at first glance that there were dozens of people gathering, but in reality there were only sixteen. Kitty, hungry as she was, didn't take a seat, for nobody had told her where she belonged. It was Peg who finally pushed her into a chair and who introduced her to the personage seated opposite her. "Miss Leacock, this is Miss Jessup's abigail, Emily Pratt."

Kitty examined the other abigail with interest. She was a woman of middle age with a pointed nose, watery blue eyes, and a head covered with corkscrew curls. The most interesting thing about her, however, was her way of carrying herself. If there were a single word with which to describe her, it would be "ladylike." The way she sat in her chair, the way she looked down her nose, the way she picked up her knife . . . all these suggested the most exaggerated gentility. In the setting of the servants' hall, it seemed to Kitty that the woman was, to use an old saying her governess was wont to use, "putting on airs."

Miss Leacock acknowledged the introduction with a mere nod, but before she returned her attention to her soup, she gave Kitty a look of thorough if disapproving appraisal. *That's quite all right,* Kitty said to herself, *I feel the same distaste toward you.*

Kitty attacked the soup with more eagerness than she'd ever shown for food in her life. And never in her life had mere cabbage soup given her such pleasure. In a moment she forgot the humiliation of the past hour and surrendered herself to the physical satisfaction that comes when real hunger is assuaged. But she was not to forget for long. Peg, who was seated just below her on her right, leaned over to her. "It wasn't right, y'know, no matter what Cook says," she whispered.

"What wasn't right?" Kitty whispered back.

"An abigail shouldn't be made t' be a servin' girl. It's . . . how shall I say? . . . beneath ye."

"Then why did Mr. Naismith make me do it?" Kitty asked the maid curiously.

The girl shrugged. "T' put you in yer place, I suppose. Everyone's sayin' y're a bit uppish."

"Oh? Why do they say that?"

"I dunno, Emily. It's just a way you have. The way ye walk, with that toss of yer braid. An' the way ye talk, too. Sorta . . . proud, y'know. Like an actress on the stage."

"Goodness! You don't mean that I put on airs, do you? Like Miss Leacock there?"

Peg blinked in surprise. "Like Miss Leacock? Oh, no! Everyone *expects* Miss Leacock t' be uppish. She don't put on airs. It's sort of natural with 'er, y' see."

Kitty bit her lip to keep from laughing aloud. "Being uppish is natural to her but not to me, is that what you're saying?"

"I s'pose that's whut I'm sayin'. But don't feel bad, Em'ly. The way you are, well, I sorta like it, myself."

"Thank you, Peg, but I don't wish to appear uppish. Do you think it would help if I kept my head down—?"

But Peg, like the rest of the servants, had turned to greet Mr. Naismith, who had entered and was just taking his place at the head of the table. "Well, that's done," he announced to Mrs. Prowne. "Not a flawless occasion, I admit, but we got through it." He sighed wearily and reached for the basket of bread. "I think this is an evening that calls for a bit of my special wine. Go up and bring me a bottle, will you, Jemmy?"

"I 'ope the mutton pâtés was satisfactory, Mr. Naismith," Cook said, setting a bowl of soup before him.

"Quite satisfactory, Cook. Mr. Toby praised them particularly. In fact, the whole dinner might have been satisfactory if a certain young person I shall not name . . ." Here his eyes roamed down the length of the table until they reached Kitty's face. Fixing his stare on her, he continued: ". . . if this certain young person hadn't behaved in the rudest and most indiscreet fashion I've ever witnessed. Howsomever, you can all be sure I shall not again make the mistake of asking her to help serve."

"Then perhaps," Kitty muttered, her cheeks burning in offended pride, "you should not have asked that 'certain young person' to help serve in the first place!"

There was a shocked murmur from the listeners, and Peg gave her a kick under the table. Mr. Naismith blinked. "What did you say?" he demanded.

"I said that perhaps I shouldn't have been asked to serve in the first place." Kitty's mind was racing with excitement. Here she was, acting the role of a servant in the midst of a group of them who were born to their roles. If she was to be convincing, she had to learn to think as they did. What Peg's words had signified to her was that servants were each assigned a very distinct rank and that their pride was affected if they were not given due recognition of that rank. Taking what she believed was Peg's hint, she lifted her chin proudly and said firmly, "I'm an abigail, after all, and not a serving wench."

The murmur grew to a gasp, but Naismith lifted one lordly hand for silence. "Are you saying, you greenhead, that I had no right to employ you at the table?"

Kitty ignored Peg's second warning kick. "Yes, that's *just* what I'm saying."

"Now see here, girl," Mrs. Prowne put in, "y're a great deal too free wi' yer tongue! Mr. Naismith has the right t' ask any one of us fer assistance wi' any task 'e chooses."

"No, 'e don't," Peg hissed under her breath. "He wouldn't of ast La Leacock t' do it, would 'e?"

"You wouldn't have asked Miss Leacock here to do it, would you?" Kitty repeated aloud.

"Will you *listen* to the chit?" Naismith demanded of the ceiling. "What have I ever done to have such creatures forced on me?"

A babble of voices broke out at once. The cook told the butler not to take on so. "Ye don't wish t' spoil yer digestion," she cautioned. Mrs. Prowne ordered Kitty to keep a civil tongue in her head. Lily asked anyone who'd listen where this green girl had come from? Jemmy, returning with the wine bottle, demanded to know what was causing the to-do. And someone else wondered aloud why Mr. Naismith didn't sack her at once! Only Miss Leacock seemed unperturbed and continued in her inimitable ladylike style to sip her soup.

The babble died down as Naismith slowly rose from his chair. "I knew she'd be trouble the moment I laid eyes on her," he said to the gods above. Then he looked at his staff sadly. "It is a shame and a curse that I can't sack the girl. But she's employed by the Birkinshaws, not by us. We must try to bear her presence for a fortnight. I know I can count on all of you to cover her indiscretions and to make the best of a bad bargain." And he turned and went toward the corner stairs.

"Wait, Mr. Naismith," Cook called after him, "ye ain't 'ad yer dinner. I roasted the chicken wi' rosemary, just as ye like it."

"Sorry, Cook," he said over his shoulder, "but I've lost my appetite."

All eyes followed him as he tiredly climbed the stairs and disappeared into his rooms. Then all eyes turned to Kitty, devastating her with lugubrious disapproval. There was absolute silence as one after the other resumed eating. Kitty felt as if she were back at school and had been put in Coventry. Red-faced and embarrassed, she requested Peg to pass the bread, but the maid seemed not to hear. "Why are *you* angry at me?" Kitty whispered to her. "I only repeated what you said."

"I didn't *mean* ye to repeat it, ye blabbermouth," Peg hissed back.

So much for our budding friendship, Kitty thought ruefully, feeling utterly alienated and alone. It was then that she noticed someone's hand holding out the breadbasket toward her. It was Miss Leacock. Kitty gaped at the woman in surprised gratitude. At least *one* person at the table had not put her in Coventry. Of all the servants at the table, Kitty would have picked the snobbish-seeming Miss Leacock as the *last* person to offer her a kindness. "Thank you, Miss Leacock," Kitty said, touched.

"Ye're quite welcome," Miss Leacock said, picking up a piece of bread and daintily spreading it with butter. "It might in-ter-est ye to know, Miss Pratt," she said in a voice that was high and clear and in which each syllable was primly and perfectly enunciated, "that I *have* served at the family table on oc-ca-si-on, although I have not been asked for se-ve-ral years. Though some here may not realize it," and here she threw Peg a withering glance, "it's an *honor* to be chosen by Mr. Naismith to wait on the family, es-pe-ci-al-ly for a young person who's new to the household."

"Oh," Kitty said shamefacedly, "I didn't know."

"How could you know," Miss Leacock said just loudly enough to be heard by everyone at the table, "when you'd been badly advised?" Here she gave Peg another look which clearly indicated where the bad advice had come from. "And now I think enough has been said on this subject. You'd better eat your chicken, Miss Pratt, before it becomes cold."

With that, *Peg* received the disapproving glances from the others that had hitherto been thrown at Kitty. But soon normal table conversation was resumed, and Kitty, having been returned from Coventry by Miss Leacock's strategem, set to her dinner with renewed appetite. Only Peg still seethed. "Ol' witch," she muttered under her breath about Miss Leacock.

But Kitty didn't pay attention. Over her chicken, she threw the "old witch" a warm smile. She was beginning to learn who, among all these alien strangers, her real friend might be.

chapter eleven

Kitty and Emily intended to exchange complete details of their evening's adventures before going to sleep, but each of them was too exhausted by the strenuous day to chat for long. While Kitty dutifully helped Emily to undress—a luxury Emily experienced for the first time in her life and greatly enjoyed—Emily reported to Kitty that Toby Wishart was a rudesby. "I thought at first that he was quite handsome, but I later came to the opinion that the fellow would not possibly make a good husband."

"Then you think my plan is a good idea, after all?" Kitty said, buttoning Emily into her own best nightgown and trying not to yawn.

"As to that," Emily replied, climbing up on the high bed and sinking back with a sigh against an enormous pile of the softest down pillows imaginable, "I can answer that question only after we see how this wild scheme turns out."

Kitty, too tired to discuss anything further, dropped an ironic little bob to her "mistress" and retreated to the narrow little room in the servants' wing to which she'd been assigned. She undid the buttons of her bombazine all by herself—and with more difficulty than she'd expected—and fell upon the lumpy cot that was to be her bed for the entire fortnight of the visit. "I'll never be able to shut my eyes on this dreadful contraption," she told herself, but no sooner had the words crossed her mind than she fell fast asleep.

It seemed as if she'd barely slept an hour before Peg roused her. "Ye'd better get dressed real quick if ye want yer breakfast," the girl warned. "Cook clears the table sharp at six."

"Heavens," Kitty muttered groggily. "What time is it now?"

"A bit after five, so, ye see, there ain't much time."

"Good God!" Kitty cried, leaping out of bed. She'd have to perform her ablutions, shine her boots, button the twenty-four buttons of her bombazine, and braid her hair all in half an hour if she was to have time to eat. She set about dressing herself with the greatest possible speed, but she was still struggling with the back buttons of her bombazine when she heard a clock somewhere strike five-thirty. She sank on her bed in dismay. Five-thirty! And she hadn't even started on her hair! She'd never make it to breakfast at this rate. And she was unbelievably hungry again. *Perhaps*, she thought, *this scheme of mine was a mistake after all!*

A light tap on her door roused her. She opened it a mere crack, for she realized it wouldn't do to be discovered in such disarray. She felt relieved to find it was Miss Leacock standing at her door—Miss Leacock, the one person at the table last night who'd behaved like a friend. "Miss Leacock!" she exclaimed in surprise. "I . . . er . . . Good morning."

"I didn't see ye at breakfast," the ladylike abigail said in the cool, distant voice Kitty remembered from the evening before, "so I wondered if ye were in some dif-fi-culty."

"Yes, I am," Kitty admitted in desperation, opening the door and letting the older abigail in. "It was good of you to come, but, honestly, I'm not worth your attention. You'll only get into trouble with Mrs. Prowne or Mr. Naismith if they catch you here."

"Ye needn't worry about that," Miss Leacock assured her in her precise, carefully enunciated syllables. "After twenty-seven years of service to her ladyship, I'm quite im-mune from scolds."

"Oh, I see. Then *that's* why everyone calls you Miss Leacock instead of addressing you by your given name as they do me."

"No, my dear, that's *not* why. They call me Miss Leacock because nobody *knows* my given name."

"Oh?" Kitty asked curiously. "Why is that?"

"Because I won't tell them. But that is neither here nor there. I came in to learn what is causing ye dif-fi-culty."

"Yes, so you did." Kitty sank down on her narrow bed and gave a hopeless shrug. "Well, then, since you're good enough to be concerned, Miss Leacock, you may as well hear the truth about me. I'm not accustomed to getting up at five. Even at school we were permitted to sleep 'til seven. Neither am I accustomed to this hideous bombazine. And I haven't even *begun* on my blasted hair!"

"No need for panic, girl," Miss Leacock said calmly. She pulled Kitty to her feet, turned her round without another word, and quickly buttoned her dress. And before Kitty could object, she started on her hair.

"This is more than kind," Kitty said with sincere gratitude. "I don't know why—"

"I re-col-lect, when I first came here, how frightened I was by the morning scramble. I don't think I would have managed without the help I received from Mrs. Prowne."

"Mrs. *Prowne?* I never would have thought . . . she seems to me to be a very unfriendly sort."

Miss Leacock smiled, the first smile Kitty had seen her give. "That was many years ago," she said. "She was much younger then. The years have given her more res-pon-si-bility and less patience. But believe me, my dear, under that frown she likes to wear, she's very good at heart. In fact, if we hurry down to the hall, I'd wager you'll find she's ordered Cook to keep some breakfast warm for you."

Kitty followed Miss Leacock out the door. "I knew I had a great deal to learn about being a servant in a great house," she said in self-accusation, "but it seems I have much to learn about *people,* too."

Miss Leacock actually laughed. "So do we all, my dear, so do we all. But you'll learn what you need in good time."

"There's something else I'll learn in good time," Kitty said with a gurgle of laughter, running ahead of the older woman and holding open the servants' hall door for her.

"What's that?" Miss Leacock asked as she passed.

"Your given name," Kitty whispered in her ear.

Emily, however, reminding herself that she was living the life of a lady, stayed abed until nine. It seemed to her that she'd slept half the day away, but even at ten, when she timidly stole into the breakfast room ravenous as a wolf, she learned from Naismith that she was the first one down. "Except for his lordship, of course," the butler added.

"Oh? Has he breakfasted already?" Emily asked, eyeing the lavish buffet spread out before her. It contained an amazing selection of edibles. The array of food seemed too varied and exotic for a mere breakfast. There were platters of muffins and biscuits, racks of toast, bowls of fruits both fresh and stewed, covered serving dishes of several kinds of ham and other smoked meats, ramikins filled with curried, poached, or shirred eggs, pots of coffee and tea, pitchers of cream and honey, assorted jellies, and trays of scones, tarts, and crumpets. It was a far, cry from the porridge and tea that was called breakfast at the Marchmont Academy.

As Naismith helped Emily to load her plate, he explained that his lordship always left early to ride around the grounds with his bailiff. "As to Master Tobias, one never knows when he'll come down. And Lady Edith and Miss Alicia take breakfast in their rooms, so you needn't delay your own on their account."

Naismith may have felt sorry for the poor young lady having to breakfast all by herself, but Emily enjoyed the peacefulness of it. She rejoiced in the freedom of having a meal without being forced to make conversation and having to guard against a slip of the tongue. She was almost finished when Toby came in. The fellow looked even more handsome than he had the night before. He was dressed in a dashing riding coat, yellow breeches, and a pair of elegant Hessians with tassels at their tops. He gave her a cursory greeting, downed a cup of coffee and a muffin without sitting down, and explained that he was off to exercise his favorite roan. Then, obviously realizing that to dash off without inviting her would be too rude even for him, he asked cursorily, "Oh, would you care to come riding, Miss Jessup?"

"I don't ride, thank you," Emily responded with icy politeness.

Toby merely shrugged. "Then I trust you'll excuse me, ma'am," he said and promptly retreated from the room.

After he disappeared, Emily left the table wondering what she was to do with herself next. She wandered about the rooms aimlessly, wishing she could spend some time at the magnificent piano but afraid of annoying the others in the household. By and by, Lady Edith made an appearance. "Alicia is feeling out of frame again," she said, seating herself in the Blue Saloon and taking up her embroidery. "I don't know what to do about that poor child."

"May I pay a call on her?" Emily asked, glad for the opportunity to have something to do.

Lady Edith smiled at her gratefully. "Oh, *would* you? A bit of diversion might be the very thing for her."

Emily ran upstairs eagerly and knocked at Alicia's door. A voice within invited her to come in, but when she entered she found that Alicia was not alone. On one side of her bed a short, balding man with spectacles and a thick mustache stood with his fingers on Alicia's wrist, taking her pulse. On the other side stood a middle-aged abigail holding a tray of medicines. Alicia smiled at Emily feebly. "Oh, Miss Jessup, how good of you to come. Miss Leacock, set a chair for our guest, if you please. Miss Jessup, this is Dr. Hugh Randolph, who so kindly comes each day to examine me. Hugh, this is Kitty Jessup, Lord Birkinshaw's daughter. It was she who made the wonderful tisane for me yesterday."

The doctor peered at her over his spectacles. "Ah, yes. Quite a miracle worker you must be to have cured Miss Alicia's migraine sufficiently to encourage her to get out of this deuced bed and go down to dinner. How do you do, ma'am?"

"How do you do?" Emily said in polite acknowledgment, although she was taken aback by his curmudgeonly manner. "But perhaps my visit is not felicitous at this time." She took a backward step. "Shall I return later?"

"No need to go on my account," the gentleman said gruffly. "I was just leaving. I don't know why this woman insists on my coming every day. It would do her more good to perform some vigorous exercise for a quarter-hour than to have me take her damned pulse."

"Oh, Hugh, please don't be cross," Alicia pleaded. "You know that I would exercise if I had the strength."

"You'd *have* the strength if you forced yourself to be a little energetic for just one week!" the doctor barked. "Come with me, Miss Leacock, and I'll give you some more of those headache powders. But don't give them to Alicia unless you deem it a dire emergency. Try warm milk or one of Miss Jessup's tisanes before you let her take the powder." He waved a warning finger in Alicia's face. "A *dire emergency*, do you hear me?"

"Yes, Hugh, I hear you. But must you go so soon? You've only just come."

"Of course I must go. I have patients who are *ill*, you know. *Really* ill. Good day, Miss Jessup." And with Miss Leacock at his heels, he strode out of the room.

Emily looked after him for a moment and then turned back to Alicia. The fragile woman was looking at the closing door with an expression of such hopeless longing that Emily almost gasped. Was poor, colorless Alicia in love with her bald, ill-tempered little doctor? "I'm so sorry," she apologized. "I interrupted your visit with your doctor."

"Oh, no," Alicia said, trying to reassure her with another feeble smile. "He was about to leave anyway. He never stays with me for more than a couple of minutes." She tried surreptitiously to wipe away a tear that dripped from one eye. "He doesn't take m-my headaches very s-seriously."

Emily sat at the edge of the bed and took one of Alicia's thin hands in hers. "Oh, I'm sure he does," she murmured comfortingly. "Perhaps he was just a bit crotchety today."

Alicia dropped her eyes. "No, he's always crotchety with me. I . . . I seem to . . . to t-try his patience. He's really a very kind, very sympathetic gentleman. You mustn't judge him by his gruffness to me."

"If he's always gruff with you, why do you believe that he's kind and sympathetic?"

"Because he was so at first, before I wore him down." She gave a small, reminiscent sigh. "He was so gentle in those days, so understanding. I think he almost . . . liked me. Now it seems as if he thinks I'm not improving just to *spite* him." She looked up at Emily and let her eyes overflow unchecked. "Doesn't he kn-know I would g-get up and *d-dance* for him if I c-could?"

"Oh, Alicia," Emily said, patting the older woman's cheeks with her handkerchief, "please don't cry. We can think of something . . ." She felt herself slipping into the familiar role so often practiced at school, the role of comforter and advisor.

"Think of s-something?" Alicia blinked up at her, hope shining like a rainbow through her tears. "What do you mean?"

"I don't know yet," Emily admitted, "but I can see you've fallen into the habit of presenting yourself to him as helpless and weak. Perhaps if one day you could surprise him with a cheery face . . . you know, Alicia, your face becomes remarkably transformed when you smile."

Alicia gaped. "Oh, Miss Jessup, does it *really?*"

"Yes, it does. I've noticed it several times. And you must stop calling me Miss Jessup if you want me to continue to call you Alicia. My name is Em—*Kitty,* if you please."

"But, Kitty, my dear, were you trying to tell me that I should *pretend* to Hugh that I feel better than I do?"

Emily knit her brow. She hadn't intended to advise Alicia to *scheme.* That sounded more like Kitty's sort of advice. On the other hand, she didn't see what harm there would be in so mild a pretense. "Just give me a little time to think. Perhaps Ki—I mean my abigail can help me think of an idea."

"Your abigail?"

"Yes. I . . . er . . . often consult her in such matters. She's a very ingenious young woman."

Alicia pulled herself up higher on her pillows and studied Emily with a cocked head. "Do you know, I'm feeling better! You've cheered me up more than I dreamed anyone could. I'm so glad you've come to stay with us, Kitty. Mama is quite right about you, you know. She said you're the sweetest young thing. I think Greg's choosing you for Toby was the best thing that's happened to this family in years."

But if Alicia and Lady Edith were taken with Emily, it was soon obvious that Toby was not. All afternoon he avoided her. Then he absented himself from the tea table. Finally, at dinner that evening, he teased her unmercifully until his brother told him sharply to cease and desist. Even then the dastardly fellow said bluntly—right in front of her!—that anyone who couldn't laugh at his taunts had no sense of humor.

When Kitty came to undress her at night, Emily recounted the dinner conversation with tight lips. "The fellow is a swine," she declared furiously. "He kept saying things like, 'I hate goodness . . . it ruins conversation,' or 'Every proper lady becomes a bore at last.' I knew he meant me, but he expected me to *laugh* at those cruel quips!"

"He does sound a beast," Kitty agreed as she undid Emily's evening dress, "but I don't see why you should take on so. He's nothing to you, and yet your hands are trembling just speaking of him."

Emily looked down at her quivering fingers. "I don't know *why* I'm so upset. I think I'm beginning to . . . to *hate* him." She looked over her shoulder at Kitty in amazement. "You know, Miss Jessup, I don't think I've ever hated anyone in my life before."

"Is that true?" Kitty shook her head in disbelief. "I've hated so many people I've lost count."

"Have you really? Who?"

"Let's see." She puckered her brow thoughtfully as she tucked away the gown and pulled out the nightgown. "There was a drawing master Mama hired when I was a little girl. He always insisted that I copy exactly what he drew, and when I dared to draw what *I* wanted, he rapped my fingers most painfully with his ruler. Oh, how I despised that man! And there was a peddler at a fair from whom I bought what was supposed to be a gold ring. I gave him every penny that I'd saved for months and months, and when the ring turned black in less than two days, I went back to find him, but of course he was gone. I'm still furious when I think of it." She raised the nightgown over Emily's head. "And sometimes I've hated Bella—"

"Bella? At school?" Emily asked, peering at Kitty in surprise as her head emerged from the neck of the nightgown.

"Yes, quite often. Especially when she tattles. You needn't look at me as if I were a demon. It's perfectly natural to hate, I think, and not so dreadful if you don't take action."

Emily's huge eyes widened in awe. "Take *action?*"

"Yes, like putting a dose of belladonna in the hated one's tea, or pushing him off a high tower."

"Goodness, how can you even *think*—?"

"I don't, really. Hating someone doesn't automatically make one a murderer, you know. Although . . ." Kitty couldn't help smiling wickedly. ". . . I have sometimes wanted to wring Bella's neck."

"I know just what you mean," Emily said, climbing into bed. "I had the urge, all evening, to slap Toby Wishart's face!"

Kitty, playing the role of abigail to the hilt, tucked Emily's comforter in all around her. "Then why didn't you?"

"Slap his face? You mean *really?*"

"Yes, why not? A slap is not a crime, you know. And the fellow deserved it, didn't he?"

"Oh, Miss Jessup, I couldn't actually *slap* someone, even if he *did* deserve it."

"Well, *I* could." She gave the pillows a last pat and went to the door. "And you could, too, given the right circumstances. It seems to me that you just don't hate him enough."

After Kitty left, Emily blew out her bedside candle and snuggled down under the covers. *Oh, yes,* she thought, *I hate him enough.* How could she help but hate him? Hadn't he made it clear to everyone that he thought her a prude and a bore? And hadn't he snored through her performance at the piano? In fact, if he continued to behave in the same odious way as he did this evening, she might very well bring herself to slap him. As Miss Jessup had said, a slap was not a crime. She smiled to herself in the darkness. Why, her palm was actually tingling in anticipation!

chapter twelve

Kitty closed the door of Emily's bedroom behind her and raised her candle high. The corridor leading to the back stairs loomed ahead of her like a dark cave. Why, she wondered, couldn't Lord Edgerton keep the corridors lit as her father did at Birkinshaw House? At home the candles in the hallway sconces burned all night. But it was probably impractical here. The corridors in this place were so long and numerous that their distance was undoubtedly measured in miles instead of feet. Even so, there should have been *some* candle sconces installed here and there. What if, stumbling about in the darkness, one should come upon a *rat?*

Holding her candle before her carefully, Kitty lifted her skirts with her free hand and proceeded with a gingerly step down the hallway. She could see the glow from the main staircase ahead of her. That, of course, was nicely lit, even though the back stairs had sconces only at the turnings. *The Wisharts are very generous about their own comfort,* she said to herself with a touch of bitterness, *but what do they care about the comfort of the staff?* The thought made her stop in her tracks and grin with satisfaction: she was beginning to think like a servant!

There was a sound of footsteps on the main stairs, and in a moment a figure appeared down the hall. It was a gentleman, and he, too, carried a candle. Kitty wondered if she was about to come face to face with her intended, but she realized at once it wasn't he. She'd gotten a glimpse of Toby at the disastrous dinner the night before, and she was certain that he was stockier than the gentleman now approaching. In another instant she could see that the gentleman was Lord Edgerton himself. Kitty peered through the shadows at him admiringly. He seemed to her to be the physical embodiment of everything

90

manly. There was something about the way he held his head, the way his step seemed to be propelled from the hip, the way his arm swung from his shoulder with a suggestion of restrained strength that fascinated her. Emily might find the revolting Toby handsome, but Kitty was convinced that his brother had something more than mere handsomeness in his face. Lord Edgerton's face had *character*.

She wondered if he would remember that it was she who'd laughed at his joke the night before. Would he stop and speak to her? An exchange of pleasantries with him would be a very satisfying way to end her day. Her blood tingled in her veins in excited anticipation.

They were now face to face. Kitty dropped a curtsey. "Good evening, your lordship," she said breathlessly.

Lord Edgerton barely glanced at her. "'Evening," he muttered abstractedly and passed by.

Kitty stood frozen to the spot. He hadn't even taken notice of her! *Blast the man*, she thought angrily, *can't he see I'm someone special? Does this deuced bombazine hide one's personality so completely?* She knew that servants were not supposed to make themselves noticed, but she was Kitty Jessup, and Kitty Jessup, even in servants' garb, was not the sort to disappear into the woodwork. It was not her way.

And then, as usually happened when she felt challenged, her brain bubbled up with a naughty and utterly irresistible idea. "*Aaaaaaaah!*" she screamed, letting her candle, stick and all, fly through the air. "A *rat!*"

"What?" his lordship asked, wheeling about. "*Where?*"

"There! Right *there!*" She ran toward him, holding her skirts high. "*Aaaah! Don't* let it *bite* me!" And she leaped up at him, knowing full well that his instincts would be quick enough to catch her up in his arms.

She was not mistaken in him. He caught her without a moment's hesitation, although he dropped his candle in the process. It, like hers, fell to the ground and went out, leaving only the dim glow from the stairway to pierce the darkness. "Good God!" he exclaimed, tottering to regain his balance while holding her against him. "Are you sure?"

"Of *course* I'm sure," she said, clutching him about the neck. "I saw its beady eyes!"

"Is that all?" he asked in some disgust. "If all you saw

were the eyes, how can you tell it was a rat? It was probably only a mouse."

"Only a *mouse*? *Only* a mouse? How would *you* like to feel a mouse nuzzle your ankle in this wretched black hole of a hallway? Besides, you can't be *sure* it wasn't a rat."

"Yes, I can. We don't *have* rats. I employ a veritable platoon of servants to keep this place free of them."

Kitty hid her face in his neck. "It felt like a rat to me."

"Did it indeed?" he asked, lifting her chin and trying to look into her face. "How can it have *felt* like a rat, may I ask?"

Kitty gave a very convincing shudder and buried her head in his shoulder again. "I could *sense* his pointy snout," she whispered with a proper touch of terror.

"Now, see here, girl," his lordship said firmly, "if I give you my word that we don't have rats, may I be permitted to put you down?"

"Only if you're certain that whatever it is is gone," she said promptly, letting her cheek brush against his.

"If it's still lingering about here after the racket you made, it's the stupidest rat in creation," he said drily.

"There! Even *you* called it a rat."

"Mouse, then. I meant mouse. Now let me put you down and find my candle. I promise not to desert you until we've ascertained that the corridor is free of any and all rodents."

He set her on her feet and bent down, feeling about in the darkness until his hand touched the candle, still in its holder. Then he started for the stairway.

"Where are you going?" she cried, clutching at his arm fearfully.

"Only to get us some light. Here, take my hand if you must."

He led her to the stairs and held his candle to the first lighted taper he came upon. "There now," he said, returning to the corridor and holding the light high, "are you now convinced that no creeping creature is lurking about?"

"Yes, my lord," she said with a meek bob. "Thank you, my lord. I'm sorry I . . . er . . . jumped up on you that way. I quite lost my head."

"Yes, you did, didn't you? I didn't know that housemaids were so terrified of mice."

"Not mice, remember," she corrected. "Rats, if you please. Rats. Besides, I'm not a housemaid. I'm Miss Jessup's abigail."

He held the candle closer to her face. "Ah, yes, so you are. Forgive me, but I seem to have forgotten your name."

"Emily, my lord. Emily Pratt."

"Well, Emily Pratt, can it be that you've never encountered a mouse at Birkinshaw House?"

"I don't come from Birkinshaw House. I come from the Marchmont Academy. And no, I never did encounter a *rat* there. Miss Marchmont keeps cats."

"So you insist it was a rat, do you?" He frowned at her forbiddingly, but she didn't miss the touch of amusement in his eyes. "Has anyone ever told you, Emily, that you have a saucy tongue?"

"Yes, my lord," she answered demurely, "I've been accused of it once or twice."

"I'm not surprised. Rats, indeed. I have a feeling that you'd have stirred up as a great a fuss if the creature had been nothing more than a spider. However, in this case, since I didn't see the creature myself, I suppose I must give you the benefit of the doubt. I'll grant that it is possible—though highly unlikely—that the creature *was* a rat. And since the slight possibility does exist, I shall help you find your candle and escort you to the back stairs."

"Thank you, my lord. That is most kind of you."

Something in her tone made him throw her a suspicious look. But after meeting her very level stare, he shrugged and picked up her candle. "Here, girl, give me your hand and come along."

He led her down the corridor, covering its entire length in no more than two dozen long strides. Clutching his hand, Kitty had to run to keep up with him. When they reached the landing of the back stairs, she released her grip and made another bobbing curtsey. "I am very grateful to you, my lord," she said. "It isn't often that the master of the house goes out of his way for a mere abigail."

"It isn't often that someone accuses me of harboring rats in the hallway," he countered, lighting her candle with his own. "I hope, girl," he added, handing her the candle, "that you won't frighten the other maids with—" He stopped short, peering at her through the added brightness of the second candle. "Wait a moment! This isn't the first time I've encountered that saucy tongue of yours, is it? It was at the table last night. Aren't you the chit who spoke French?"

"Well, yes, my lord, I was that *'chit,'* but I don't exactly—"

"You're a strange sort of abigail, I must say."

Kitty wondered if she'd gone too far. "S-Strange, my lord? Because I know a little French?"

He looked at her intently. "Yes, I would say you're a bit strange. You're very glib in English, too."

His suspicious expression warned her that things were coming very close to a crisis, but Kitty was nothing if not inventive in a crisis. "That's because I'm not always going to be an abigail," she improvised smoothly. "Miss Marchmont, at the academy, is training me to be a teacher."

"Oh, I see." His lordship, accepting her words as a perfectly logical explanation of her peculiarities, studied her with renewed interest. He was not surprised that she had aspirations beyond her present situation; even yesterday, when she'd laughed aloud in the dining room, she'd seemed to him to be gifted with an intelligence and spirit beyond what one usually found in a housemaid. And now, in the candlelight, with her cap askew on the most glowing hair he'd ever seen and the flame of the candle reflected in a pair of laughing eyes, she appeared to him to exude a pixieish, almost magical charm. "A teacher, eh?" he remarked, suddenly finding himself quite willing to dally for a bit. "Is that what you wish for your future?"

"Yes, I think so." She was quick to recognize the spark of interest in his eyes, and she felt her pulse quicken. Was it relief that he was no longer suspicious of her, she wondered, or was it something more? "Teaching is a promising career for someone like me, don't you agree?" she asked, hoping to hold his attention for a little while longer. "I'd earn both independence and respect."

"But what about happiness? Do you think teaching will make you happy?"

"I can't tell about that. Not yet."

He smiled down at her. "Most girls your age dream of

finding themselves a handsome young husband, not independence and respect."

"Husband, faugh!" she exclaimed with so violent a toss of
her head that the orange-red braid flipped like a horse's tail. "I
shan't think of marriage for *years*. Besides, I don't think I'm
suited for it."

"Why not? You certainly *seem* suited for it."

"Oh, no, not I." Her eyes twinkled enticingly in the
candlelight. "I'm much too flighty."

One of his eyebrows lifted in amusement. "But not too
flighty for teaching, eh?"

This gave her pause. Her face fell. "Are you saying that
you don't think I'd be suited for teaching?"

"It's hard to say on so short an acquaintance. But if first
impressions are significant, I would think not."

"Really, my lord?" she asked, pretending to take offense.
"Why not?"

"Anyone who throws herself into a strange man's arms
with such wild abandon does not seem to me to have the
steadiness of character necessary for teaching."

"It *wasn't* a strange man's arms!" She turned her luminous
eyes up to his face and added softly, "I knew it was you."

There was something in her voice . . . in those eyes . . . that
made him catch his breath. The girl was captivating. If it
occurred to him, somewhere deep in his mind, that this surge
of feeling was completely inappropriate for the master of a
noble household toward a servant who was no more than a
child, he did not let the thought surface. He simply permitted
himself to enjoy the sight of her and indulge in what was
nothing but harmless banter. "I hope your pupils will not be
little boys," he teased.

"Oh? Why do you say that?"

"Because in your presence they will never be able to concentrate on their books." He continued to stare down at her,
noting the tiny freckles scattered over her nose and the fullness of her mouth that seemed curved into a tiny but permanent smile. Aware that he was in some way hypnotized, he
nevertheless had no desire to shake himself loose. Either the
candlelight was having a peculiar effect on him, he decided,
or the girl was a witch.

"Is that meant to be a compliment, my lord?" she asked, the corners of her mouth turning up even more.

"I suppose it is." He shook his head admiringly. "Do you realize that there must be more than a thousand ringlets escaping from your braid? Here, hold this!"

The order confused her. "What?"

He didn't answer but merely thrust his candle into her hand. Then, still feeling spellbound, he slowly tilted her head up and straightened her crooked cap.

She blinked, completely disarmed by the sweetness of the unexpected gesture. "Thank you, my lord," she murmured.

They stared at each other for a moment until he shook himself awake. "Now, *why* did I do that? You're only going to bed anyway."

She put a hand up to her cap. "I'm sure I couldn't say, my lord."

"No, I didn't think you could." He peered at her a moment more and then blinked to break her spell on him. In a manner that said that this business had gone quite far enough, he took his candle from her hand, said a brisk good night, and set off down the hall. But after taking three strides he stopped. "Tell me the truth, Emily Pratt," he said, turning back for a final look at her, *"was* there a rat?"

"Yes, my lord," she said with utmost sincerity, "there certainly was."

He grinned. "A really big one, eh?"

"Oh, yes, my lord. E*nor*mous." And with another bobbing curtsey, she turned on her heel and pranced off down the stairs.

chapter thirteen

The next morning dawned rainy and cold. Emily, standing at the window of her sumptuous bedroom and gazing out at the grim, gray sky, found herself wishing that she were back at Miss Marchmont's school. At school her days, even dreary days like this, were full of activity. Here at Edgerton, luxurious as it was, there was almost nothing for her to do except to feel wretched.

Of course, there was no real reason for her to feel wretched. What difference did it make that the revolting Toby didn't like her? What did his opinion matter, anyway? He was nothing to her, not in her real life. If she'd met him as herself, as Emily Pratt, he would have taken no more notice of her than he would of a housefly crawling on the wall. What made it more humiliating, however, was that even at her best—wearing Miss Jessup's loveliest gown and playing the piano in her very best form—she had put him to sleep. But why should she feel humiliated? The blame was more his than hers. After all, even Lord Edgerton himself had admired her that night, and anyone could see that his lordship had more intelligence and taste in his little finger than the odious Toby had in all his body! Besides, in little more than a week this adventure would be over, and she would never again lay eyes on Tobias Wishart. Why could she not dismiss him from her mind?

Wishing to avoid the unpleasant feelings that Tobias Wishart managed to stir up in her, she determined to banish all thoughts of him by concentrating, instead, on Alicia. She sat down on the window seat and reviewed in her mind the scene in Alicia's bedroom the day before. Remembering Alicia's woebegone expression when Dr. Randolph had left her room,

Emily was again struck by the obviousness of the woman's adoration of her doctor.

When Kitty arrived to help her dress, Emily recounted to her all she'd learned about Alicia's situation. "I think she truly cares for her doctor," Emily explained, "but everything she does seems to irritate him. It's almost as if her illness were a constant reproach to his medical abilities."

"But the doctor feels she isn't truly ill, isn't that what you said?"

"Yes. It *does* seem as if her condition is all in her mind. Of course, one can't be certain. Doctors have been known to be wrong. That's why I'm not sure I did the right thing in advising her to pretend to feel better."

"I think you gave her the very best of advice," Kitty said firmly. "Perhaps, if she pretends long enough, the pretense will become real."

"That's what I hoped when I said it," Emily admitted, "but what if she really is more ill than the doctor believes?"

"Then she'll be too ill to keep up the pretense for long. I don't see that there's anything to lose. When the doctor arrives today, let her greet him sitting up in a chair. That should give matters a cheerful start. I say, Emily, why don't you bring her my Prussian-red dressing gown to wear? It will give her cheeks a glow."

"Oh, Miss Jessup, *may* I? It's so good of you. That robe will be perfect!" She clapped her hands in enthusiasm. "And I'll curl her hair with a hot iron, and . . . and perhaps she'll let me rub a bit of blacking on her lashes, and—"

"Just a minute, my girl," Kitty said, holding up a warning hand. "Remember you're *not* an abigail. I cautioned you before that you'd have to stop 'doing' for people."

Emily's excitement faded. "Oh, dear, I *did* forget. I never dreamed that not *doing* for people would be so difficult." She paced about the room for a moment but then looked across at Kitty with a challenge in her eyes. "But wait, Miss Jessup! Wouldn't *you* be doing something to help Alicia if you were in your rightful place?"

"In my rightful place I probably wouldn't have even *noticed* Miss Alicia's predicament." She sighed ruefully. "It's strange, but acting as your abigail is making me see that I've been a very self-centered creature all my days."

"Now, Miss Jessup, that's not so. At school everyone thought you the most generous of friends. You were always sharing your things and buying sweets for everyone, and—"

"That was nothing. I always had more pin money than I needed. It's what's inside one that counts, and in my inside, I'm afraid, there was never much thought of anyone beside myself. Just this morning, when Miss Leacock came for me, it occurred to me that..." Kitty's face suddenly lit up. "Wait, Emily! *I* know how we can prettify Miss Alicia. We can ask Miss Leacock to do it!"

"Miss Leacock?"

"She's Lady Edith's abigail. And she dresses Miss Alicia, too. I can deliver the dressing gown to her and tell her you sent it. I'll explain your scheme to her. I'll say that everyone knows Kitty Jessup is a schemer; it will all be quite in character. I think Miss Leacock will be delighted to bring a little color into Miss Alicia's life."

Emily threw her arms about her friend. "Oh, Miss Jessup, that will be just the thing! I don't know how to thank you!"

Kitty, having already rummaged through the clothes chest and pulled out the dressing gown, bustled to the doorway with it. "You might thank me, *Miss Jessup*, by calling me Emily. I'm *Emily*, remember?"

Emily spent the morning pacing through the downstairs rooms, wondering how Alicia was faring. She kept herself from going up to call on the bedridden woman, fearing that she would find herself tempted to curl Alicia's hair or rouge her cheeks. *Emily,* she told herself, *you have to stop thinking like a maid-of-all-work if you are to get through this visit without giving yourself away.*

Lord Edgerton discovered her in the empty drawing room, staring longingly at the piano. His lordship was in the worst of moods. He'd been out with his bailiff to inspect the work being done to modernize his experimental dairy farm (a project in which he'd been interested for several years), but he'd been driven indoors by the icy rain. Not only had the weather interrupted his personal plan for the day but it presaged a long delay in the exterior work on the buildings. He was in the act of ripping off his riding gloves when his eye fell on her. "What is this, Miss Jessup? Are you alone again?" he demanded, unable to mask his irritability.

Emily started. "Oh! Your lordship! I didn't see . . . g-good day to you," she stammered, dropping a little curtsey.

"Why is it that I never see you with company, ma'am? You must be finding your stay here very dull indeed. I really must apologize to you. I've never known my family to be quite so inattentive to their guests before."

"No, please, my lord, there's no need to apologize. I don't expect everyone to dance attendance upon me every moment of the day."

"Not every moment, no. And not everybody. But one would think that by this hour *someone* would be down." He took a deep breath to ease his frustration. "There's no need to tell me that Alicia is, as usual, indisposed. But can Mama still be abed? And where the deuce is Toby?"

"This is just the sort of morning one *should* stay late abed," Emily assured him soothingly. "May I send for Naismith, my lord, and order some tea for you? You must be chilled through."

His irritation drained away, and he gazed at her admiringly. "You are so good-natured, Miss Jessup, that you put me to shame. Thank you. Tea would be most welcome, particularly so if you join me. But tell me, my dear, why do I never see you at the piano? Surely a talent like yours must have been developed by hours of practice. Don't you care to practice here?"

"I would love to practice here," Emily admitted, "especially since I've never before played on so fine an instrument. But I was afraid I would disturb the household with my noise."

"Disturb the household? Don't be foolish, child. The walls are so thick that the sound couldn't carry very far. And as for your 'noise,' as you call it, I fear that the only disturbance would be that everyone would feel tempted to gather round the door to listen to your music instead of attending to business. Please, Miss Jessup, I pray you, make use of the instrument whenever and for so long as you like."

They had their tea, after which Lord Edgerton excused himself. She must have flown to the piano immediately after he turned his back, for he heard her first chords before he'd closed the door behind him. He paused for a while at the door listening to her rendition of a Beethoven sonata before forcing himself to depart. He had a mission that could not be postponed.

A moment later he stalked into Toby's bedroom, tore the covers from the bed, and yanked the stupefied Toby to his feet. "You dashed bobbing-block," he swore between clenched teeth, "where is your breeding? Have you no manners at all?"

"Greg? Somethin' th' matter?" Toby asked, blinking and swaying on unsteady legs. "What've I done now?"

Edgerton glared at him and then let him fall back on the bed. "It's what you *haven't* done, you cursed jackanapes! Why aren't you *courting* the girl? Every time I come across her, the poor chit is *alone!* If she were merely an ordinary guest in this house, she'd have a right to expect more attention than she's been given, but the girl is more than that. She expects to be your *betrothed,* confound it! What must she be thinking? If this is the sort of neglect she has to endure in the *courting* period, what can she be expecting of the *marriage?* That you'll send her an occasional letter from distant parts and pay her a visit every Christmas?"

"Is it my fault she's a bore?" Toby muttered in sullen self-defense.

"She is *not* a bore. She is just a bit shy. You can't expect a young girl without experience to shine in strange surroundings, especially when you've made it clear you're disappointed in her. She needs drawing out, that's all."

Toby ruffled up his hair with despairing hands. "Dash it all, Greg, I don't know *how* to draw her out!"

"That's rubbish. You've plenty of experience flirting with females. Just spend some time with her and see what happens."

"How can I spend time with her? She don't *do* anything."

"What do you mean by that? What have you asked her to do that she couldn't?"

"She don't play cards, for one thing. The girl admitted to me that she'd never even played silver-loo!"

"She's cozening you. Lord Birkinshaw's daughter never played silver-loo? Impossible!"

"But that's what she said. And when I offered to go riding with her yesterday, she said she didn't ride."

"Didn't ride?" Greg's brows rose in astonishment. "That really *is* rubbish! Birkinshaw once told me that at the age of *twelve* the little minx stole a gelding from his stables and, dressed up like a tiger, raced the animal through the five-o'clock crush at Hyde Park so skillfully that the Regent sent an offer to hire her for his own stables. When he heard that the impressive tiger was none other than Birkinshaw's daughter, he invited the child to ride with him the very next morning."

Toby threw up his hands in a gesture of utter confusion. "Then why did she say she didn't ride?"

"I don't know. There's a great deal about Miss Kitty Jessup that puzzles me, I admit. Perhaps Birkinshaw said some idiotic thing to her to make her fearful of us. We'll get to the bottom of it one of these days." He sat down beside his brother and put an arm over his shoulder. "But in the meantime, Toby, do your best to entertain the girl. Talk to her. Take her riding, even if she says she doesn't ride. Tell her you'll teach her. If you make her feel at home, she'll be more likely to show her true colors. It's already plain to me that she's out of the ordinary. If you give her a chance, she may make it plain to you, too."

Toby made a face. "I'll give it a try, Greg. But if it would come to pass that *I* find her out of the ordinary, it'd be a blasted *miracle!*"

chapter fourteen

Emily had been playing Beethoven for more than an hour, completely absorbed and happy, when something—a breath, a slight movement, a change in the air—made her aware of another presence in the room. Startled, she whirled about on the bench. "Oh," she said, stiffening, "it's you."

The intruder was Toby, ensconced in a high-backed easy chair, his feet raised on an ottoman and his hands tucked comfortably behind his head. "Don't stop on my account," he urged. "Go on with your playing."

"No, thank you," she said, getting up quickly. "I've quite finished."

"That's not so." He, too, got to his feet. "You've got to learn not to tell so many whiskers, my girl. If you hadn't discovered my presence here, you would have gone on playing for some time, wouldn't you? Tell the truth, now, Miss Jessup. Wouldn't you?"

She put up her chin proudly. "Perhaps I would. But if we're going to tell the truth, then you can't pretend you wish to sit there and listen to me play, can you?"

"*Really* the truth?" He rubbed his chin ruefully. "Well, then, I admit that I ain't musical and that I don't go out of my way to attend concerts and musicales. And I really *abhor* being stuck for an evening listening to a gaggle of females sing in their high, quivery sopranos while their mamas beam and beg 'em to sing 'just one more little tune, my love.' But I've been sitting here for quite some time listening to you, and I must say that I was very impressed with how quick your fingers dance over those keys and how grand the sounds are that you bring out of that old instrument."

"Thank you, sir," Emily said with a slight, acknowledging bow, "that was the kindest thing you ever said to me. But how

103

much time was the 'quite some time' that you've been listening?"

"About fifteen minutes," Toby said. Then he shrugged. "Well, perhaps it was ten."

"Or perhaps five?"

He grinned. "Very well, five."

"Five minutes can be a long time for someone who isn't musical to listen to Beethoven, so I'll spare you any more. If you'll excuse me, sir, I shall leave you in peace."

He reached out and took her arm. "Don't go yet, Miss Jessup. I've come down particularly to seek your companionship."

She looked at him suspiciously. "Have you stopped speaking the truth so soon? I'm quite aware that you've been avoiding me for two days. You've told me to my face that you find me a bore. So why have you suddenly come seeking my companionship?"

He grimaced ruefully. "Must I tell the truth again?"

"It usually is best."

"Well, then, the truth is that Greg ordered me to."

"That's what I thought." She tried to ease her arm from his grip. "There was not the least need for your brother to coerce you, sir. I am perfectly content with my own company. Please consider yourself absolved from your obligations to me, and let me go."

"I will, of course, if you insist. But I wish you'd relent and sit down with me. We'll make a strange marriage if we can't even speak to one another."

Emily felt her cheeks blanch. "M-marriage?" she stammered.

His eyebrow rose. "Yes, marriage. Nuptials. Wedlock. Does my speaking the *words* frighten you? Or is it the thought of the actual *deed* that turns you pale?"

"I . . . I don't know." She turned a pair of frightened eyes up to his face. "You are so . . . blunt. I didn't expect . . ." She paused and bit her lip.

"Didn't expect me to mention it? Good God, Miss Jessup, didn't you think we'd even *talk* about it? Why do you think you're *here?*"

Her eyes fell. "Well, perhaps I *should* sit down with you after all," she said with a surrendering sigh.

He led her to the armchair he'd been sitting in and gallantly handed her into it. Then he perched himself on the ottoman. "There, that's better. Now, then, shall we jump right to it and talk about our marriage, or would you rather make some inocuous chit-chat first? Come, come, Miss Jessup, say *something*." When she still didn't say anything, he leaned forward and added encouragingly, "I know one thing we can speak of right away, and that is your name."

She threw him another frightened glance. "My name?"

"Yes. Do you expect me to call you Miss Jessup until our wedding day, or may I begin to call you by your given name? It seems to me we'd make real progress toward a more comfortable intimacy if we call each other Toby and Kitty."

Emily shifted in her seat. She knew she had to say something, but she didn't have any idea of how to conduct this interview. What was her attitude toward the marriage plan supposed to be? Was she to behave as if she accepted the wedding intentions with enthusiasm or as if she was only reluctantly acceding to the authority of her parents? Or should she act as if she had every intention of rejecting the plan in the end? *Good heavens,* she asked herself, *why hadn't she and Kitty discussed these questions before?* Meanwhile, Toby was sitting before her with his brows arched expectantly, waiting for a response. "I have no objection to your calling me Kitty," she said cautiously.

"Good," he said, "but—?"

"But?"

"I heard a *but* in your voice. What else did you want to say?" He waited a moment, but when he got no response, he jumped to his feet in annoyance. "I don't know why you're so afraid to say what's on your mind, Kitty. We Wisharts are not monsters, you know. We won't eat you."

"I know that. You must understand that it is difficult for me to speak of our . . . our marriage when I know that you don't desire it."

"But I *do* desire it," he said, seating himself again.

"You must be joking! You know you don't like me at all."

Now it was his eyes which fell. "I wouldn't say that, exactly. I like you well enough right now . . . now that we're being honest with each other like this."

"If we're being so honest, then admit that you'd never have chosen me if you were left to your own devices. You certainly can't believe that we'd suit."

"I'm not sure what I believe. Perhaps we might."

"What folderol! Name *one way* in which we might possibly suit! We've already eliminated music . . ."

He shrugged. "And games. And sports. But there are more important things that bring a man and wife together. Building a home . . . having babies . . ."

Emily gasped. "Babies!" The thought of having Toby's babies brought a surge of color to her cheeks.

"Good God, you're blushing," he exclaimed, teasing. "You *are* a prude."

"Yes, I am! Babies, indeed. How can you speak of having babies with a woman you don't even like?"

"That's jumping to a conclusion much too early in the game, my dear. I might like you a great deal in that way. Having babies together is certainly one way in which we might suit very well. We haven't tested ourselves in that direction yet."

"*Tested* ourselves? How could we possibly test ourselves?" Then, with a sudden gasp, she stared at him with revulsion. "Unless I misunderstand you, sir, you are making an utterly vulgar suggestion. So vulgar that I shall have to leave this room at—"

He chortled. "You *do* misunderstand me, Kitty. I only meant that we haven't tested our compatibility at *kissing.*"

Color flooded her cheeks again. "K-kissing?"

"Kissing. You have heard of it, I trust? One presses one's lips to the lips of one's betrothed . . . or one's sweetheart . . . and if the sensation is a pleasant one, the pair may consider themselves to be 'suited' for marriage in one of the most important ways."

"Bosh! No one can interpret so much from a mere kiss," Emily said decidedly, trying by an air of sophistication to cover her earlier gaffe.

"A *mere* kiss, miss? If one can call a kiss 'mere,' one hasn't been properly kissed at all. Here, let me show you."

And before she knew what he was about, he got to his feet, pulled her to hers, slipped an arm about her waist, and planted a very substantial kiss on her mouth.

In no way could that kiss be called *mere*. A better word, she realized much later, might be *provocative*. The first sensation it provoked in her was confusion. She'd never been held in a man's arms before, much less been kissed, so it took some seconds for her to grasp what was happening. When the confusion cleared, and she realized she was being very soundly kissed, she felt positively thrilled, for the sensation was even more intoxicating than she'd imagined in her girlish dreams it would be. But by the time he let her go, another, much more provoking and unpleasant sensation had taken over—humiliation. A proper lady, she told herself, would not be manhandled like this by a proper gentleman, certainly not in the gentleman's own drawing room. Whether the impropriety was Toby's or hers she was not sure, but she *was* sure that she should never have permitted such a thing to occur. He must hold her cheap to have done this to her.

Humiliation brought tears to her eyes. She pushed away from him and turned her back. "How d-dared you do such a th thing?" she demanded, her voice shaking.

The fellow actually laughed. "How *dared* I? I didn't think that question had been asked for a hundred years, except in those dusty, old-fashioned novels."

"You can certainly find innumerable ways to insult me," she cried, wheeling on him. "First you k-kiss me as if I were n-nothing but a vulgar little *doxie*, and then you c-call me old-fashioned. Well, I know what Ki—what a *real* lady would do to you now! She'd *slap your face!*" And Emily lifted her hand and swung at him with all her might.

He caught her wrist in midair. He gripped it in a painful, viselike hold and bent her arm back behind her until she had to fall against him to keep him from breaking it. His face was so close to hers that she thought the beast was going to kiss her again. But he only grinned. "I don't permit *anyone* to slap me, ma'am, not even the little chit who's going to be my wife."

"Your *wife?*" She wrenched herself from his hold. "I will *never* be your wife! I wouldn't marry you if—"

"Please don't say what I think you're going to say," he laughed, watching her stalk to the door. *"Please* don't say it!"

But she couldn't be stopped. She glared at him from the doorway and spat the words out as though nobody in the whole world had ever said them before. *"I wouldn't marry you if you were the last—"*

"I know, I know," he groaned mockingly. "If I were the *last man on earth."*

chapter fifteen

Kitty had been quite right about Miss Leacock's willingness to "prettify" Miss Alicia. Not only did she agree (with the restrained enthusiasm her excessively ladylike character permitted) to the scheme, but she invited Kitty to assist her. The two appeared at Miss Alicia's door precisely one hour before the doctor was due to arrive, armed with the Persian-red dressing gown, a curling iron, a small coal brazier, a pot of rouge, a vial of Honey Waters, and a box of Ivory powder. There were many more ointments, powders, and beauty-enhancing artifices they could have brought, but as Miss Leacock said, "we mustn't overdo, not this first time."

Miss Alicia did not, at first, show any enthusiasm for their plan for beautification. She claimed to be too weak to sit up, much less to dress or to "do up" her hair. But Kitty insisted that her mistress would be much offended if her gift of the dressing gown were not put to use. Miss Alicia, not wishing to hurt the feelings of the visitor who'd shown her so much kindness, finally agreed to allow Miss Leacock to drape her in the robe. The dressing took a great deal of effort and was accompanied by many sighs and groans, but when Miss Leacock held up a mirror to Miss Alicia's face and declared that it was "truly as-ton-ishing how the color manages to brighten your complexion," Miss Alicia looked almost pleased with herself and declared that she felt a great deal better.

Taking that declaration as an opening to push Alicia into agreeing to other adornments, Kitty urged the bedridden woman to permit her to curl her hair "just the way I did Miss Jessup's this morning." Alicia graciously acquiesced, and Kitty reached for the curling iron, which Miss Leacock had already set warming in the brazier in which she'd piled some glowing coals from the fireplace. Never having handled a curling iron in her life, Kitty didn't realize that the handle, also made of iron, became almost as hot at the tip when it had been heating in the coals for any length of time. Ignorantly grasping the handle in a firm grip, she received a painful shock. She dropped the iron with a shriek and began to hop about the room, shaking her hand vigorously to ease the burn.

"Good God, girl, you didn't pick it up without the holder, did you?" Miss Leacock muttered, thrusting a thick pad into her hand. "How could you be so for-get-ful?"

"Sorry," Kitty said, wincing in pain. Bravely trying to behave like any ordinary abigail to whom such accidents were undoubtedly commonplace, she picked up the curling iron with the pad and set it back in the brazier. Miss Leacock, evidently not intending to make a to-do over Kitty's scorched palm, returned to her task of dabbing Miss Alicia's face and neck with a wad of cotton soaked in the Honey Waters. Kitty, realizing with some chagrin that abigails' minor injuries were not going to be given the sympathy and loving care that a nobleman's daughter might expect in similar circumstances, blew a cooling breath over her throbbing palm, gave it one last shake, and set to work attempting to curl Miss Alicia's hair.

She was working on the third curl when Miss Leacock looked up from her own work and began to watch what the younger abigail was doing. After a moment, and with a strange look in her eye, she took the iron from Kitty's hand. "I think, Emily," she said with quiet firmness, "that *I* shall do Miss Alicia's hair myself, since I am more fam-*il*-i-ar with what she likes. You may wash her with the aromatic lotion, if you please."

When the work on the coiffure was completed, Miss Leacock suggested that Miss Alicia permit them to powder her face and black her lashes. The suggestion was immediately rejected. "You know what damage the tiniest use of cosmetics does to my delicate complexion, Miss Leacock," Alicia reminded her, waving away the paints and powders with a shudder. But a last look at herself in the mirror that Miss Leacock held up for her brought a smile to her lips. "You've done my hair very well, Miss Leacock. Very well. I like the curls you've arranged to fall over my forehead. It almost makes me seem a bit..." She gave a tiny giggle as she tried to think of an appropriate word. ". . . well, frivolous." But, as usual with Miss Alicia, her cheerfulness was a fleeting emotion; one dark thought or another always came along to cloud the little gleams of sunshine in her life. "Oh, dear," she said, her smile dying away, "you don't think Dr. Randolph will find the curls *too* frivolous, do you?"

"Oh, no, Miss Alicia, it's not in the *least* fri-vo-lous," Miss Leacock assured her.

"I'd wager Dr. Randolph finds them so attractive he'll accept your invitation to tea, just to see them again," Kitty ventured.

Miss Leacock threw her a look that said she was going too far. But Miss Alicia only looked thoughtful. "Invitation to tea?" she echoed faintly. "Why, I've never *dared*—"

"But of course you haven't," Miss Leacock murmured soothingly, plumping up her pillow. "He would never come to tea unless *you* were coming down. And he knows that you almost never feel well enough to do so."

"Yes, that's quite true," Miss Alicia agreed with a sigh.

The subject was dropped. But by the time Dr. Randolph arrived, the two abigails had propped Miss Alicia into a sitting position (by piling up an additional four pillows behind her back), tied the neck ribbons of the dressing gown into a charming bow at her throat, and (by dint of a great deal of coaxing) pinched her cheeks into a faint glow of pink.

The doctor was so startled at the sight of her that he gaped. "Well, well," he remarked, his face lighting up, "what have we here? Have you stumbled on some miraculous cure?"

"No, of course not," Alicia said, blushing. "I only put on this—"

"Miss Alicia followed your advice," Miss Leacock interrupted smoothly, "and did not take a single headache powder since you left. I do believe her health is taking a turn for the better."

"And about time, too," the doctor said, crossing to the bed and taking his patient's narrow wrist between his fingers. "I told you often enough, Alicia, that if you stopped relying on these medications you would feel better. And now look at you! One day of restraint and you're looking five years younger."

"Five years—!" Alicia smiled beatifically. "You cannot mean it, Hugh!"

"Of course I mean it." Still holding her hand, he sat down on the edge of the bed. "Now, when have you ever known me to offer Spanish coin?"

At this point, Miss Leacock and Kitty tiptoed from the room. As soon as they'd closed the door behind them, Kitty clapped Miss Leacock on the back, gleeful despite the burning pain in her palm. "I'd say that went very well, wouldn't you?"

But Miss Leacock didn't return her smile. "Never mind that," she said, frowning at Kitty with narrowed eyes. "Who *are* you, miss?"

Kitty's high spirits were immediately quenched. "Who *am* I? Wh-what do you mean?"

"Ye're no abigail, Emily Pratt. I've never yet met an abigail who didn't know how to handle a curling iron. I'd hazard a month's wages on your being some sort of im-pos-ter."

Kitty looked at her accuser with wide-eyed innocence. "But, Miss Leacock, I *told* you I'm not really an abigail. I was maid-of-all-work at the Marchmont Academy. Miss Jessup just hired me for a fortnight. She's keeping me as abigail until her visit here is over, and then I'm to return to the academy."

Miss Leacock shook her head. Taking Kitty's two hands in hers, she said, "No maid-of-all-work has hands like these. These hands haven't scrubbed floors or emptied slops in all their ex-is-tence. Are you going to tell me who you are and what ye're up to, or shall I tell Mr. Naismith that ye're some sort of humbug?"

Kitty winced. "Tell Mr. Naismith? You *wouldn't!*"

The abigail crossed her arms over her chest decisively. "I would and I will."

Kitty eyed the older abigail accusingly. "I thought you were my friend."

"One can't be friends with someone who has secrets."

"But you have a secret from *me,* don't you? And yet I wish to be *your* friend."

Miss Leacock drew herself up in offense. "What secret?"

"Your given name."

"Oh, pooh! That's a mere trifle . . . and not at all the same thing!"

"What if I swore to you that my secret is as trifling as yours? Would you trust me and stay silent a little while?"

"I don't know, Emily. I don't see how such a secret could be trifling. You might very well be up to something dreadful, like robbing the family."

"That's stuff and nonsense. Do I look like a robber to you?"

The abigail studied her intently. "Well, no, but—"

"If I give you my word that—"

At that moment Miss Alicia's door opened and the doctor emerged. "Ah, there you are, Miss Leacock," he said, beaming at her over the spectacles that always seemed to slip halfway down his nose. "I wish you to tell Lady Edith for me that I found Miss Alicia much improved. Perhaps her ladyship can encourage her to take some exercise while she is feeling so much better. Something simple, like a parade through the picture gallery or a stroll through the gardens on the next balmy day. I know it's too much to expect her to do any bending or stretching, but any little exertion might bring her to a more normal way of life. In any case, tell her ladyship that I'm encouraged. I'm *very* encouraged." He adjusted his spectacles, put on his beaver, and started down the hall. "Oh, yes," he added, glancing back over his shoulder, "and tell her, too, that I've accepted Miss Alicia's invitation to return later today, to tea."

"Good *gracious*," Miss Leacock exclaimed in an awe-struck whisper, staring after the doctor's retreating form, "he said he's coming to *tea!* She actually asked him to tea!"

"See? I knew it would work," Kitty said in triumph. "We make a good team, don't we, Miss Leacock?"

"I was beginning to think so," she answered, eyeing Kitty dubiously.

"Are you still suspicious of me? Good heavens, Miss Leacock, anyone can see I'm no criminal! I give you my *word.*" Kitty's tone and expression were convincingly earnest. "If I swear to you that I'm up to no harm, that my secret affects nobody but me, and that I will reveal it to you very soon, will you keep still about me 'til the end of our visit here?"

Miss Leacock sighed in surrender. She didn't really wish to bring trouble on the girl's head, for she was becoming quite fond of her. Besides, she found the younger woman very persuasive. "If you will swear that you're up to no harm . . ."

"I swear it on my honor," Kitty assured her.

"Very well then. I'll hold my tongue for a while. But how soon—?"

"How soon will I tell you?" Kitty laughed and planted a kiss on the older woman's cheek. "Right after you tell me your full name."

chapter sixteen

Kitty, excited by her success with both Miss Alicia and Miss Leacock, scurried to Emily's room to tell her the news. She knocked at Emily's door and heard a muffled sound within that might or might not have signified permission to enter. Puzzled, she opened the door carefully and stepped over the threshold. To her surprise, she found Emily rising hastily from the bed and making a feeble and completely unsuccessful attempt to staunch the flow of tears from her eyes. *"Emily,"* she exclaimed, quickly closing the door, "whatever is amiss?"

"Everything," Emily stated flatly, taking a deep breath and dashing the tears from her cheeks with the back of her hand. "I've brought everything c-crashing down on our heads."

Kitty crossed the room to her side. "It can't be as bad as that, even if they've found you out." With complete composure, she put an arm about Emily's waist and led her to the bed.

"They didn't find me out," Emily said, sinking down on the edge of the bed and expelling a trembling breath, "but it's the next worse thing."

Kitty sat down beside her. "If they didn't find you out, there *is* no next worse thing."

"Yes, there is. I've r refused him, you see."

"Refused him? Refused *whom?"*

Emily turned to stare at Kitty in surprise. "Why, Toby, of course. Whom did you think?"

"Oh, *him."* She made a waving motion with her hand that consigned Toby to eternal limbo. "Who cares about him?"

"Who *cares?* Good heavens, Miss Jessup, he fully expected to *marry* me . . . er . . . you!"

"I don't give a fig for his expectations. Don't tell me you were wasting your emotions weeping for the abominable Toby

115

Wishart!" She looked at Emily curiously. *"Were* you weeping for him?"

Emily looked down at the hands locked together in her lap. "No, I wasn't. I was weeping for myself. He . . . offended me, you see . . . deeply offended me."

"What, *again?* I say, Emily, I hope you slapped him this time."

Emily threw a quick, guilty look at Kitty's face. "No, I . . ." She shook her head and dropped her eyes again. "I'd rather not speak of it. But I must tell you that it was when he spoke of our . . . your marriage that I lost my head. When he brought the matter up, I became utterly flummoxed. You hadn't instructed me in what to say if the subject came up, you see. I didn't know if you wanted me to pretend to accept him, to say that this wedding was being forced on me, or to reject him. But then, when . . . when matters got out of hand, I . . . I told him I wouldn't have him even if he . . ." She twisted her fingers together tightly to keep them from trembling. ". . . if he was the l-last man on earth."

"Did you really say that?" Kitty asked, wide-eyed. "I didn't think anyone ever said those words in real life."

Emily covered her face in shame. "Well, I d-did."

Kitty could see that her friend needed comfort, but it seemed to her that Emily was unduly upset. "Why are you taking on so?" she asked. "I think it's perfectly *splendid* to have told him that, for it's nothing but the truth."

Emily slowly raised her head. *"Is* it the truth, Miss Jessup? Are you sure you don't want him?"

Kitty blinked. "Why on earth do you think we're enacting this masquerade in the first place?"

"I know why you *began* this enterprise, but that was before you met him. Now that you've seen him, don't you feel even a *little* less sure? After all, he *is* very handsome and d-debonair . . . and ch-charming, in his way . . ."

"I thought you said he's a rudesby," Kitty reminded her, watching her face through narrowed eyes.

"Well, yes, he behaves like a rudesby to me—horridly so! —but I . . . I think it's because I don't know how to . . . to handle him. Perhaps I bring out the worst in him."

"Are you suggesting that I might do better with him? That *I* might find him debonair and charming?"

"Yes, I think it very possible."

Kitty got to her feet, put her hands on her hips, and looked down at her friend with critical affection. "Do you want to know what *I* think, Miss Emily Pratt? I think you are in the gravest danger of falling in love with the fellow! I don't know why it is that the most innocent females always are attracted to the greatest bounders, but it seems to me that's just what's happened to you."

"Miss Jessup, *no!*" Emily cried, her eyes widening in horror. "I *can't* be!" And, throwing herself across the bed, Emily burst into sobs again.

Kitty, alarmed and contrite, sat down and leaned over her prostrate friend. "Don't take on so, Emily, please don't," she begged, patting the other girl's shoulder. "I wasn't really serious. You know how I make jokes about everything. Please don't cry."

Emily took a few deep breaths, brought her sobbing under control, and rolled over. "I'm a g-goose," she said, wiping her eyes again, "but it doesn't m-matter any more, in any case, because we'll be leaving now."

Kitty blinked. "Leaving?"

Emily sat up. "Yes, of course. Since I've refused him, there's no longer any reason for us to stay, is there?"

"No, I suppose not," Kitty muttered, feeling suddenly deflated.

Emily sat up, her spirits buoyed by the prospect of the end of the pretense that she'd been living for the past few days. "It will really be a most satisfactory finish to this adventure," she pointed out. "You'll have accomplished your aims without ever having been unmasked."

But as Emily's mood rose, Kitty found hers plummeting. She'd been immensely enjoying her stay here at Edgerton and was looking forward to the remaining days of her adventurous fortnight. She didn't want the adventure to end so soon. "Don't you think we should remain until my mother and father come to take us back?" she asked feebly.

"No, I don't think so at all. Why should we?"

"Well, we have no carriage, for one thing . . ."

"I'm certain that Lord Edgerton would provide one if I asked him. I can go to him and say that since we've discovered that Toby and I don't suit, there seems no purpose in our remaining together for the full fortnight. I can suggest that he provide us with a carriage at his earliest convenience."

"Yes," Kitty agreed reluctantly, "I suppose . . ."

It was now Emily's turn to stare at Kitty. "Good heavens, Miss Jessup, you sound as if you don't wish to leave. Don't tell me that you *want* to remain here until we're discovered! Can you really wish to endure the torture of being unmasked, of facing the accusations, the anger, the recriminations, the scolds, the punishments, the *shame—!*"

"Enough!" Kitty held up her hands in self-protection. "You've said enough to score your point. But we can't be hasty. First I must be certain that the Wisharts consider your refusal of Toby's offer to be final. Then I must decide where I'm to go from here. You can go back to school, but I can't, since Papa has withdrawn me. And I don't know what the effect will be on him if I appear unexpectedly on the Birkinshaw doorstep. Give me a day or so to think the matter through."

Kitty left Emily's room so distracted that she forgot to mention the success of the prettification of Miss Alicia. This latest turn of events had taken complete hold of her mind. It had all happened too abruptly for her to ascertain her best course of action. She needed to think, and the best place for that, in the circumstances, was her little room in the servants' quarters. There was barely an hour before she had to help Emily dress for tea, but she might get a little time to herself if she could make her way to her room before anyone discovered her. She had not been an abigail for long, but the few days had been long enough for her to learn that a servant was not given much time to herself. She knew that if Mrs. Prowne discovered her, she might very likely set her to polishing brass; if Mr. Naismith came upon her, he'd surely order her to set the tea table; or if Miss Leacock found her idling, she might very well suggest that "idle hands make bare feet," and that she'd make better use of her time pressing out Miss Jessup's morning robe. Only with a great deal of luck would she manage to elude them all.

She hurried down the hall toward the back stairs, hoping desperately that no one would discover her, but a footstep behind her caused her to peep over her shoulder uneasily. Fortunately, it was only Jemmy, the footman. She acknowledged his presence with a quick nod and hurried on her way.

But Jemmy would not be dismissed so easily. The new abigail had attracted his attention from the first, and this was the first time he'd encountered her alone. "Wait, little Em'ly," he said, running to catch up with her.

"I'm in a hurry," she said, not pausing.

"Whatever it is kin wait fer a bit," he said, grasping her arm. "I want t' talk to ye."

"Let go of me, Jemmy," she ordered curtly, "or you'll find yourself in trouble."

"Ye're worth a bit o' trouble," he grinned, pulling her close to him. And before she could utter a word, she felt a sharp nip on her posterior. She froze for a moment in astonishment. Why, the looby had *pinched* her! She'd felt it right through her bombazine, two stiff petticoats, and a thick pair of under-drawers!

She gasped. "Why, you . . . you blasted *bobbing-block!* Who gave you leave to take such liberties?"

The footman leered. "It's a rare pleasin' backside ye 'ave, see," he explained, quite unabashed.

"Oh, is it indeed?" Kitty demanded furiously. "Well, then, let's see how pleasing you find *this!*" And despite the pain that still throbbed in the palm of her hand, she let him have a sharp crack across the cheek.

"*Ow!* Ye damned she-cat!" he bawled, stung.

Mr. Naismith, emerging at that moment from her lady-ship's room where he'd been receiving her instructions for the serving of a rather special tea this afternoon, could barely believe his eyes at the sight in the corridor. That two members of his staff could hold an altercation in this part of the house was unheard of! "What sort of goings-on are *these?*" he demanded in an irate whisper. "This would be bad enough belowstairs, but this, I remind you, is the *front corridor!* His lordship's own bedroom ain't a step away, and the main stair-way's just ten yards behind. What do you think you're doing here?"

Jemmy rubbed a hand over his reddened cheek. "That little cat landed me a facer," he said sullenly.

"I might've known," the butler sighed, turning his eyes

upward. "Trouble goes along with her like it was her perfume."

"Is *that* what you've got to say?" Kitty demanded, too enraged to lower her voice. "Aren't you going to ask that jackanapes *why* I landed him a facer?"

"Hush, girl!" Naismith ordered in an undervoice. "Do you want the whole family to hear? I ought to drag you downstairs to face his lordship. P'rhaps *he'd* know how to scare the devil out of you!"

"Perhaps he would," a voice remarked from behind them. The three turned around to find Lord Edgerton regarding them curiously. "What's the to-do here, Naismith? Is there—Ah! Good afternoon, girl. Emily, isn't it? Don't tell me you've seen another rat."

"You might say so, my lord," Kitty responded promptly, glaring at Jemmy pointedly.

"Do you know this girl, my lord?" Naismith inquired. "If so, it won't surprise you to learn that she causes a to-do wherever she goes."

His lordship tried not to smile. "No, it doesn't surprise me. *Did* she discover another rat?"

"I don't know anything about rats, my lord. She evidently was molesting the footman here—"

Kitty exploded. "*I*? Molesting *him*? Of all the—!"

"Be *still*, girl!" Naismith hissed through clenched teeth. "Wait 'til you're spoken to!"

Kitty forced herself into submission. Furious as she was, it wouldn't do, she warned herself, to forget that she was playing the role of a humble household employee. She bit her tongue and lowered her eyes, but not before she noticed that Lord Edgerton was watching her with amused interest.

Lord Edgerton turned to the footman. "How, may I ask, Gerald, did this little slip of a girl molest you?"

"She slapped my face, m'lord. 'Ere, ye can see the mark of 'er hand, I wager." And he removed his own hand to reveal a large, red welt on his cheek.

His lordship's brow rose. "The girl must be a great deal stronger than she looks," he murmured. "Well, Emily, what have you to say for yourself?"

"He deserved it," she responded with alacrity. "I slapped him after he molested *me*."

Naismith snorted. "Gerald had been in our employ for seven years, my lord, and in all that time I've never known him to molest anyone."

His lordship studied each face in turn. "Tell me, Emily, just *how* did he molest you? Can you show us a red mark comparable to his?"

"No, I can't. I have one, I'll be bound, but in a place that's too private to reveal."

Edgerton almost laughed aloud. "Are you saying, you minx, that the idiot pinched your bottom?"

"I would not wish to express myself quite so vulgarly, my lord, but that is the gist of my accusation. And I don't find it nearly so amusing as you do."

Naismith turned quite red. "Watch your *tongue*, you disrespectful jade!" he hissed with apoplectic wrath. "I won't have you speaking to his lordship in that saucy way!"

"That's all right, Naismith," Lord Edgerton said, trying to be conciliatory. He was finding a good deal of enjoyment in this contretemps himself, and he didn't wish his butler to take the matter so seriously. "I've been the victim of Emily's disrespectful tongue before. She assures me that such sauciness, though not appropriate for an abigail, is very useful for a teacher, which she hopes one day to become. So perhaps we can excuse her."

"Excusing her is your privilege, my lord," Naismith said with icy disapproval, "but I would not advise it."

"No? What would you advise, then?"

"That you send 'er packing, my lord. Back to the Birkinshaws. Let them deal with her as they see fit. We can easily provide Miss Jessup with another abigail while she is here."

"But I don't see how we can do so before we've gotten to the bottom of this matter. We haven't even asked Gerald if he pinched the girl." His lordship turned to the frozen-faced footman. "Well, Gerald, are you guilty of this heinous crime?"

"No, m'lord," Jemmy answered, his expression turning innocent as a babe's. "I never touched 'er."

"Why, you lying *dastard*," Kitty cried, running at him with fists clenched, "I'll—!"

"Calmly, calmly, little firebrand," his lordship said, catching her up in his arms. "We can't let this matter degenerate into fisticuffs."

Kitty, squirming and wriggling in his hold, tried to kick herself free. "Just let me at him! Put me *down,* dash it all! The deuced liar. . . . I'd like to scratch his eyes out!"

"I won't put you down until you control your temper, my girl. And if you don't do so by the time I count to ten, I shall drop you down the chute into the coal hole, where I have no doubt you'll find rats aplenty! There, that's better. Now, do I have your word that you'll indulge in no more outbursts?"

She only half believed that he would carry out his threat, but even half a conviction was enough to cool her ire. She nodded meekly. "Yes, my lord."

He set her on her feet and waited while she straightened her apron and adjusted her cap. Then he cleared his throat. "With two completely contradictory stories, we seem to be at an impasse here. But I must agree with Naismith that the word of a fellow who's given seven years of exemplary service must be credited above that of a newly arrived wet goose with a saucy tongue."

"Well, of all the unfair—!" she blurted out, stung.

"Silence!" he ordered. "You gave your word there would be no more outbursts."

She opened her mouth to remonstrate, but one look from his no-longer-amused eyes stilled her tongue.

"Thank you for your support, my lord," Naismith said. Then he gave the footman a surreptitious poke in the ribs. When there was no response, he added with a touch of annoyance, "And Gerald thanks you, too, I'm sure."

"Oh, yes, m' lord," Jemmy said hurriedly. "Thank ye, m' lord."

Naismith now fixed his reproachful eyes on Kitty. "Shall I send this baggage back to the Birkinshaws, my lord?" he asked.

"No, I think not. If you have no objection, Naismith, I'd like to give her another chance."

Naismith had no choice but to bow his acquiescence. "As you wish, my lord." He snapped his fingers at his underlings, signaling them that the interview was over and that they were to go about their business. Jemmy, after throwing a barely perceptible look of triumph at Kitty, quickly melted away down the hall.

But Edgerton had caught the look. "I would like Emily to

remain here for a moment," he told the butler. "You may go, Naismith."

The butler bowed and soon disappeared down the stairs. Kitty, furious that his lordship had not supported her, put up her chin and eyed the master of the house with unflinching disdain. "I don't see that there's anything more to be said, my lord," she declared icily.

The look of amusement returned to his eyes. "I take it that in your opinion I did not show the wisdom of Solomon in my judgment," he remarked.

"Far from it," she retorted.

"Not so far from it, if you consider all sides. I knew perfectly well that you'd been pinched. But I could not undermine my butler's authority in front of his staff, could I?"

"Why not, if he's in the wrong?"

"He did not believe he was, and since the point couldn't be proved, it seemed best not to humiliate him."

Kitty pouted. "It was easier to humiliate me, is that what I'm to conclude?"

"You, my girl, are as utterly beyond humiliation as a duchess. I have never in my life come across a servant with so little humility. That's why I asked you to remain behind. I want to warn—"

"You asked me to remain so that you could *scold* me?" she interrupted in chagrin. "I thought it was to *apologize!*"

Edgerton's eyebrows rose. "Good God, girl, what a tongue you have! You *should* have been a duchess. Why on earth should I apologize? *I* didn't pinch you."

"That's true, you didn't. Well, then, my lord, say what you have to say."

"Ah! Then I have your permission, ma'am, to proceed?" he asked with a derisive bow.

She gave an answering curtsey. "Yes, my lord, do go on."

"Very well, but this is serious, my girl. Naismith is obviously very annoyed with you, and I can well understand it. I know that you'll say that this afternoon's incident was not your fault, but evidently there have been others that were. I myself was a party to two of them. I'm afraid, Emily Pratt, that you have a way about you that is not appropriate for your position. You've been here only a few days, but already you've come to my notice more than the housemaids I've employed here for years. I've indulged you thus far because you're clever and quick, but Naismith has made me see that I may have encouraged you in your propensity for insubordination. If you are to remain employed in this household, I suggest that you try for a bit more docility."

She lowered her head and stared at her shoes like a chastised child. "Yes, my lord," she said with all the docility she could muster.

"Mmm," he mused, staring at her suspiciously. Everything about her at this moment—her stance, her lowered eyes, the chastened tone of her voice—bespoke obedience, but there still remained about her an aura of an untameable spirit. Docility was just not in her nature. "Oh, bother!" he muttered under his breath. How had he become embroiled in this business anyway? "All right then, Emily, run along. Just remember that if Naismith has any more difficulty with you, I won't have any choice but to—"

"I know," she said, making a little *moue*. "Drop me down the coal chute with the rats." She gave him another quick curtsey. "Good day, my lord."

He watched her hurry off down the hall, the red-gold braid flapping against her back. She seemed to him to be an utterly delicious, charming creature, and he hated having had to take an avuncular tone with her. He was struck with an overwhelming desire to say something to her to soften the severity of the scolding he'd just delivered. "Emily," he called, striding after her, "one thing more."

"Yes, my lord?"

"Don't be too upset about the footman pinching you. It's just that you're too delectable." He grinned down at her with what he hoped was an air of paternal fondness. "If I were the footman, I might very well have pinched you, too."

"If *you* had done the pinching, my lord," she said, the saucy gleam returning to her eyes, "I might never have felt the urge to slap." And with a last laughing glint from her eyes, she scampered off.

He turned toward his office, smiling at the presumptuous daring of the girl. "The deuced little chit was *flirting* with me," he said to himself as he walked down the hall. "What a little vixen!"

It was too bad he hadn't met her at another time in another place. If he'd been younger . . . if she'd been a duchess . . .

He sighed. Life was only rarely structured as a man would like. If the world were a proper place, this little maidservant *would* have been born a duchess. She was perfect for the role. In fact, in a more logical world, she would have been Birkinshaw's 'wild, trouble-making minx' of a daughter, and the daughter would have been the abigail. The little maidservant fit Birkinshaw's description much more closely than her mistress. One could much more easily imagine *her* stealing her mother's emerald brooch or riding her father's stallion across Hyde Park than the quiet girl whose spirit only seemed to come alive at the piano. If anyone was a wild, trouble-making minx it was—

Greg Edgerton stopped in his tracks as the truth burst on him like a lightning bolt. Of course! It would explain every inconsistency! Everything about Miss Jessup that had been troubling him, and everything about the saucy little abigail that was incongruous, could be made logical by a very simple adjustment: one needed only to switch their identities. If Emily Pratt was really the Birkinshaw chit, and the quiet Miss Jessup was really Emily Pratt, then everything that had been happening since they arrived would make more sense. That was it, of course! He didn't know why the minx had done it, but he suddenly knew, as surely as he knew his own name, that the abigail was Kitty Jessup! *The mischief-making minx and her abigail had traded places!*

chapter seventeen

Greg Edgerton had been fatherless since the age of fourteen and had, by this time, become accustomed to taking charge of all matters in his household. When decisions had to be made, everyone in the family deferred to him. When something was amiss, it was left to Greg to set to rights; when something was confused, it was left to Greg to straighten out. Setting things to rights and straightening things out had become a habit with him. Therefore his first reaction to the confusion of the Jessup affair was that it was up to him to set the matter straight.

But a second reaction quickly followed. *Why not let Toby straighten out this coil himself?* he thought. It was just the sort of prank Toby might have devised if he'd been in the girl's place. Toby would undoubtedly take devilish delight in setting the matter to rights. Greg had no doubt that Toby would be greatly relieved to learn that his betrothed was indeed the wild-spirited girl she was reputed to be. And in the process of setting matters to rights, Toby and his bride-to-be would develop a bit of intimacy that would scarcely have been possible if they'd met in the ordinary way. Developing a feeling of intimacy with that roguish little imp would be a most delightful experience for his brother. Greg almost envied him. *Dash it all*, he thought, *I do envy him!*

Perhaps it was this feeling of envy that caused Greg to hesitate. Although he didn't know why, he found himself unwilling to reveal the truth to his brother just yet. Before he embarked on this course of action, he needed to give the matter some additional thought. For one thing, he was peculiarly reluctant to give the girl away. He was enjoying the feeling of being the only one in the household (besides the false Miss Jessup and the true one) to know the truth. And for another thing, he wasn't certain *why* Miss Jessup had embarked on this deception. He would certainly like to know what her intention was. Perhaps it would be wise to defer any action until he discovered just what her motive was. *No*, he concluded, *I won't tell Toby just yet.*

The most obvious motive for Kitty Jessup's masquerade, he reasoned, was that she wanted to look Toby over carefully before committing herself to the betrothal. If that *was* her reason, perhaps he should give her that opportunity. The chit had gone to a great deal of trouble to contrive this scheme. Why not watch and wait . . . and see how it would turn out? If in the end she decided she liked Toby well enough to submit to the betrothal, Greg couldn't help wondering how the minx would go about revealing her true identity. And conversely, what would she do to extricate herself from this coil if she decided that she *disliked* him? Greg found himself greatly fascinated by the possibilities, and he decided that he would not cheat himself of this delicious opportunity to watch the developments from the vantage point of his new awareness.

The next couple of days proved disappointing to him. He saw nothing of the real Kitty at all. Naismith was evidently keeping a close watch on the girl and occupying her with so many tasks belowstairs that she had few opportunities to show her face in those areas of the manor where Greg might come upon her. For the first time in the two decades that Naismith had been in the family's employ, Greg found himself wondering if the butler might be too severe with his staff. If he didn't catch a glimpse of the mischievous abigail soon, he'd be forced to ask Naismith the whereabouts of the dungeon in which he was hiding her.

Meanwhile, however, other household matters were beginning to come to Greg's notice. One was that his sister was leaving her bed and coming downstairs with surprising frequency. During these appearances, Alicia's conversation was remarkable for its lack of complaints and its diminishing reliance on descriptions of symptoms. At tea, especially when Dr. Randolph was present, it struck Greg that his sister was looking almost pretty!

A second matter that caught Greg's attention was his brother's attitude toward Miss Jessup—the *false* Miss Jessup, as Greg now thought of her. Though Toby still teased the girl unmercifully, his taunts were far less cruel than they'd been at first. In fact, they often seemed to Greg to be more flirtatious than unkind, but the girl didn't seem to find them so, for she often paled and turned tearful when he twitted her. Greg was sorry to see her so upset. She was a lovely creature who didn't deserve to be made unhappy.

The sham Miss Jessup was evidently exerting a beneficial effect on all of them. Alicia hinted that it was Miss Jessup who'd instigated the change in her "condition," Mama was charmingly animated in her company, and Toby seemed to be much less bored by being at home than was usual for him. In addition, the girl's evening performances on the piano were a rare treat for them all. Even Toby began to sit still for them and to watch her with astonishing attention. Greg couldn't help wondering where the real Miss Jessup had found her and how she'd convinced so upright a young lady to participate in this deception.

Emily, having no idea that Lord Edgerton was observing her with new eyes, was conscious only of her increasing discomfort whenever Toby was present. Every time he came into a room in which she sat, she felt herself tremble. If he said something to her unexpectedly, she jumped. She didn't know why he had so devastating an effect on her. A little scene that had occurred the previous afternoon was typical: Toby had been bound indoors by rain for the third day in a row and, having discovered her sitting on the window seat in the Blue Saloon staring mournfully out at the leaden sky, had asked her (in a tone she interpreted as bored desperation) to play a game of skittles with him. "It will help pass away a few hours," he said, shrugging.

Emily was not flattered by the implication that he was seeking her companionship as a last resort. "Isn't that a child's game?" she asked in her most superior manner, intending to give him a proper set-down. "One would think that at your advanced age you'd have outgrown your interest in it."

"Yes, one would, wouldn't one?" he replied lightly, ignoring the insult and fondly tweaking a curl of her hair. "But you know I'm just a boy at heart."

"Yes, that's quite true." She brushed his hand away. "A boy of not more than twelve."

"If I *were* a boy of twelve, you'd not refuse me, would

you? I'd go bail you're the sort who's invariably kind to dumb animals and helpless children."

"You sir, are far from helpless, even if your mental age *is* no more than twelve." She rose regally. "But, since I *am* a kind sort, I'll agree to play skittles with you for a bit."

Chuckling triumphantly, he led her to a large billiard room in the west wing of the house. The room, which had been Toby's playroom in his childhood, was now rarely used. Emily had never seen it before. She stopped in the doorway and looked about her with interest. There was a billiard table in the far corner, a huge toy chest under the windows, and a structure of climbing bars and ropes against the wall to the right of the doorway where she stood. But what caught her eye at once was a rocking horse standing in lonely splendor in a dark corner. Never in her life had she seen so beautiful a plaything.

While Toby went promptly to the toy chest to remove the nine pins and wooden balls that the game of skittles required, Emily crossed the room to the rocking horse and gazed at it admiringly. It had evidently been carved by a true artist, for everything from the flare of the nostrils to the arch of the braided tail had been shaped with loving care. Even the colors of the paint—the dark red of the horse's coat, the rich black of the mane, and the blues, greens, and gilts of his saddle and appurtenances—managed to exude a magical glow despite the fading caused by the dust of years. "Oh!" Emily breathed. "How lovely he is!"

"Lovely?" Toby, kneeling on the floor near the windows where he was setting up the nine pins for the game, looked up in surprise. "It's only my old rocking horse. One would think you'd never seen one before."

"Not one as beautiful as this."

He got up and went to her side. "Good God, girl, you look positively wistful. Do you want to ride him?"

She smiled and shook her head. "No, of course not. I was only thinking how much my little . . . that is, how the little girls of Miss Marchmont's lower school would love a plaything like this."

"Then let's send it to them. I'll have Naismith see to it."

Emily gasped. "Oh, no! I didn't mean—! I couldn't let you

give it away. You should keep it for your own children . . . the ones you'll have some day."

He grinned down at her. "You mean *our* children, don't you?"

She felt her heart give a sudden thump. "I don't mean anything of the sort," she answered, turning a deep red.

His smile broadened as he took her arm to lead her to the skittle alley he'd set up. "Don't trouble yourself about it, my dear. I'll send the horse to your Miss Marchmont, and when we have our first child, I'll have a new rocking horse made . . . so magnificent that it will put this one to shame."

"I wish you would stop talking fustian," she murmured, putting a hand to her burning cheek.

It was not until after she'd beaten him soundly at skittles that the color in her face returned to its normal pink. Later, when she learned from the butler that the horse had been sent to the Marchmont Academy that very afternoon, she was almost moved to tears. And, as additional evidence of Toby's devastating effect on her, the recollection of his words, ". . . *when we have our first child,*" kept echoing in her ears through half that night.

Fortunately, the next day dawned bright and sunny. Everyone in the household was cheered by the change in the weather. Edgerton set out early to supervise the renewed work on the dairy farm. Lady Edith took a stroll through the gardens. Alicia permitted Miss Leacock to dress her in a becoming yellow morning gown and actually came down to breakfast. And Emily sat down at the piano and played with enthusiastic energy for two hours. When she finished, she turned on her seat to find Toby, in his riding clothes, sitting before the window watching her. "How long have you been listening this time?" she asked.

"Since you started."

"But that was two hours ago!" She narrowed her eyes in disbelief. "You *couldn't* have been sitting here for two hours."

"Oh, but I was. I've been waiting to ask you to ride with me, but I didn't want to interrupt."

"Then you've quite wasted your morning," Emily said with a touch of malicious satisfaction. "I've told you before I that I don't ride."

"Yes, so you said. But come anyway. I'll teach you. Every well-bred young lady should ride, you know."

She shook her head stubbornly. "I don't even have a riding costume."

"Shame on you, Miss Kitty Jessup. That really *is* a whisker."

"Are you calling me a liar?" Emily demanded, taking immediate offense again.

"I'm afraid I must. You see, I sought out your abigail and told her to get your riding clothes ready. She said she'd do so at once. So, miss, you obviously *do* have riding clothes."

Emily colored. "You had no right—!"

"Please, Kitty, let's not quarrel. It's a lovely day for riding. Do go up and change. Your abigail's waiting to dress you right now. You may as well say yes, ma'am, for I don't intend to take no for an answer."

Emily hesitated and then shrugged in reluctant agreement. She had been wondering if she could endure spending the rest of the day wandering through the chilly rooms, all of which she'd explored many times already. This outing would at least bring some variety to her day. "Very well," she said, striding purposefully to the door, "but I warn you, Toby Wishart, that if you find me a bore in the drawing room, you'll find me much worse on a horse."

Kitty, while helping her into the riding dress, tried to allay her fears. "Sitting a horse is as easy as pie," she declared, "so long as you don't become tense. You mustn't allow the horse to sense that you're fearful."

"But I'm more than fearful," Emily asserted. "I'm terrified."

"There's absolutely no need to be. Just sit easily, hold the reins with a light hand, and keep the animal to an easy canter. Tell Toby you don't wish to gallop today."

"But even with an easy canter I could fall, could I not?"

"You won't fall. One isn't thrown by a horse that only ambles along. And if you should feel unsteady, just take one hand from the reins and grasp hold of the pommel. That'll make you feel secure, I promise you."

That advice, and the sight of her face under the charmingly feathered, tilted-brim riding cap, gave Emily the courage she needed. She joined Toby in the front hallway, and when she saw the appreciative gleam in his eyes at her appearance in riding garb, her confidence soared. She strolled out to the stables with him, feeling almost jaunty.

Toby, remembering his brother's claim that the girl was really a superb rider, chose a spirited mare for her. "You'll like Carlotta, Kitty. This black-coated charmer was named for her Spanish sire, Carlos El Maligno, an evil-hearted devil of an animal. She inherited his wonderfully springy step."

"I'd rather have a slug," Emily muttered, eyeing the dancing horse dubiously.

Toby laughed. "We don't own a slug, I'm afraid. You'll have to make do with this beauty."

He helped her up, and they set off down the bridle path at an easy gait. Emily felt a moment of terror at the unexpected height of the horse, but once she became accustomed to sitting so high above the ground she was able to relax. Carlotta seemed perfectly docile, and after a little while Emily decided that Kitty had been right; riding a horse was not so difficult.

To her great surprise, Emily began to enjoy herself. It was lovely to be so comfortably seated in this gently rocking saddle, her skirts draped gracefully over the horse's side and her silk neckerchief whipping out behind her in the wind. She felt like a noble lady in an Arthurian romance, riding out in stately elegance toward some great adventure. She glanced over at Toby. He seemed so handsome and manly astride his prancing steed that he fit perfectly into her imaginary romance. He was (at least momentarily) her Gawain, her gallant knight, a medieval hero ready to ride into danger at her behest or joust with a fierce foe for her honor. At that moment he met her eye. Holding his prancing gelding in tight rein so that he could keep abreast of her, he threw her a warm smile, as if he knew —and shared—her secret thoughts and felt the same pleasure she was feeling.

A surge of joy swept through her at what she saw in his eyes, but she quickly looked away lest he see too much in hers. Instead, she drew in a quick breath and looked about her. The view from atop the mare was new to her and amazingly beautiful. The fields stretching out before her were rimed with frost and seemed to shimmer in the sunlight like a silver sea. The horses' breath turned to mist in the cold and rose up to blend with hers. The air was crisp and clear, tingling her cheeks and the tips of her ears, and the wind was just sharp enough to bring an effervescence to her blood. She'd had no idea, until this moment, that a ride on horseback could be like this.

But Toby, not really the gallant knight she was imagining him to be, was not the sort to endure a sedate amble for very long. "Let's race over that rise to the home woods," he suggested eagerly.

"No, thank you," Emily said, waking abruptly from her daydream, "I don't care to gallop today."

"Nonsense, my dear. This is a perfect day for racing. You needn't fear that I have too much advantage over you, you know. I've given you one of the fleetest animals in our stable. And to prove that I'm more than fair, I'll allow you a fifty-yard lead."

"But I told you, Toby, that I really don't ride."

"You also told me you didn't have a riding costume. I don't know why you insist on telling me such rappers. I have it on excellent authority that you're a *ripping* horsewoman."

"It's not a rapper, Toby, I swear! This is the first time I ever—"

"Well, let's see about that, shall we?" Toby, with a roguish grin, lifted his riding crop and whipped it across the mare's flanks. Carlotta, daughter of Carlos El Maligno, shivered to life and set off in a headlong gallop across the field as if possessed of the evil spirit of her forebear. She disappeared over the rise in a trice, but not before Toby caught a glimpse of Emily's terror-stricken face. *Good God*, he thought, his heart clenching in panic, *have I made a terrible mistake?*

He spurred his mount instantly in pursuit, but he heard her scream before they'd gone a yard. He raced at breakneck speed across the field, but as soon as they flew over the rise, he saw the sight he'd been dreading and brought his horse up short. She lay face down on the ground before him, absolutely unmoving. "Oh, *God*," he moaned as he flung himself from his mount, "I've killed her. Dear God, don't let me have killed her!"

He knelt beside her, heart pounding and hands trembling. He stared at her for a moment, afraid to touch her. One of her arms was buried beneath her and the other was flung out over her head. Her hat was lying a few feet beyond her outstretched fingers, and her hair, which had been pinned into a neat bun, had loosened and fallen in a twisted rope over one shoulder. Her silk scarf lay limply across her back, quivering in the wind. It was the only sign of movement he could detect.

He bent over her. "Kitty?" he whispered into her ear. "Kitty?"

There was no response, but a little wisp of mist floated from her almost-buried nose. She was breathing! Gently he turned her over. She groaned softly but did not open her eyes. He lifted her head and shoulders from the ground, bracing her back with his arm and resting her head on his shoulder. "Please, Kitty, say something," he pleaded. "Be the sweet little kitten that you are and tell me you're all right!"

Her eyelids fluttered, and her eyes slowly opened. She focused her gaze on his face, but the expression in her eyes was vague and disoriented, as if she were deep in a dream. Then, to his astonishment, her lips curved in a slow smile and two lovely, vertical dimples appeared in her cheeks. She lifted one hand like a somnambulist to his face and traced the line of his jaw with one finger. "Gawain . . ." she breathed.

"Gawain? I ain't Gawain." He searched her face fearfully. "Who the devil's Gawain? Good God, the fall must've rattled your brains! Don't you know me, Kitty? Look at me, girl! Don't you recognize me at all!"

She blinked her eyes and groaned. The face of the handsome knight of her dreams was transforming itself into that of Toby Wishart, with his roguish eyes and self-indulgent, thick-lipped mouth that had so often in the past few days mocked her unmercifully. But now those eyes looked painfully distracted and the mouth was twisted into an agonized grimace. She realized all at once that she was lying on the ground, that he was holding her in his arms, and that his distraction had something to do with her. Slowly, as if her brain were functioning under water, everything drifted back to her. The ride, the horse's sudden dash over the hill, the fall . . . it was all returning to her consciousness. And she was becoming aware, too, of a painful throbbing in her forehead and excruciating soreness in various parts of her body. She wanted to close her eyes and sink back into the foggy nothingness from which his voice had roused her, but the agony in his face touched her and kept her from sinking into a swoon. "I know you, Toby," she managed to whisper.

He gave a convulsive shudder and clutched her to him. "Oh, you darling girl," he muttered into her neck, "you *know* me! Thank God!" And, in blessed relief, he lifted his head and kissed her with an intensity of feeling he didn't even know he possessed. He felt himself trembling all over. Never had he kissed a woman in quite this way. Was it relief, he wondered, that had set him shaking like a schoolboy, or was this something else?

Emily, bruised and shaken though she was, couldn't help noticing that this kiss of his was quite different from the last. When he'd kissed her in the drawing room, he'd been very much in command of the situation. This time the arms with which he clutched her were quivering with an emotion over which he seemed to have no control. She, too, wondered if this reaction of his was merely relief that she hadn't been seriously injured or something much more significant. "Oh, *Toby*," she gasped, wide-eyed, when he released her, "what is it? Did I frighten you so dreadfully? There's no need to tremble so, really there isn't. I'm only bruised."

"Are you sure? Try to move your arms and legs." Without taking his supporting arm from her back, he got to his feet. "Here, let me help you up. Can you stand?" And with the greatest solicitude, he gently lifted her and set her feet on the ground.

She felt dizzy and sore but she was certain nothing was broken. "There. I'm standing. And I shall be able to walk back if you give me an arm. So you needn't look at me any longer with that stricken look."

"Do I look stricken? If I do, it's because this was all my fault. I thought . . . Greg said he was certain you'd been riding since childhood. I don't know how he can have made such a mistake. But I'm not trying to place the blame on his shoulders. It is all mine. When you told me you didn't wish to gallop, I should've listened to you. I don't know how to apolo—"

"It's not necessary," Emily said, cutting him short. She realized all too well that her lie about her true identity was more to blame for this accident than his whipping the horse. "I . . . forgive you."

"I don't know why you should," he muttered in self-re-proach, abruptly lifting her up in his arms, "for I don't forgive myself."

"Heavens, Toby," she protested, "what are you doing? Put me down!"

"It's more than a mile to the manor house from here. The least I can do is carry you home." He shifted her higher upon his chest and started off. "After a fall like yours, you must be put to bed and checked by Dr. Randolph."

"But you can't carry me all that way. Please, Toby, I am quite well enough to—"

"Be still, woman, and don't be forever arguing with me. I can put my breath to better use than to banter with you, you know. You ain't a featherweight."

But in truth he was enjoying the weight of her in his arms. He was sorry, when they came to the door, that he had to put her down. It was only his concern for the whereabouts of the horses that made him release her on the doorstep. "Will you be able to manage the stairs on your own? If you can, I think I'd better get back and see if I can find the horses."

"Yes, thank you, Toby, do go on. I shall be fine."

He held the door for her and watched her pass him by. "Kitty?"

She turned back curiously. "Yes?"

"It's the most astounding pass. I never expected . . . but I do believe . . ." He threw her a sheepish grin. "What would you think if I told you I was falling in love with you?"

She felt her heart give a little lurch in her chest. "In *love* with me? *Are* you, Toby?"

"I think so. Would it please you if I were?"

The look on his face was so surprisingly, sincerely, boyishly eager that it stirred her deeply. For a moment she forgot who she really was. "Yes. Oh, *yes*," she breathed, fix-ing her wide eyes on his face. But the truth of her deception was never far from her consciousness, and she immediately realized the necessity of retracting. She sighed a long, linger-ing sigh. "If only . . ."

"If only . . . ?" he prodded.

She stared at him for a moment, longing to throw her arms about his neck. But she wasn't Kitty Jessup, and she had no right to let this scene go on. "If only I were . . . someone else.

You mustn't let yourself fall in love with me, Toby. You mustn't!"

"Why not? Is it that you've fixed your affections on some other fellow?" His smile gave way to a sudden glower, and he strode into the Rotunda and grasped her hands. "Look at me, Kitty! Is it that Gawain fellow you named in your delirium? Is it he who stands between us?"

She gave a gurgling laugh that was half a sob. "Oh, Toby, you *are* a fool! Gawain was one of King Arthur's knights of the round table."

"Oh, is *that* who he was?" Toby, not a bit abashed at his ignorance, exhaled a relieved breath. "Well, I don't see why you should laugh. I told you I ain't bookish. But if this Gawain is only some dead fellow in a book who can't possibly be a rival, then I don't see why I mustn't fall in love with you."

"Take my word for it, Toby. You mustn't."

"But *why?*"

"Because," Emily said, dropping her eyes and slowly turning away, "I am the wrong girl for you. The very wrongest girl in all the world."

chapter eighteen

At the very time that Emily was falling off her horse, Miss Leacock was making a revelation to Kitty in the sewing room. The sewing room was a small, cozy place where the fire was always burning, where the ironing board was always set up, and where a tired abigail could find refuge. It was shabbily cheerful, with two high windows through which the afternoon sun slanted in cathedral-like majesty. One of the walls was covered with little spokes that held spools of thread of every color imaginable. The room also contained a worktable (which stood against the wall under the windows), a number of shelves containing fabrics and button boxes, and a padded mannequin of Lady Alicia's form on which a half-made blouse of ecru silk was presently pinned.

Kitty liked this room best of all the rooms in the servants' quarter, but what pleased her most of all were the room's two armchairs. Worn and ragged though they were, they were thickly upholstered and very comfortable. There was also a padded footstool set between the two chairs, large enough to hold two tired pairs of feet. Since only Bess, the resident seamstress, and the two abigails ever used the sewing room, it became a convenient hideaway when the busy maids needed a moment to put their feet up.

Miss Leacock and Kitty met there almost every afternoon, for it was the place where they mended small tears in their mistresses' gowns, pressed out their petticoats, and did whatever other little chores were necessary to prepare the ladies' dinner clothes for the evening. On the afternoon that Miss Leacock made her revelation, she was sitting on one of the armchairs, her feet up on the footstool and her hands busily fashioning a lace collar with only a crocheting needle and a spool of white thread. Kitty stood at the ironing board struggling mightily in her attempt to press out the flounce along the hem of a blue muslin gown that Emily would wear that evening. Between the soreness of the burn on her palm and the fullness of the flounce, she was having the greatest difficulty. Nevertheless, she managed to glance across the room several times, admiring the dexterity with which Miss Leacock managed her crocheting needle and the beauty of the lacy concoction that seemed to emerge from her fingers like magic.

Neither one of them spoke for a long while. Then, out of the silence came Miss Leacock's voice. "The name is Thisbe, you see," she remarked without preamble.

"What?" Kitty gaped at her stupidly, unable to make sense of the remark, which seemed to be part of a conversation that Miss Leacock had been conducting with herself.

"You said ye'd tell me your story if I told ye my name. Well, my name is Thisbe."

"Thisbe? Like the Thisbe who was supposed to be eaten by a lion but later perished for love of Pyramus?" Kitty bit her lip to keep from laughing. The image that flashed through her mind of the decorous Miss Leacock fleeing from the lioness on her large bare feet with her corkscrew curls bouncing was ludicrous indeed. But it wouldn't do to tease the abigail; she was evidently very sensitive on the subject. "It's a very romantic name," Kitty said soothingly. "I don't see why you're ashamed of it."

"I'm not ashamed of it. It's just that it doesn't suit me." She gave an embarrassed giggle. "Thisbe Leacock. It makes me sound like a Vauxhall Gardens fancy piece."

Kitty blinked. "What's a Vauxhall Gardens fancy piece?"

The older abigail's fingers ceased their work as she looked up at Kitty in surprise. "Good gracious, girl, you *are* an in-no-cent. Have ye never heard of pets of the fancy? Ladybirds? *Chères amies?*"

"Yes, of course I have," Kitty said with more confidence than she really felt. "A pet of the fancy is . . . well, like an opera dancer, is she not? A woman of loose character? The sort who's offered a *carte blanche* by a gentleman who is unhappy in his marriage?"

Miss Leacock resumed her crocheting, smiling to herself at the girl's obvious innocence. "Yes, or who doesn't wish to marry at all."

"Oh, I see. Then a Vauxhall Garden fancy piece is such a woman who is found at Vauxhall?"

"At Vauxhall, or Castle Tavern or one of a dozen other places." She glanced across at Kitty with a mischievous gleam. "Lily says that Lord Toby had one of them tucked away at Limmer's Hotel, but that his lordship discovered her and bribed her to disappear."

"Toby Wishart kept a *mistress?*" Kitty queried, shocked. "What a deuced loose fish the fellow is, to be sure!"

"I don't know," Miss Leacock demurred. "He's not so different from most of the men in his circle. Keeping a mistress is not at all unusual."

"It's not?" Kitty gaped at the other woman for a moment and then resumed her ironing, her brow wrinkled thoughtfully. After a long while she looked up again. "Has . . . does his lordship keep a f-fancy piece?" she asked, trying to make the question casual.

"Oh, I don't think so," Miss Leacock responded promptly. "A very proper gentleman, his lordship. Though I suppose one can't be certain. He was once engaged to Miss Helen Inglesham, and she, ye know, was the most e-le-gant of females. A man who chooses someone like Miss Inglesham isn't the sort to keep a mistress."

Kitty resumed her ironing with angry vigor. "Then why didn't he marry the so-elegant Miss Inglesham?"

"They were to be married three years ago this fall, but it was the time that Miss Alicia was taken with her first spell. We all thought she was on the verge of death. The wedding had to be postponed. Then, when she recovered, Lord Edgerton decided to go abroad to study the French system of dairy farming. He was gone so long that Miss Inglesham must have believed he'd lost interest. She married the Earl of Glenauer and now has two babies."

"Oh." Kitty carefully replaced the iron on the coal brazier and frowned down at the flounced gown. "Do you think his lordship is . . . sorry?"

"I don't know. A thing like that . . . it's hard to say."

"What was this Inglesham woman like?"

"Oh, very lovely. Tall and willowy, ye know, with the most graceful fingers. I remember when she came here to visit—I was helping to serve the tea that day—I remember that she picked up her cup with such delicacy that I couldn't take my eyes from her bea-*ut*-i-ful hands."

"Mmmmph!" Kitty grunted, involuntarily looking down at her own hands, which were far from bea-*ut*-i-ful. The right, with its burnt palm, was bandaged with a worn and begrimed handkerchief, and the left, after only one week of household labor, was already becoming red and rough. "If Lord Edgerton is the sort who seeks out elegant ladies with graceful hands," she snapped, pulling the evening dress from the board in irritation and stalking to the door, "he's not the man I took him for."

"Goodness, what did I say to set ye so off the handle?" Miss Leacock inquired in surprise. "And where might ye be going so ab-rupt-ly? Ye can just take yerself back here and sit down. You have to keep your part of the bargain."

"Bargain? What bargain?"

"You said ye'd tell me your name if I told you mine. Well, I've told ye. Why do ye think I revealed it to ye if it wasn't to get something in return?"

"You know my name," Kitty said evasively. "It's Emily Pratt."

"It may be," Miss Leacock retorted, "but there's more to yer story than that."

Kitty shook her head. "I'm sorry, Miss Leacock, but it's too long a story to tell you now. I have to bring this gown to Miss Jessup's room. We'll talk about it sometime soon, I promise."

The older abigail frowned. "How soon?"

"In a few days. I give you my word to reveal all to you in a few days." And before Miss Leacock could protest, she whisked herself out of the room.

Miss Leacock shook her head in annoyance, put aside her crocheting, and was starting to rise from her chair when the door opened again. It was the young abigail, poking her head round the door and peeping in. Miss Leacock sat back and asked hopefully, "Changed yer mind, Emily Pratt? Have ye decided to make yer con-fes-sion?"

"No, not that. Only to tell you that you're wrong about your name." She threw the older woman an affectionate grin. "If you ask me, the name Thisbe Leacock is positively bea-*ut*-i-ful."

chapter nineteen

Emily's climb up the stairs proved more difficult than either she or Toby had anticipated. A stabbing pain in her hip made itself noticed at the first lift of her foot, and when she clutched the bannister to support herself, she almost cried out from the even greater pain in her shoulder and arm. By the time she reached the top, her whole left side was throbbing. She managed to reach her bedchamber by clinging to the hallway wall, but as soon as she stepped inside the room and closed the door, she fainted away.

It was Kitty who found her. She'd come up intending to help Emily change from her riding clothes to the newly pressed dinner gown. Terrified at the sight of her friend sprawled unconscious on the floor, she first tried to bring her round by calling her name and patting her cheeks. When this method failed, she forced herself to be calm and searched through the bottles on the dressing table for the sal volatile. One whiff of the salts brought Emily back to consciousness. Kitty, awash in guilt for having encouraged Emily to ride, couldn't seem to keep her knees from trembling uncontrollably. Nevertheless, she helped her friend onto the bed and gingerly removed her boots. Then, remembering that she'd heard Miss Leacock remark that Dr. Randolph was expected again this afternoon to take tea, she raced downstairs to see if he was still on the premises.

She caught him at the doorway, attended by both Mr. Naismith and Miss Alicia. While the butler helped him into his caped overcoat, Alicia hovered about, clutching his doctor's hat and medical bag while awaiting the opportunity to say a private farewell. Under normal circumstances, Kitty would have remained hidden in the background to observe the coy glances exchanged between the doctor and his now-favorite patient, but at this moment she was too alarmed about Emily's condition to hold back. "Dr. Randolph," she cried, bursting in on the little group, "you must come at once!"

Mr. Naismith glared. "You've not had permission to *speak!*" he hissed. "Can't you ever—"

"You don't understand! Em—er, Miss Jessup's taken a tumble from her horse! I found her fallen senseless on her bedroom floor!"

The doctor did not have to hear more. It did not even occur to him to question the illogic of someone's falling from a horse onto a bedroom floor. He snatched his bag from Alicia's hand and ran immediately to the stairs, with Kitty close behind. Naismith, well able to distinguish between major and minor problems, did not bother to reprimand the abigail again. Instead, he hurried after them, knowing that his assistance might be needed upstairs. Alicia wavered on her feet for a moment, as if she, like poor Miss Jessup, would faint dead away, but love had so strengthened her character that she quickly got hold of herself. "Alicia," she said to herself aloud, "you will be strong!" With that, she squared her shoulders and followed the others up the stairs.

Kitty and the others entered the bedroom to give the doctor whatever assistance he required. Kitty helped to remove the white-faced Emily's clothes and, during the doctor's examination of her bruises, squeezed her hand when the injured girl cried out in pain. After a thorough going-over, the doctor lifted Emily's head from the pillow and discovered a smear of blood. Kitty saw the smear, too. "Oh, my God!" she cried. "Look!"

Alicia clutched the bedpost. "It's *blood!*" she gasped, whitening. "She's bleeding *profusely.* I think I . . . I'm going to *swoon!*"

"You will *not* swoon," the doctor snapped, throwing Alicia a quick glance of reproof. "The girl has a minor laceration here on her scalp. Scalp wounds tend to bleed rather freely. No need to make a fuss." He examined Emily's head, bound it round with a length of gauze bandage, and settled her back on her pillow. "Now, Naismith and I are going to have to set a bone," he announced, rising from his place at the side of the bed.

"A bone?" Kitty gasped, exchanging looks of consternation with her white-faced friend. "What bone? Is it . . . broken?"

"I shall tell you the details in due time," the doctor responded with what Kitty thought was infuriating terseness. "Alicia, you and the abigail are to wait outside."

"Yes, Hugh, if you wish it," Alicia said, looking chastened and ashamed. "I'm sorry if I behaved foolishly a moment ago."

"No need to apologize," the doctor said, softening. "I don't know why the sight of blood causes such consternation among the uninitiated. But you must learn to observe bleeding with dispassion, my dear, if you intend—" He stopped himself in midsentence and blushed.

"Yes, Hugh . . . I forgot," Alicia mumbled, blushing also.

Kitty took no notice of this interesting little exchange. "May I not stay?" she begged the doctor.

Mr. Naismith growled and looked skyward. "You heard the doctor, did you not? Wait outside!"

"It's all right, Emily," the white-faced Emily said, trying to give Kitty an encouraging smile. "I'll be all right."

Kitty and Miss Alicia waited anxiously in the corridor outside Emily's door, both of them too absorbed in their own thoughts to engage in conversation. Kitty's mind was racing about, trying to decide how this latest calamity might affect Emily's and her own precarious position in this household. She felt strongly that Emily's accident was the last straw in a series of mishaps that had been occurring during the last few days. Everything about this adventure was turning out to be more complicated and troublesome than she'd expected. In the first place, her position as abigail, which seemed a great lark when she'd begun, was now a daily drudgery. She didn't mind attending Emily (who was not at all a demanding mistress), but her other tasks were becoming a heavy burden. She was expected to keep her mistress's room heated, which meant she had to carry buckets of coal up from the cellar and empty the ashes three or four times daily; she had to help the upstairs maids make up beds and dust the bedrooms; she had to wash and iron undergarments, petticoats, sashes, camisoles, or nightclothes almost every day; she had to take her turn serving at the servants' meals; and if Mr. Naismith or Mrs. Prowne suspected that she had an unoccupied moment, they found some task—like cleaning the wax from the candleholders, polishing the lavaboes in all the bedrooms, shining the crystal of the dining-room chandelier, or sweeping the hall carpets— to keep her busy. By bedtime she was so tired that she fell instantly asleep despite the lumpiness of her mattress and the narrowness of her dreadful cot.

In the second place, the burn on her hand had blistered, the blisters had burst, and the palm was now red and raw. Instead of healing, it was becoming more and more painful each day. She had complained about it at first, asking Mrs. Prowne to excuse her from carrying the coal scuttle, but the housekeeper had accused her of trying to malinger, so she never mentioned it again. Miss Leacock had dusted her palm with a medicinal powder and wrapped it with gauze after the blisters had burst, but since then Kitty had been reluctant to draw further atten- tion to it. It seemed to her that the housemaids on the staff were all strong and hardy girls who, when they *did* become ill, bore their ailments with admirable stoicism. She wanted to be as strong as they. To be forever crying about a little burn would be behaving like the spoiled child she used to be. Therefore she padded the palm of her hand with a folded handkerchief, bound it with another, and merely gritted her teeth when the pain became severe.

The third troublesome situation had to do with Emily's re- quest that they cut this visit short. It was a very sensible re- quest, and in the light of the other problems, Kitty realized perfectly well that it was just what they ought to do. Emily was obviously becoming enamored of the odious Toby Wis- hart, and the best thing for her would be to leave. Emily's suggestion had other advantages as well: if they left at once, Kitty would no longer have to slave away belowstairs, Emily could get over her infatuation, and Lord Edgerton would never have to learn what a dreadful liar and trickster she, Kitty Jes- sup, really was.

But *there* was the rub. Gregory Wishart, Lord Edgerton. If Kitty took Emily's advice and went away, she would never see him again. Nothing she'd suffered in the past several days pained her as much as that thought. She didn't know when or how it had happened, but she'd somehow lost her head over Lord Edgerton. He'd become someone special to her. She hated to admit it, but the most appropriate word for her condition was *obsessed*. She thought about him constantly. It seemed to her no man existed who was more handsome, witty, kind, wise, or, in a word, wonderful. She found herself hoping, during every waking moment (and even in her dreaming ones), that he would cross her path. She peeped down every corridor, looked constantly over her shoulder, found any possible excuse to go upstairs to the family's part of the house, just to catch a glimpse of him. Any day which failed to grant her that glimpse was an overwhelming disappointment.

This obsession with the master of the estate in which she was living as a servant was the fourth, and probably the greatest, of all the troubles that had beset her until Emily's fall. She knew that an obsession such as she had for Lord Edgerton was bound to lead to pain for her. In the long run, no good could come of it. When his lordship discovered who she really was, he'd be as angered and disgusted with her as her parents would. As an upstart little servant girl she held a bit of charm for him, but as the spoiled, troublemaking daughter of Lord Birkinshaw she could not expect him to feel anything but revulsion. After all, his only interest in Kitty Jessup was as a possible wife for his brother. She was certainly not the sort he would ever consider for himself. Miss Leacock had described the sort of lady he wanted; that tall, willowy, elegant creature with the beautiful hands was nothing at all like Kitty Jessup.

As long as her identity remained undetected, she could hope to see him, speak to him, find ways to tease and irritate and flirt with him. But once the truth came out, it would be all over. That was why her every instinct cried out to remain. Her time for happiness was so short. There was less than a week left to her. These few remaining days were all there would ever be of her association with his lordship.

But now there was this last straw—the accident that had happened to Emily. And it was all Kitty's fault. She had to face the facts: everything was going wrong. If, miraculously, Emily proved not to be badly hurt, Kitty promised herself that she would take Emily's advice and arrange to leave Edgerton Park as soon as possible. Besides being the most sensible solution to the coil she'd created, it was the best way to make amends for the suffering she'd caused her friend. "Don't let any bones be broken," she prayed silently.

Though the doctor soon emerged to inform them that indeed no bones were actually broken, his news did not encourage Kitty to hope for the prospect of a quick departure. "The young lady," he informed the two females waiting in the corridor, "has sustained a dislocated left shoulder, a severely bruised hip, several scrapes and contusions on her left arm and leg, and a laceration on her head which, though it bled profusely, is really only a minor injury. There are no signs of concussion. I've reset and bound the shoulder, cleaned and medicated the open wounds, and administered a laudanum sedative. Only time will do the rest. She's to spend a few days in bed, and her arm will have to be carried in a sling for several weeks." He took his hat from Alicia's hand and clapped it on his head. "For the rest of today," he ordered, turning to the abigail, "Miss Jessup must be left to sleep undisturbed. You are to watch over her all night, understand, to administer laudanum if she wakes and is in extreme discomfort. She is to have no visitors and is not to go downstairs or even leave her room. As for tomorrow, I shall call in the morning and we shall see."

In his abrupt fashion, he turned and made for the stairs, Alicia following hurriedly in his wake. Mr. Naismith, however, hung back and took Kitty's arm, preventing her from going in to Emily's room. "Hold on there, miss," he said in a hissing whisper. "I'm not at all certain you're up to sickroom duty. Per'aps I should ask Miss Leacock to take your place."

"No, please, Mr. Naismith," she answered earnestly, "I promise to do my very best for her, really I shall. I'll sit beside her all night. I won't let myself drowse for an instant! She'll be much more pleased to see my face when she wakes than a stranger's, I swear she will. Please?"

Mr. Naismith made eyes at the ceiling and relented. "Very well," he said, wagging a finger under her nose, "but if you go wrong in any way, it's the finish of you."

Kitty entered the bedchamber, closed the door quietly, and went over to the bed. Except for the bandage around her forehead and the remaining pallor of her cheeks, Emily looked quite normal. Her breathing seemed regular and untroubled, and her expression was not that of a person in great pain. Kitty, relieved, closed the drapes to blot out the light of the setting sun, lit a small candle to give herself enough light in which to observe the slumberer, drew up an armchair near the bedside, and sat down for the night's vigil.

She'd just settled into the chair when there was a knock at the door. She opened it just a crack. Toby stood outside, tapping a foot impatiently. He was disheveled from the top of his unruly hair to the bottom of his mud-spattered boots, and his face was tight with distress. "Let me in!" he ordered.

"Sorry, sir, but the doctor said—"

"The devil take the doctor!" he growled, pushing the door back and forcing his way past her with such angry strength that she fell back against the wall. He strode across the room, but when he caught sight of the dimly lit figure lying unmoving on the bed, he stopped short.

Kitty, regaining her balance, ran up to him. "Please, sir, don't wake her. The doctor told me most particularly. . ."

But Toby wasn't listening. He was no longer aware that she was there. He was staring down at Emily's white face with a look of horror in his own. "Oh, my poor, sweet little kitten," he muttered in a choked voice. To Kitty's utter astonishment, he sank down on his knees beside the bed and lowered his head until it rested on the bed beside Emily's bandaged shoulder. "What've I done?" he asked himself thickly. "My love, what've I done?"

Kitty's throat tightened with unshed tears. She was both profoundly shocked and profoundly moved to see the rakish, wild, sportive Toby Wishart brought so low.

But after watching him for a moment, she felt uncomfortably like an intruder. On tiptoe, she backed out of the room and carefully, silently, closed the door on the private scene within.

chapter twenty

If Kitty expected Toby to recover his composure and emerge from the bedchamber within a short time, she soon discovered her mistake. The grandfather clock at the end of the corridor chimed the half hour and then the hour, but the door remained closed. Another half hour passed. Kitty became bored with pacing up and down the corridor. She began to wonder if she should return to the bedside and eject the young man bodily. After all, the doctor had said no visitors. And what would Mr. Naismith say if he came by and discovered her out here in the hallway instead of inside at the injured girl's bedside where she was supposed to be?

The question had barely crossed her mind when she heard a step behind her down the hall. If it was the butler, she was doomed. She couldn't duck into the bedroom now, for she'd surely already been seen. She wheeled about and peered down the hall. But the figure approaching was not Mr. Naismith. It was Lord Edgerton himself.

He came down the hallway with a quick, purposeful stride. "Ah, Emily," he greeted her, his brow knit worriedly, "good evening. I've just come in from the dairy and only just heard about the accident. Is Miss Jessup badly hurt?"

"I don't think so, my lord," Kitty replied, dropping a little curtsey. "A dislocated shoulder and several bruises. Contusions, Dr. Randolph calls them. But no bones broken, he said."

"That, at least, is a relief. I'm very sorry this has happened. May I go in and see Miss Jessup for myself?"

"I don't think so, my lord. Dr. Randolph said she was to have no visitors today."

"Oh, I see." The amused look that was missing from his eyes on his arrival now returned. "Is that why you're pacing about out here? To keep visitors away? Shouldn't you be inside, keeping an eye on your mistress?"

"Yes, my lord, but, you see, your brother is with her now."

"Oh, he is, is he?" Lord Edgerton's eyebrows rose in mock displeasure. "How is it that he's permitted to visit and I am not?"

Kitty lowered her eyes, the very epitome of modest virtue. "I don't usually care to tell tales, my lord, but in self-defense I must confess that he forced his way in."

"Did he indeed? The blasted rudesby!"

She flicked him an enigmatic glance. "Yes, I've heard him described so."

"Oh? Have you?" He studied her with an intent interest. "Is that what you think of him?"

"It is not my place to make judgments of my betters," she responded primly. "In all fairness, however, I must admit that he seemed very upset by Miss Jessup's accident."

"I should hope so. And he's still in there, I take it. How long has he kept you out here?"

"Over an hour. But he isn't keeping me here. It was my own decision to leave the room. It didn't seem proper for me to . . . er . . . to be an observer of his distress."

"Well, you may not wish to be an observer of it, but I do," his lordship declared, and he turned and opened the door.

The sight that met his eyes caused him to stop in his tracks on the threshold. Toby was still on his knees beside the bed, but he'd laid his head upon Emily's pillow and was gazing at her face with a look that could only be called adoring. Lit by the single candle on the nightstand, their faces surrounded by shadow, the scene looked exactly like a painting by a master of French Romanticism, a dark canvas with only the faces shining in an amber glow. If the scene *had* been a painting, it would have been given a title of mythic significance, like "Eros et Psyche" or "La Nuit de l'Adoration."

Lord Edgerton could do nothing but blink in amazement. After a moment, he silently backed out and closed the door with the same care Kitty had shown earlier. "Good God!" he exclaimed in a hushed whisper. "Was that *Toby?*"

Kitty, remembering all the nasty things Toby had said to Emily at first, did not understand what had caused this apparent change in him and was still suspicious of his motives.

"He's your brother, my lord," she pointed out tartly. "You should know."

His lordship looked down at her with one eyebrow raised. "Even the accident to your mistress hasn't sweetened your sharp tongue. I warned you to guard against that tendency, didn't I? Haven't you taken my good advice to heart at all?"

"Oh, *yes*, my lord," she assured him with almost-convincing earnestness. "Very much to heart. Mr. Naismith hasn't scolded me *once* since you lectured me the other day."

"What?" he asked suspiciously. "Not once?"

Kitty guiltily remembered the butler's last words to her just a short while ago. "Well, perhaps once," she admitted.

He guffawed. "What a sauce-box you are, girl! If I had the sense I was born with, I'd send you packing. Have you had tea?"

The abrupt change of subject confused her. "Tea, my lord?"

"No, of course you haven't. Neither have I, so I told Naismith to leave a tray in my study. Come along and have a cup with me."

"Thank you, my lord, you are most kind. But I don't think I should leave my post."

His lordship shook his head in despair. "You really are incorrigible. When your master tells you to go, it is your duty to obey. Can it be that you are unfamiliar with the word obey? It means to follow instructions, to comply with orders, to submit to those in authority—"

"But, my lord, Mr. Naismith said that if I left this post it would be the finish of me."

"And, knowing you, he was quite right to say it. But since you've already left your post to my brother, and since my brother seems in no hurry to desert it, I think it permissible to take a little time for tea."

"But what if Mr. Naismith should discover—?"

"You can trust me to deal with Naismith if it becomes necessary. Now, come along, girl, and let me hear no more arguments."

He set off down the hall without further ado. Kitty, looking appropriately meek, followed obediently. But her pulse raced with excitement at the realization that he wished to spend a bit more time in her company. Her inner excitement, added to the necessity of running to keep up with his long-legged stride (which he made no attempt to slow down to accommodate her), caused her to arrive at his study door in a state of extreme breathlessness.

He opened the door and stood aside for her. "Oh, what a lovely room," she exclaimed, pausing in the doorway.

It was indeed an impressive room. The ceiling was high, and the three multipaned windows, which covered the entire wall opposite where she stood, climbed the full height of the room. Books lined two of the other walls while the third held the fireplace and an awesome array of paintings. A huge, eight-legged desk, covered with ledgers and papers, stood before the window, and a library table (on which the tea tray had been set) dominated the center of the room. Two armchairs before the fireplace completed the furnishings.

Lord Edgerton gave her only a moment to look about her. "I'm delighted that you approve, my dear," he said drily, "but if you insist on keeping me standing here holding the door for you, we shall never get our tea."

"Oh . . . I'm sorry," she murmured, stepping inside.

"Make yourself comfortable, girl." He made a sweeping motion toward the armchairs near the fire. "I'll pour the tea."

But she didn't sit down. Instead she crossed the room and stood studying the various portraits on the wall. She decided that the portrait right over the fireplace, of a heavyset gentleman in a red velvet frock coat with gold buttons, had to be the late Earl of Edgerton, for he had Toby's thick lips and a look of the present Lord Edgerton about the eyes. A portrait of a slim girl in white was Lady Edith in her younger days. And another, showing the same girl, now not quite so slim, seated on a chaise with a baby in her arms and two children standing beside her, was the most interesting painting of all. "Oh, what a darling little boy you were," she remarked, staring at the likeness closely.

"I can't imagine how you recognized me," he said, coming up to her with a brimming cup. "I couldn't have been more than ten when that was painted."

Unable to tear her eyes from this representation of his younger self, she reached for the cup without looking, jostling it in its saucer. The hot liquid spilled over, wetting the bandage on her hand and causing a sharp pain on the already raw palm. *"Oh!"* she cried out, wincing, and dropped the cup and saucer.

"Good *God*," his lordship exclaimed in horror, "what's *this?*"

Kitty reddened in embarrassment. "Oh dear," she murmured, bending down and trying desperately to mop up the spilled tea with her apron, "I'm so clumsy. Please forgive . . . the cup isn't broken, but I'm afraid the saucer—"

"I'm not concerned about the china, you idiot!" he barked, grasping her arms and lifting her to her feet. "What have you done to your hand?" Without giving her an opportunity to object, he took her hand in his and pulled off the makeshift bandage. When he saw the red, raw, discolored palm he winced. "Damnation!" he muttered under his breath. "How did this—?"

"It's nothing, my lord," Kitty said, trying to pull the hand from his grasp. "It's only a little burn."

"A little *burn?* The deuced wound's almost *festering!* I'll have Naismith's head for this!"

"No, please!" she begged, placing her other hand gently on his arm. "It's not his fault. He doesn't even know about it."

Her gesture softened him a bit. "Very well, we'll talk about that later. For now, we must do something about this . . . this mutilation. Wait here. I'll be right back." He stalked to the door and then turned back to her. "You heard me, miss! I expect you to remain right there where I left you. You are not to leave this room for any reason whatsoever. For once in your unruly life you are to *obey!* Do I make myself clear?"

"Yes, my lord," she said with a deep, ironic curtsey. "Whatever you say, my lord."

Her lack of seriousness made him grit his teeth in irritation. "I don't know how you managed to reach the ripe old age of—what is it? Seventeen?"

"Eighteen, my lord."

"Eighteen, then. I don't know how you've managed to survive so many years. I'm surprised someone didn't murder you long ago." And he slammed out of the room.

She stared at the door for a moment and then looked down at her blemished palm. It was indeed an ugly wound. Now that she knew it was finally going to be attended to, she could admit to herself that it looked putrid. With a shudder, she thrust the hand behind her back and turned her mind to other things. She strolled about the room, glancing at his lordship's books and rifling through the papers on his desk. But nothing caught her interest until she chanced upon a miniature in a silver frame that had been placed in a position of importance in the center of one of the bookshelves (where, she noted, it could easily be seen by anyone seated at the desk). It was a portrait of a lady whose face bore no resemblance to anyone in the household. She was tall and graceful, with soft, blonde curls framing a delicate face. And even in miniature, Kitty could detect that the lady had long, elegant fingers.

She picked it up and carried it to the fire to take a closer look. But before she'd crossed the room, the door opened. Lord Edgerton entered, carrying a tray on which he collected two bowls, several rolls of gauze bandage, some vials and jars, and a pair of scissors. "Ah, you're still here," he said, placing the tray on the library table. "I must admit I would not have wagered a large sum on finding you. Come here to me, if you please."

Hiding the hand holding the miniature in a fold of her skirt, she gingerly approached the table. Without warning, he lifted her up and sat her upon it, surprising her so greatly that she dropped the miniature. He bent down and picked it up. "What's this?" he inquired.

"I saw it on one of the bookshelves and wished to take a closer look. I hope you don't mind." She bit her lip nervously, but kept her eyes fixed on his face. "She is very . . . lovely . . ."

"Mmmm," his lordship grunted indifferently, putting the painting aside and sorting through the items on the tray.

Kitty, perched as she was on the table, was face to face with him. She took a deep breath and looked him squarely in the eye. "Is it your Miss Inglesham?"

"My Miss *Inglesham?*" He stared at her, agape with astonishment. "Wherever did you hear about *her?*"

"Backstairs gossip." Kitty shrugged. "One of the maids mentioned her."

Edgerton snorted. "That, my inquisitive child, is a painting of Lady Matthieson."

"Oh." There was a pause while his lordship poured some evil-smelling lotion from a vial into one of the bowls. Kitty knew she should let the matter of the portrait drop, but she could not. "Was Lady Matthieson someone *else* you loved?" she asked brazenly.

Edgerton frowned at her in annoyance. "Someone else I loved? You are implying by that question that I once loved Miss Inglesham. If your backstairs gossips told you that, it is a perfect example of the inaccuracy of that sort of information. I may have been taken by Miss Inglesham at first, but I soon found her an insipid bore. I had to hide myself abroad for months to disentangle myself from that relationship. And as for Lady Matthieson, *she* was my great-aunt Mathilda. She is said to have run off to America with a captain of the Royal Guard. If my calculations are correct, and if she's still alive, she is now about ninety-three years of age. I hope that answers your question."

"Well, almost," the incorrigible girl persisted. "I would just like to know, if she is only your elderly aunt, how it is that her picture stands framed in silver in a place where you can see her every time you lift your eyes."

"Because, Miss Curiosity, it's a Gainsborough, and I happen to like the work very much. Are you satisfied now?"

"Yes, my lord," she said, lowering her eyes meekly.

"Good. In that case, we can finally turn our attention to the more important matter of your hand."

He took her wounded hand in his. She kept her face turned away as he bathed and cleaned the wound, cut away dead skin, and painted her palm with a caustic liquid that made her gasp. After that the worst was over. As he covered the entire area of the burn with a soothing ointment, he resumed the conversation. "I've answered all *your* questions, girl, so perhaps you'll answer mine. How was it that you and 'one of the other maids' were discussing Miss Inglesham?"

Kitty had the decency to blush. "I . . . we . . . she just happened to remark that you were once . . . betrothed to her."

He cocked an eyebrow at her. "Just *happened* to remark? Out of the blue?"

"Not exactly."

"Then how, exactly?"

Her color deepened. "The subject came up when we were . . . er . . . speculating about your . . . er . . . oh, blast, I can't tell you!"

"What? The intrepid Miss Emily Pratt afraid to speak up? Come on, girl, I won't eat you. What were you speculating about?"

Kitty put up her chin. "About whether or not you keep a fancy piece in London as your brother does," she blurted out with bravado.

Edgerton choked. He was in the act of folding a length of gauze into a thick pad, but her answer so shocked him that everything he was holding fell from his hand—the pad, the roll of gauze, the scissors, and all. It took a good deal of restraint to keep himself from guffawing, but he was afraid that a laugh might be a sign of encouragement to the abominable chit. "My *word*," he muttered as he bent to pick the things up, "is that the sort of thing you talk about belowstairs?"

"Well, you must admit the subject is an interesting one."

"That's no excuse. Interesting or not, it's an unfit subject for innocent girls." He reassembled his material and continued to fashion the gauze pad. "I still don't see how Miss Inglesham's name came into the discussion," he remarked, knowing full well that he'd be wiser to let the matter drop.

"It came up when Miss . . . when the other maid said that any gentleman who'd been betrothed to someone as lovely as Miss Inglesham was not likely to keep a fancy piece."

"Ah, I see." He placed the thick pad gently on her palm and began to secure it to her hand with a long length of bandage. "I seem to have misjudged you, Emily Pratt. I would have thought you too innocent even to know what a fancy piece was."

"I'm not a child, you know," she said, drawing herself up in offended dignity. "It's a mistress, is it not? Someone to whom a gentleman offers a *carte blanche*. And that means that she has a free hand to spend as much of his money as she wishes, in return for favors, of course. Am I right?"

"Quite right," Edgerton said, biting back a grin. *This is indeed Birkinshaw's irrepressible daughter,* he told himself. There was no mistaking it. But if Birkinshaw were privy to this shocking conversation, he would no doubt call Edgerton out! Edgerton knew he should reprimand the girl, but he couldn't do it. He was finding her naughty innocence completely entrancing.

"You see, I *do* know a good deal," the girl was continuing, "although I *didn't* know—until that conversation with the other maid—that you gentlemen find your mistresses in Vauxhall Gardens."

"Oh, not only in Vauxhall, my dear," he said, teasing. "'We gentlemen' find them in all sorts of places."

"Do you really?" she asked, wide-eyed. But suddenly her face fell, and she dropped her eyes. "Oh. I suppose that means that . . . that you *do* . . . k-keep one." She looked up again hesitantly. "*Do* you?"

This time he couldn't hold back a hearty laugh. "Do I keep a mistress? Somehow I *knew* you would have the temerity to ask that question. But if you think I shall ever bring myself to answer it, you've underestimated your man."

But she did not seem chagrined by his answer. Instead she was studying him absently, as if her mind had leaped to another idea. "Where else might a gentleman find a mistress?" she inquired.

"Good heavens, girl, I hope you're not expecting *me* to educate you in these matters!"

"No, but . . ." She cocked her head like a curious little sparrow. "Might a gentleman find one in his own house? Among the *servants?*"

"See here, you irrepressible minx," he said, wavering wildly between laughter and indignation, "are you suggesting that I might be guilty of seducing one of the housemaids?"

"Only wondering if you would *consider* it," she retorted, her eyes dancing. "If you would, I myself might very well—"

"Emily Pratt, you go *too far!*" he barked, appalled. His amusement died abruptly. He was furious with her for her disgraceful suggestion and furious with himself for having encouraged it. "If I were your father, I'd lock you in your room and throw away the key." He picked up her wounded hand, which he'd dropped sometime during this unprecedented conversation, and resumed winding the bandage around it.

"Then you won't consider—"

"Enough!" he snapped, glaring at her in avuncular disapproval. "This conversation has gone beyond the bounds of decency. Let us drop this subject, if you please, once and for all."

"Very well, my lord," she said with a sigh.

"Reprehensible chit!" he muttered under his breath. "Now I see what Birkinshaw meant—"

"What did you say?" she asked, taken suddenly aback. "Did you say . . . *Birkinshaw?*"

Lord Edgerton wanted to bite his tongue. "No I did not," he declared firmly. "You are now bandaged, and you may go."

"Thank you, my lord," she murmured, studying him closely. She'd feared, for a moment, that she'd given herself away, but if he knew who she was he certainly would have disclosed it. She'd probably not heard him properly. She was still safe. "It was very good of you to trouble yourself like this for me," she said with real gratitude. "Now, if you'll only help me down—"

"Speaking of taking trouble, girl," his lordship said, tossing the soiled washcloth and the remaining bandages and medications back on the tray, "I should have thought that someone on the staff would have doctored you long before this. Can you give me one good reason why you didn't report this to Naismith or Mrs. Prowne? Are they so forbidding that you were afraid to tell them?"

"No, not at all. It was just that I burned myself in such a stupid way. I picked up the curling iron without a holding-pad, you see. I don't know how I came to do something so foolish. Everyone knows that the handle gets as hot as the iron and that you have to hold it with a pad. I was ashamed to admit my stupidity, that's all."

He picked up her now-thoroughly-padded and bandaged hand and stared down at it. "And so you simply went on dusting and sweeping and ironing and carrying scrub-buckets and such?"

"Yes," she admitted, gazing down from her perch at his bent head.

"What a little fool you are!" he murmured. But his voice, at variance with his words, was more tender than she'd ever heard it. For some reason it made her pulse quicken and her heart pound tensely.

He, on his part, suddenly felt tense, too. He lifted his head and stared at her, startled by a sharp constriction in his chest. He didn't know if it was the result of the improper banter they'd just exchanged or the unusual closeness of her face, but this impish girl who had so enchanted him that night in the corridor seemed now to be infinitely more bewitching. Not only did he see the same pixie charm of her freckled nose and pointed chin that he'd seen before, but now he discovered in her hazel eyes and firm jaw a depth of character he hadn't noticed earlier. This little chit was every bit as wild, unpredictable, and troublesome as her father had claimed, and she'd arranged to embroil them all in a wickedly mischievous deception of which he utterly disapproved, but he had to admit that the girl, having set herself that course of action, had executed it with determination, wit, and true courage. It couldn't have been easy for her to play such a lowly role, to endure the scoldings of the butler and the snobbery of the other servants, to withstand the blandishments of the amorous footman, to deny herself the luxurious life she'd been accustomed to, and to labor from morning to night on menial tasks she never before attempted. And she'd done it with a hand whose flesh was seared raw! It was difficult not to admire her for it.

Her face was very close, so close that he couldn't help realizing how very beautiful that face had suddenly become in his eyes. At first he'd found her adorable, but not beautiful. *When had the change occurred?* he wondered. He tried to find the answer, but his mind was not functioning normally. The allure of her full mouth was irresistible, and without thinking of what he was doing, he put his arms about her waist and pulled her to him. The irrepressible little wench seemed not at all dismayed but fitted herself against him, slipped her arms about his neck, and pressed her lips to his.

He closed his eyes, tightened his hold on her, and kissed her hungrily. For a long, delicious moment he pushed away his awareness that he was behaving like a cad . . . that this was the girl he'd pledged to his brother, that she was a mere child —seventeen years his junior—and that he was supposed to be convinced that she was a servant in his employ. On all three counts, kissing her was despicable. Even while surrendering to the sweet intoxication of the experience, he hated himself. After much too brief a wallow in depravity, he forced himself to regain his self-control. He released her and loosened her hold on him.

Kitty, overwhelmed, emitted a tremulous sigh. Her eyes slowly opened, and she gazed at him in wonder. "Oh, my!"

she breathed, awestruck. "Does that mean . . . you *will* make me your mistress?"

"No, it does *not!*" he shouted, putting a shaking hand to his forehead. "How did I ever get myself in such a fix?"

"But why not?" Kitty asked, her face falling. "Did I not kiss you properly?"

Edgerton winced. "There was nothing wrong with how you kissed me, you goose. But no kiss, no matter how sublime, can be considered *proper* between us."

"Proper, pooh! Who cares about propriety?"

"Listen here, my girl, you are being excessively silly," he said impatiently, feeling a powerful surge of sympathy for poor Birkinshaw. He realized for the first time that Birkinshaw's problems in raising this willful, impulsive girl were far more difficult than his with Toby. "You don't know what you're suggesting. You're speaking of things you know nothing at all about . . ."

But Kitty wasn't attending. The only thing on her mind was her need to know the extent of his feelings for her. She wanted some proof that he cared for her, and she didn't concern herself with anything beyond the desire for him to declare himself. It was that desire that drove her on. "Is it the *carte blanche* that worries you?" she asked bluntly. "I promise not to take advantage of that. I can be very thrifty if I set my mind to it."

He shook his head in exasperation. "Will you *stop* this, girl? I will not make you my mistress, and that's final!"

Kitty's heart sank. "You do not l-love me, then?" she asked, her mouth trembling pathetically.

Edgerton felt another sharp constriction of the chest. How easy it would be, and how delightful, to tell her that he loved her, adored her, wanted her desperately, body and soul. But even if he hadn't pledged her to his brother, even if he could convince Birkinshaw that he was not too old for her, even if he could make himself believe—and he could not—that what she felt for him was more than mere infatuation, he was not the man to take advantage of her youth and innocence. "There can be no talk of love between us," he told her quietly. "It would be to no purpose."

"Because I'm a housemaid?"

He sighed. "No, dash it all! Because you're a *child!*"

"I'm *not* a child! I'd wager there are hundreds of mistresses even younger than I."

"Emily Pratt, what you need is a good shaking! You're not the sort to be a . . . a fancy piece—*anyone's* fancy piece!—so put that idea out of your head once and for all!"

He took a few angry turns around the room, and then, feeling calmer, he turned back to her. The sight of her sitting in woebegone despair on his table, her legs dangling listlessly below, cut him to the quick. "This has been all my fault, my dear," he said, taking her bandaged hand in his. "I don't know what came over me. Believe me, I don't make a habit of kissing the housemaids."

"It d-doesn't m-matter," she said, trying to revive her pride despite the two tears that spilled from her eyes and dribbled down her cheeks. "I'll und-d-doubtedly recover."

"Within a month, I'd wager," he said with a rueful smile. "Meanwhile, Emily, I'd like you to forgive me and to forget everything we said and did in this room this evening. Will you try to do that, please?"

Kitty looked down at the hand he held. "I'll t-try, if you wish," she said, utterly crestfallen.

He lifted her down and set her on her feet. "Very well, then, go on your way."

He watched her walk slowly to the door. "Good evening, my lord," she said glumly from the doorway.

"Yes, yes, good evening," he muttered, waving her away.

"Thank you once again for t-treating my burn," she added in a brave attempt to show him that she bore him no rancor.

"Ah, yes, that reminds me," he said in the firm, strong tone of voice befitting the master of the household, "you're not to do a single chore until that hand has healed. Tell Naismith those are my orders."

She dropped one of her ironic little curtseys. "Yes, my lord."

He narrowed his eyes. "I mean it, miss! The fact that we exchanged some intimacies here this evening doesn't give you license to be disobedient. If I catch you so much as lifting a bowl, I *will* throw you down the coal hole."

chapter twenty-one

Back in London, Kitty's parents were complacently awaiting word from Lord Edgerton that their daughter's betrothal to his brother had been arranged. Although Hermione Jessup, Lady Birkinshaw, had promised her husband (on pain of withdrawal of all spending privileges for a month) not to say a word to anyone about the match until Edgerton said it was a *fait accompli*, she did permit herself the luxury of making plans for the elaborate wedding breakfast she intended to give when the time came. She daydreamed about the gowns she would order for her daughter and for herself. She tried to estimate the number of crates of champagne they would need to serve the two hundred guests she intended to invite. She even went so far as to speak (secretly of course) to the manager of Gunthers, the famous patisserie in Berkeley Square, about the design of the wedding cake.

It therefore came as a cruel shock when she overheard some dreadful gossip concerning her prospective son-in-law. She was attending her regular Tuesday afternoon tea-and-whist party at Countess Lieven's when the usual gossip over the cards turned to the subject of young men of the *ton* who kept their doxies in permanent rooms at Limmer's Hotel. "It's an utter disgrace," Lady Upton declared, taking in a trick as she spoke. "Lord Jarmies has installed his fancy piece there, and so has Francis Tarrington. And Beatrix Simmons suspects that her prissy-faced son keeps his *chère amie* in rooms at Stephen's Hotel in Bond Street, where Beatrix might run into her any time she visits her milliner!"

"Shocking!" declared Lady Westbrook, shaking her head with such vigor that the corkscrew curls over her ears danced. "We shall see these libertines parading their game pullets up St. James in broad daylight before long."

162

"I wouldn't be a bit surprised. There's an on-dit circulating about that Sir Lucas Farling, who's seventy-eight if he's a day, has taken up with a Castle Tavern wench not yet eighteen," Lady Upton said in disgust. "The disreputable old lecher!"

"Speaking of Castle Tavern wenches," Countess Lieven remarked as she rearranged the cards in her hand, "my brother told me that young Wishart's taken up with one of them, too. Which shows that the young can be as revoltingly lecherous as the old."

Lady Birkinshaw paled. "Did you say Wishart? *Toby* Wishart?"

"Yes. Edgerton's younger brother. Are you acquainted with him?"

"No," Lady Birkinshaw answered awkwardly, keeping her eyes fixed on her cards, "but I think I've heard Birkinshaw speak of him."

"No doubt," the countess said drily. "The boy has often provided the ingredients for scandal-broth."

Lady Birkinshaw felt faint. "I suppose so," she murmured, "but surely the on-dits concerning him were only of boyish pranks, were they not?"

"Not this time." Countess Lieven, laughing at the tale she was about to reveal, threw out a card. "They say he put his doxy up at Limmer's last month and then left her to stew while he went down to Suffolk to rusticate."

Lady Birkinshaw put a shaking hand to her forehead. Surely her husband could not be such a fool as to give their daughter in marriage to so dastardly a creature! "The story sounds like a hum to me," she declared bravely. "The boy's barely out of school, is he not?"

"Schoolboys can be the most disgraceful of all," Lady Upton said in her obnoxiously decisive manner. "And Toby Wishart has already made himself known as a loose screw."

The countess nodded in agreement. "Dreadful scamp. Gotten himself into all sorts of scrapes. Hermione, dear, do play your card. It's your turn."

Lady Birkinshaw discarded without looking. "Yes, but none of the scrapes that Birkinshaw told me of were more than mere waggishness," she protested, hoping against hope that the countess's story was exaggerated.

"Your husband evidently doesn't gossip as much as my

brother William," the countess laughed. "William told me that Wishart chose a girl who was decidedly lacking in tact. When he was called down to rusticate in Suffolk, it seems he left her without funds. Well, the doxy—I think my brother says she goes by the picturesque name of Lolly Matchin—made quite a vulgar row about it until Edgerton paid her off."

"Good God!" Lady Birkinshaw muttered under breath. "What have I done?"

"You've made a mistake, that's what you've done," Lady Upton chortled, picking up the trick. "I knew you weren't thinking when you discarded that jack of clubs. That mistake, my dear, has cost you the game!"

But whist was the last thing on Lady Birkinshaw's mind. She made her excuses as soon as she could and hurried home. She could hardly wait to give her idiotic husband a piece of her mind.

Lord Birkinshaw, however, was not to be found anywhere in his home. He'd gone to his club, of course. The fact that Lady Birkinshaw should have expected such to be the case in no way eased her frustration. To make matters worse, he didn't return home until well past midnight. By that time his wife was in a rage. "You thoughtless, impulsive, brainless *nincompoop,*" she greeted him the moment he stepped in the door, "you've really done it this time!"

Poor Lord Birkinshaw had imbibed a large share of White's liquor stock and was feeling very woozy. "Don' know what y'r jawin' about, m' love," he mumbled, "but tell me all about it in th' mornin'. I'm off t' bed." With that, he pecked her cheek and stumbled cheerfully toward the stairs.

"Stand where you are!" his wife ordered in the dulcet tones of a sergeant of the guard. "You will *not* go to bed tonight. Instead, you will order the carriage, and we will set off for Suffolk. I've had Jenkins pack your bag already, so there's nothing to keep us from starting out at once."

"Startin' out f' *where?*" he asked, peering at her from a pair of utterly bewildered eyes.

"Suffolk. The Edgerton place. That's where."

"But, my love, we can't go t' Suffolk tonight. It's pas' midnight. Besides, it'll be snowin' before mornin', if I'm any judge. Air smelled like snow t' me."

"I don't care about the hour or the weather. We must go

right now to save our daughter from the dreadful fate you wished upon her."

"Drea'ful fate? Wha' drea'ful fate is that, m' dear?"

"Confound it, Thomas Jessup," his wife exploded, throwing up her hands in disgust, "I might have known that you'd be soused just at the moment when I need you most!"

His lordship drew himself up in offense. "Not soused. Just a wee bit vertig'nous. Jus' tell me slowly 'n' calmly . . . what drea'ful fate's befallen our Kitty?"

"It hasn't befallen her yet," his wife said impatiently. "We must hurry and *keep* it from befalling her."

"Yes, m'love . . . but *what* mus' we keep from befallin' her?"

"*Marriage* is what. Marriage! Toby Wishart must not be permitted to marry Kitty!"

Lord Birkinshaw pursed his lips and tried to concentrate. "Marriage? But . . . th' matter's all settled, ain't it? Can't stop it now. Gave m' word. Gave m' *hand,* hang it all! Settled!"

Lady Birkinshaw rounded on him in fury. "I don't care about your word or your hand! We are going to Suffolk to bring our daughter *home,* do you hear me? We are going whether you will it or not, whether it snows or not, or whether you gave your word or not!" She picked up a bonnet which had been lying on a nearby chair and clapped it on her head. "I will not have my daughter wed to that *cad!*"

His lordship gaped at her. "Are y' speakin' of young Wishart? He ain't a cad. A bit of a scapegrace, perhaps, but not a cad. After all, he's only a boy!"

"That's just it," his wife declared, snatching up her cloak with one hand and grasping his arm in a viselike grip with the other. "Just barely of age and already the fellow is reputed to be a . . . a damnable *libertine!*" She pulled her poor, confused husband after her to the door. "I can't speak for you," she added as she dragged him, stumbling, out into the cold, "but I, for one, would rather break my word than permit my daughter to wed a man who, even before his twenty-first birthday, has already become a dastardly *lecher!*"

chapter twenty-two

Emily dreamed that she was about to perform Beethoven's Sonata Opus 31, Number 3, in an enormous drawing room filled with hundreds of people. She'd taken her place at the piano, a hush had fallen over the crowd, she'd flexed her fingers and was about to place her hands on the keys when, suddenly, her left arm refused to move. She couldn't lift it high enough to reach the keyboard. Something seemed to have imprisoned her arm right at the shoulder. She writhed and moaned and tried to free herself but to no avail. The expression on the faces of the people in the audience changed from polite expectation to disdain. Some of them laughed. She struggled harder to free her arm. "I can play it," she pleaded. "If you will just be patient—!" But her arm would not come loose. The crowd began to jeer. "Kitty can't play a note!" they shouted. "Not a note. Kitty can't play."

"Let me go!" she cried, twisting herself about desperately. *"I'm not Kitty!"*

But they kept calling "Kitty! Kitty!" until the din was unbearable.

"Stop calling me that!" she screamed at them so loudly that she woke herself up.

She opened her eyes to a darkened room. Someone was bending over her, calling her name. "Kitty," he urged with worried tenderness, "wake up!"

"Toby?" Her voice was thick with sleep. "Is that you?"

"Are you in pain, my love?" he asked, stroking her forehead. "I can give you a dose of laudanum if you are."

She shook her head. "No, thank you, I'm all right."

"You were moaning in your sleep, so I thought—"

"I'm fine really. What are you doing here?"

"Just watching over you. I made your abigail go to bed. She looked a little red about the eyes."

Emily rubbed her eyes. "That was good of you, sir. Very kind."

His eyebrows rose. "Sir? We're back to *sir?*"

"Very well, then, Toby." She tried to sit up. "I assure you, Toby, that there's no need to stay. I don't need watching over."

"Here, let me help you," he said, sitting down on the edge of the bed and propping her up so that her back rested on his shoulder. "I *like* watching over you, you know. You're beautiful when you're asleep."

"Don't be so silly," she said, blushing. "You shouldn't be watching me sleep. You shouldn't be here at all."

"Yes I should. I'm the one who got you into this fix, and I'm the one who's going to help you get well."

Emily frowned. "Is *that* why you're here? Doing penance? How many times must I tell you that the accident was not your fault? And I'm only a little bruised. I shall soon be all over it. So you may take your unnecessary guilt and go to bed."

"Do you really believe that I'm here doing penance?" he asked, brushing back her sleep-tousled hair with his fingers. "Have you forgotten what I told you this afternoon when I left you at the door?"

Emily sighed deeply. "I haven't forgotten. You said you may be falling in love with me."

"Did I say that? If I did, it was only because of shyness." He bent his head and put his lips on her forehead. "There is no 'may be' about it, my girl. I *am* in love with you."

She couldn't help smiling. *"Shyness?* You haven't an ounce of shyness in your makeup."

"Yes, I have. You make me shy." He took her chin in his hand and tilted her head toward him. "You are so much above me in every way that I'm in constant awe of you."

Her smile faded. "You mustn't say that, Toby. It's not true at all. When you learn the truth, you'll discover that it's you who are above me."

"I don't know what you mean," he said, his brows knitting together. "You've said something like that before. What truth is there to discover?"

"The truth about *me.*"

"Confound it, what's the mystery? What truth? *Tell* me!"

She shook her head. "I can't, Toby. It's not my secret to reveal."

He looked down at her, puzzled. "Is it some skeleton in the family closet? A mad uncle? A feeble-minded brother? A drunken sot of a cousin who makes scenes at the family dinners?"

"Oh, Toby, you clown, don't make me laugh. It hurts."

"I'm sorry, my love. I'll try not to. But if it's none of those things, then—"

"I wish it *were* one of those things. But this is even worse."

"Worse? What could be worse? Unless—" He gasped, clapped a hand to his forehead in exaggerated alarm and groaned. "Oh, horror of horrors! Unless—can it be that you're hideously disfigured somewhere under your clothes?" His eyes laughed down at her, but his expression remained one of horrified revulsion. "Aha, that's it! You have a huge and ugly strawberry mark on your left thigh!"

She bit her lip but couldn't hold back the giggles that shook her sides painfully. "Please, Toby," she gasped, "you said you wouldn't make me laugh."

He turned serious at once. "I'm sorry, my love. But I have to make you see that even if there *is* a secret, it can't make any difference to my feelings for you. Do you think there is anything you could tell me that would make me stop loving you?"

"You mustn't even *start* loving me, Toby. You mustn't."

"Yes, so you've said. But you're too late." And to prove it, he bent his head and kissed her gently.

"Oh, Toby!" she moaned, holding him off with her good arm. "Don't—!"

He let her go, placed her carefully against the pillows, and rose. "If you really want me to hold back, then you must explain why," he said reasonably.

She lowered her head. "I can't."

"You don't trust me, is that it? Or you don't love me enough. Come to think of it, you've never said you love me." He sat down on the edge of the bed and took her hands in his. "Do you?"

She looked at him tearfully. "Please, Toby, don't make me—"

"Do you?"

She pulled her hands from his grasp and buried her face in them. "Yes, I do. I *do!* More than I can s-say!"

"Then we have no problem. We'll be married, just as our families wish."

She lifted her head, stared at him hopelessly for a moment, and then turned her head into the pillows. "No, we won't," she said flatly.

"But why not? Why won't you *tell* me?"

She didn't look up. "Let's not go round and round the same circle, my dear. Just . . . go away."

"Go *away?*" he echoed furiously. "Is *that* all you can say to me?"

"Yes. That's all. Except that I'm . . . very tired."

He threw up his hands in frustration. "Very well, if that's what you wish, I'll go. Shall I help you lie down first?"

"No, thank you."

"Shall I fix you a laudanum mixture to help you sleep?"

"No, thank you."

"Shall I send for your abigail?"

"No, thank you."

"Why don't you say 'No, thank you, *sir*'?" he demanded angrily.

She turned her head toward him, her face stained with tears. "I'm terribly s-sorry, Toby. I wish . . ."

"Yes, so do I." He clenched his fists and thrust them into the pockets of the riding breeches he still wore. "You know, I always thought that falling in love . . . *really* falling in love . . . would be a marvelous thing to happen to me. I always wanted to fall in love. But it turns out to be a lot like falling off a horse. It hurts all over."

"Yes," came a small voice from the bed. "I know."

He shut his eyes in pain. "Then, for God's sake, why—?"

She gave a small sob. "One of these days . . . s-soon . . . you'll understand."

He stormed to the door. "No I won't. You can give me a hundred explanations—a thousand, even—for why this is happening to us, but I'll never understand. Never, as long as I live."

He threw open the door, crossed over the threshold, and

made as if to slam the door with a good, loud crash. There was nothing that would give him more satisfaction at that moment than making a noisy, stormy, angry exit. But a glance at the dimly lit figure lying motionless on the bed stayed his hand. He gave her one last look and closed the door quietly behind him.

chapter twenty-three

Ever since Toby Wishart had dismissed her from her post at Emily's bedside and sent her to her bed, Kitty had been trying to cry herself to sleep. The feeling of misery, which had overwhelmed her when she'd been dismissed from Lord Edgerton's study, had worsened while she'd been sitting at Emily's side with nothing to do but watch her friend sleep. With nothing else to occupy her mind, she'd reviewed the entire incident in Lord Edgerton's study, and she soon realized that she'd made a terrible fool of herself. She'd been hideously hoydenish and vulgar and had embarrassed his lordship and herself. He was a man who was drawn to elegant ladies with graceful hands, and she had behaved like a trollop. She'd never be able to look the man in the face again.

Sleep had been eluding her for two hours or more when there was a tap at her door. It was Peggy with a message from Toby, requesting that she resume her vigil at Miss Jessup's bedside. "I'll sit up fer ye, if y're too weary," Peg offered kindly after getting a glimpse of Kitty's reddened eyes.

"That's all right, Peg, I'll go," Kitty said. "I can't seem to fall asleep anyway."

She slipped quickly into her bombazine and hurried up the stairs. She opened Emily's door stealthily to keep from waking her, but Emily was not asleep. To Kitty's astonishment, she found Emily with her face buried in her mound of pillows and her shoulders shaking with sobs. "Emily! Good heavens! Are you in pain? Please, love, don't cry. I'll fix a laudanum drink for you and you'll feel better in a trice."

Emily raised a hand and made a negative gesture. "Everyone wants t-to ply m-me with l-laudanum!" she wailed into the pillows. "I don't *want* any damned laudanum."

"Emily!" Kitty gasped, shocked. At school all the girls

171

used naughty words at some time or other (and when they were caught Miss Marchmont administered the soap herself), but no one had ever heard Emily Pratt swear. "What's come over you? I know you've had a bad fall, and you must be suffering greatly, but—"

"This has nothing to do with the deuced fall!" She tried to turn herself about and sit up, but the stiffness of her hip made her swear again. "D-damnation," she muttered, still choked with tears, "I can't even s-sit up by m-myself."

Kitty helped her into a sitting position and piled up the pillows behind her. "Oh, poor dear, you look terrible," she exclaimed. "What on earth—"

"If I l-look terrible, it's all your f-fault!" Emily blubbered, feeling about for her handkerchief under the pillows.

"My fault?" Kitty eyed her with surprise while her hands searched her apron pocket for a handkerchief. "What have I done?"

"I should n-never have agreed to change p-places with you! Never! If only I had r-remained at s-school, as Miss M-marchmont wished me to! Or kept my p-position as your abi-gail. But no . . . you had to force me to ch-ch-change places with you!"

"I'm sorry, Emily, truly. I never should have done it." She found a handkerchief, pulled it out, and handed it to her friend. "But what is it that's happened to upset you so?"

Emily stared at the handkerchief. "There, you *see?*" she cried, holding it up before Kitty's face. "It used to be *I* who had the apron p-pocket and who supplied everyone with hand-kerchiefs and pins and n-necessaries. You're turning into me, and I'm turning into y-y-*you!*"

"Just because I had a handkerchief in my pocket? I think, Emily, that you're a little over-agitated. Not that I blame you, considering the day you've had. But you mustn't permit one bad day to put you in a pucker."

"Heavens, you even *sound* like me! That's just the sort of thing I used to s-say at the school! It was always *I* who would c-calm the hysterics. Now *I'm* the hysteric!"

"Hush, my love, you're not a hysteric. Come, let me help you lie down. You can drink a soothing draught of laudanum and get a good night's sleep. You'll feel ever so much better in the morning."

"If anyone mentions laudanum again I shall scream!" She blew her nose vigorously and dashed away the last of her tears. "It's not the sprained shoulder that worries me, or the blasted hip, either. It's what's becoming of me."

"You know, Emily, if you keep this up, I shall take offense. If you are becoming more like me, I fail to see why it should so upset you. What's wrong with me, may I ask?"

"Nothing. I'm very fond of you . . . and admire you, too. But that doesn't mean I wish to *turn into you*. I can't afford it, you see. I was perfectly content with the prospect of teaching school and playing the piano and living out my life at Miss Marchmont's." Her face crumpled and the tears began to flow again. "I didn't w-want to wear silk d-dresses and eat fine d-dinners and *f-fall in l-love!*" she wailed.

"Oh, so *that's* it," Kitty said knowingly. "Toby's at the bottom of this."

Emily, weeping into the handkerchief, merely nodded. Kitty sat down beside her and patted her shoulder until the weeping subsided. Then, when Emily at last became calm, Kitty washed her friend's face, brushed her hair, and settled her back against the pillows. "I *am* sorry, Emily," she said, sitting down beside her on the bed. "When I first concocted this scheme, I thought I'd considered all the eventualities. But I never anticipated *this*."

"No, of course you didn't. One can't anticipate all the possibilities. That's the trouble with scheming. One can never be certain how things will turn out."

"Yes, you're right. My scheme has been unfortunate for both of us. But I've learned my lesson, Emily. I've concocted my very last scheme."

"Has it been unfortunate for *you?*" She peered at Kitty suspiciously. "I don't see why. Surely Lord Edgerton will not wish to have you for a sister-in-law after he learns what you've done. That part will be just as you planned, will it not?"

"Yes, I suppose so," Kitty agreed ruefully. "Lord Edgerton will not only not wish to have me for a sister-in-law . . . he'll not wish to have me for *anything*."

Emily didn't understand the answer, but she didn't really heed it because a dreadful thought crossed her mind. "Good gracious, Kitty, you haven't changed your mind about Toby, have you?"

Kitty snorted. "Just because it's bellows to mend with you, my dear, doesn't mean the whole world feels likewise. I haven't changed my mind. You may find Toby Wishart a paragon of manhood, but he seems a callow youth to me."

"Callow youth?" Emily was so affronted that she lifted herself erect, disregarding the pain it caused her. "How can you say such a cruel thing?"

"I can say it, Miss Pratt, because it's true. We servants hear a great deal belowstairs, you know. You have no idea of the gossip that's exchanged over the dusting."

"You've heard some gossip about Toby, then?"

Kitty hesitated. "Are you certain you want me to tell you? It may hurt to hear it."

"Oh, dear! Is it as bad as that? Well, if it is, perhaps it will cure me. Fire away."

"Then here goes. I've been told on very good authority that he kept a mistress in London."

"A *mistress?*" Poor Emily turned quite pale. "I don't believe it!"

"There's no need to look like that, you Puritan. I understand that such a thing is not uncommon among the fashionable set. Besides, he doesn't keep her any longer."

Emily sank back upon the pillows. "A mistress! That is the most revolting—! I knew he was roguish and somewhat fast, but I never *dreamed . . .*"

"Don't think of him any more, my dear," Kitty advised, lowering the pile of pillows behind her and covering her gently to her neck. "He doesn't deserve your tears. Go to sleep now. In a few days, when you are feeling more the thing, we'll make plans to go away. In a month or so we'll both have forgotten all about this experience."

Emily turned her head away. "I don't think I'll forget it *ever,*" she said sadly. "Not as long as I live."

Kitty blew out the candle. *Oh, Emily,* she said to herself, *neither will I.*

Emily, alone in the dark, felt utterly miserable in body and spirit and couldn't fall asleep. She had never considered herself to be really happy at Miss Marchmont's school, but she now realized that her life there had been quite pleasantly contented. And when she was free to practice the piano, she'd felt as close to happiness as she ever expected to be. But now she yearned to return to the modest contentment she used to have. What made her present misery almost unbearable was her realization that even when she returned to the school her former contentment would be out of her reach. She was doomed to yearn forever for something—some*one*— she could not have.

She tried to tell herself that she couldn't really love Toby Wishart. He was a rudesby and a spoiled child. He'd been sent down from Cambridge. He didn't really like music. He was not well read. He even had kept a *mistress!* Of all the horrid things he'd done, that was the horridest! There was nothing about him that matched her vision of the man she dreamed she'd one day love.

But the truth was that she *did* love him. In their last few times together he'd been so different. He'd been kind and loving and tender and even *sensitive*. Perhaps *that* Toby was the real one. Perhaps, if they'd been able to wed, she could have made him into the fine person he could be. *Oh, my dear,* she wept in the wee hours of the morning, *you'd be a better man with me!*

But healthy spirits do not wallow in misery forever, and Emily was a young woman with a healthy spirit. She was determined to find a way to lessen the depression that weighed upon her. The best way to do that, she decided, was to get away from this house as soon as possible. Kitty had promised that she would make plans to leave in a few days, but Emily didn't want to wait so long. It was then that Emily sat up with a shocking realization: she didn't *need* Kitty to scheme her own escape. She could devise her own scheme!

By the time the light of dawn crept around the edges of the draperies, she had worked it out. She got out of bed and threw the draperies open. She was astonished to discover that it had snowed during the night and that the landscape was covered with a thick white blanket. She couldn't be sure, but there seemed to be almost a foot of snow on the ground. And it was still falling. This certainly was a setback for her plans.

She sat down on the bed and reconsidered. Perhaps she should wait for Kitty after all. Kitty was so wonderful at overcoming setbacks and obstacles. But that was just it! If she wanted to behave like Kitty, she'd have to learn to overcome the obstacles herself! Would *Kitty* let a snowfall deter her? Never!

With renewed determination, she pulled herself to her feet, hobbled to the clothes chest, and pulled out the warmest garments she could find. It took her a long time to dress herself, for she could only use one arm, and every movement brought a sting of pain. But by the time the clock in the hallway struck eight, she was fully clothed. Then she sat down and wrote a farewell note to Kitty.

She'd barely finished when Kitty herself arrived with her breakfast on a tray. Emily slipped the letter under a book and gave Kitty a nervous good morning.

"Don't good morning me," Kitty scolded. "What are you *doing* out of bed?"

"Well, I'm feeling much better, you see, so—"

"You *must* be feeling better," Kitty remarked as she set down the tray. "However did you manage to do yourself up?"

"It wasn't easy," Emily admitted. "I've quite exhausted myself. I don't think I want anything to eat this morning, Kitty. If you don't mind, please take the tray away. And if anyone wants to visit with me, tell them I'm resting."

"I'd be happy to oblige, ma'am," Kitty said with a bob and a wink, "but you'll have to see the doctor. I saw him coming up the stairs. When he sees you out of bed, he'll surely kick up a dust."

But the doctor's reaction was admiring rather than angry. When he saw his patient up and dressed, he smiled at her proudly. "Y're a remarkable young lady, Miss Jessup," he said, taking her pulse. "I didn't look to see you up and about for at least a week."

"I'll get her back to bed right away, Dr. Randolph," Kitty offered, "and I'll keep her there by force if I have to."

"No, no," the doctor said, "that's not necessary. I'm no great believer in mouldering away in bed. Let her stay up and dressed as long as her body allows it. If the pain becomes too pressing, she'll know to lie down."

After the doctor departed, Emily convinced Kitty (by using every ounce of tact she possessed) that she wished to rest quietly—and alone—for the remainder of the morning. As soon as she was alone, Emily propped the note to Kitty on the mirror of her dressing table, pulled out from the wardrobe the cloak she'd worn on her arrival, pulled on a pair of heavy gloves, and hobbled to the door. She was about to open it when someone tapped again. "What is it, Kitty?" she asked uneasily. "I told you I'm resting."

"It's I, my love," came Lady Edith's voice. "May I come in? I must speak to you."

Emily, frustrated beyond words by this latest obstacle, looked about her frantically. She quickly thrust the cloak under the bed, pulled off the gloves and crammed them into the pocket of her dress, and opened the door. "Lady Edith!" she said in breathless greeting. "Good morning. Do come in."

Her ladyship returned a feeble smile. "I'm sorry to disturb your rest, my love," she said, "but I most urgently require your assistance. A dreadful thing has happened. Alicia is in hysterics, Hugh is in a fury, and I am at my wit's end. It isn't that I *blame* you, of course, but—"

"Blame *me*, your ladyship?" Emily noticed that Lady Edith's voice was unusually tremulous, that her hair was in disarray, and that her shawl was slipping from her shoulders. Realizing that Lady Edith was in a more perturbed state than she herself, Emily became more calm. "Have I done something wrong?"

Lady Edith, with an agitated shrug, hitched her shawl higher on her shoulder. "You could not have realized . . . it is not your fault. But perhaps you could come and speak to her. Or to him. Or to Greg. Perhaps Greg might think of some way to straighten it all out. Would you, my dear?"

"I'd do anything you wish, my lady, but I don't understand just what it is you're asking me. Perhaps it would be better if you sat down and told me just what has happened from the beginning."

"No, no, there isn't time," her ladyship cried, seating herself on the bed anyway. "It's Hugh, you see."

"Dr. Randolph? Has something happened to him? I saw him only a few moments ago, and he seemed perfectly fine."

"Yes, I know. That's how it all started, when he came in to examine you and found you up and dressed. He admired you so greatly for that. So greatly!" The agitated woman pulled an already-sodden handkerchief from the bosom of her dress and sniffed into it. "Then he went to see my poor, darling Alicia, who had one of her migraines again and had decided to remain in bed this morning. When he questioned her, she admitted that it wasn't terribly severe, and *that* seemed to set him into a terrible temper. He ranted and raved quite unmercifully. It was simply dreadful. Alicia's migraine is fully blown now, I can tell you."

"Her migraine put *him* in a temper?" Emily asked, confused.

"Because of you, you see. He feels that if you, who are suffering *real* pain, could get out of bed and dress yourself, then *she*, who he claims has only *imaginary* pain, should have the character to do the same."

"But doesn't he realize that imaginary pain can be just as real to the sufferer as physical pain?"

Lady Edith blinked at her blankly for a moment, and then a beaming smile dawned on her face. "Oh, my *dear*," she exclaimed, clapping her hands together, "that's so *true!* How well you've hit on the nub of it! I knew you were a treasure the moment I laid eyes on you. You're just the one to help us. Can you come down and tell that to Hugh? Perhaps you can convince him not to cry off."

Emily gasped. *"Cry off?* Does that mean . . . are you saying that Alicia and Dr. Randolph are actually *betrothed?*"

"Well, not actually. But haven't you noticed that the two of them have been smelling of April and May of late? We, Alicia and I, have not wished to announce anything yet, but Alicia believed that Hugh was on the verge of speaking to Greg. To ask permission to court her." She dabbed at her cheeks in a futile attempt to staunch the flow of tears. "We were so *blissful,* Alicia and I. To speak frankly, my love, we'd given up hope of Alicia's every marrying. Hugh may not be a magnificent catch, as these things are measured, not having a title or even great wealth, but she does love him so." She sniffed into the handkerchief once more and gave her shawl another hitch. "So will you come, my love, and see if you can set things straight?"

Emily hesitated. She didn't see what she could do to help poor Alicia, but it seemed heartless not to try. On the other hand, she was determined to execute her plan for escape. However, she supposed that a brief delay wouldn't make a significant difference. "Very well, my lady," she said, pressing the anxious mother's hand, "if you think I can be of use . . ."

Lady Alicia threw her arms about Emily in an emotional embrace, causing so great a shock of pain in the girl's shoulder that she almost cried out. "Oh, my love, it's just as I've always said. You *are* a treasure!"

chapter twenty-four .

Lady Edith had managed to keep the perturbed Dr. Randolph from storming off the premises by prevailing on him to drink some hot tea before venturing out into the snow. He had just finished when Lady Edith led Emily into the breakfast room. "There, now, tell him how wrong he is," she said with her customary tactlessness.

"I say, ma'am," the doctor objected, "ye didn't drag this poor, bruised creature all the way down the stairs just to involve her in this matter! Have ye no conscience? No *pity?*"

"That's all right, doctor," Emily said soothingly. "I'm—"

"It's you who have no conscience and no pity, Hugh Randolph," Lady Edith declared, her neck reddening in resentment, "or you wouldn't have left my daughter lying on her sickbed so distraught!"

"I only came down to—" Emily began.

"Distraught? *I* left her distraught?" the doctor snapped. "She made *herself* distraught."

"I only came down to—" Emily began again.

"I suppose *you* had nothing to do with it, is that what you're saying?" Lady Edith demanded.

"—to ask you to reconsider," Emily continued, attempting to instill an air of calm into the discussion. "After all, Alicia is—"

"Yes, that's what I'm saying! She had the migraine before I arrived."

"But only a mild one. It's entirely *your* fault that it's now so much worse," Lady Edith whined, sinking into a chair.

"Alicia *is* a bit delicate, you know," Emily put in. "She needs—"

"I fail to see how I can be blamed. If I've told her once I've told her a thousand times that if she had enough mettle not to surrender to them, the migraines would disappear by themselves."

"You've no *sympathy,* that's what's wrong with you," Lady Edith declared. "The child feels pain, even if you believe it to be imaginary. Tell him, Miss Jessup. Tell him what you told me."

"What I said, Dr. Randolph, is that—"

"The *child?*" Dr. Randolph shouted, shaking a finger in her ladyship's face. "Your daughter is almost thirty! How can you call her a child?"

"—is that imaginary pain—"

"She's *my* child, and I can call her what I like!"

Emily sighed. "Imaginary pain—"

"That's just the trouble. You treat her like a child. How can she be expected to grow up—"

"*Stop* it!" came a voice from the doorway. They all looked round to find Alicia standing there, white-faced and furious. Despite her obvious distress, she'd taken the trouble to don Kitty's becoming robe and to dress her hair. "How dare you all discuss me in this vulgar way?"

"I'm sorry, my love," Lady Edith said contritely. "I was only trying to help."

"Help?" the doctor said with heavy sarcasm. "That sort of help is like a crutch for a leg in which the break has already healed."

"And what, pray," demanded Alicia, "do you mean by that?"

"I mean, miss, that you should be helping yourself, not leaning on your mother."

"I do *not* lean on my mother!" Alicia said.

"There's nothing wrong with a young, unmarried woman seeking the support of her mother," Lady Edith pronounced at the same time.

"What's all the shouting about?" said a new voice from the doorway. This time it was Toby. He strolled into the room and made for the buffet. "Have you all lost your wits?" he asked without real concern. But at that moment he noticed Emily. "Kitty! What on *earth*—? What are you doing out of bed?"

Three voices answered at once. "Your mother dragged her down," the doctor muttered.

"I needed her assistance," Lady Edith said.

"I came to help Alicia," Emily said quietly.

"You all *have* lost your wits!" Toby snarled furiously. "Have you forgotten that this poor girl was tossed from her horse only yesterday?" He strode across the room and lifted Emily up in his arms. "You, my love, are going back to bed right now!"

"Toby!" Emily gasped. "Put me *down!*"

"You needn't baby the girl, Wishart," the doctor said. "She's not made of glass."

"Did he call her his *love?*" Alicia asked her mother, momentarily distracted from her own cares by her delight at Toby's words.

"How can you worry about that *now?*" her ladyship asked querulously. "You have other things to think about."

"There! You *see?*" Dr. Randolph, turning to Alicia, pointed an accusing finger at her mother. "The moment you have a thought for someone else, she brings your attention back to your own selfish concerns."

"My daughter doesn't have a selfish bone in her body!" Lady Edith cried.

"I know she doesn't. It's *you* who are making her so absorbed in herself," the doctor accused.

"Hugh Randolph!" Alicia cried. "How can you speak in that horrid way to my mother?"

Lady Alicia drew forth her handkerchief. "He calls *me* selfish, when it is *he* who hasn't an iota of sympathy for you, Alicia."

"I don't *need* sympathy for her," Dr. Randolph shouted, quite at the end of his patience. "I *love* her."

"Do you indeed?" came a new voice. This time it was Lord Edgerton in the doorway. Having spent a sleepless night tossing in hopeless longing for a little minx he had no right to love, he'd gone out to clear his head by riding his horse through the soft, new-fallen snow. Now, feeling a great deal refreshed by the ride, he stamped the snow from his boots as he surveyed the noisy assemblage in the breakfast room with a great deal more amusement than he could have summoned an hour ago. His eyes flitted from Toby (standing at his right with the false Miss Jessup in his arms), to his mother (who was trying with her usual lack of success to wrap her shawl about her shoulders, while Dr. Randolph and his sister gaped at each other over her head). "This is the first I've heard of any love matters," he remarked calmly. "As head of the house, shouldn't I have been the first to know?"

"I was going to tell you, Edgerton," the doctor said uncomfortably, "but your sister and I have reached a bit of an impasse here."

"More than a bit, I should say," Alicia muttered tearfully. "He believes me to be too delicate to be a doctor's wife."

"Perhaps she *is* too delicate," Lady Edith said sullenly. She was beginning to wish that Dr. Randolph *would* cry off. It had occurred to her only a moment ago that she might not enjoy having a son-in-law who disliked her.

"Do *you* think you're too delicate, Alicia?" Edgerton inquired interestedly.

"I don't know. I suppose it's up to Hugh to decide that. He *is* my doctor, after all."

"Well, Randolph? What is your medical opinion?" Edgerton asked.

"You know my medical opinion. Your sister is perfectly healthy. But she must be made to believe that herself. She's had too many years listening to her ladyship tell her how delicate she—"

"Ahem!" This latest interruption was made by Naismith, who had been standing in the doorway for the past few seconds trying to get his lordship's attention.

"Not now Naismith," his lordship said, much too fascinated with the goings-on in front of him to brook any distraction. "Are you suggesting, Randolph, that if she were married and living under less indulgent influences, she might more easily blossom into robust health?"

"It is certainly a possibility," Dr. Randolph said, eyeing Alicia with hopeful speculation.

"That's a manly, decisive response for you," Toby remarked disdainfully.

Lord Edgerton turned his attention to his brother. "I suppose *you* have a manly, decisive response to the question of why I find you standing in the center of your mother's breakfast room with an innocent young lady in your arms."

"As a matter of fact, I do," Toby retorted promptly. "I—"

"Put me down, Toby, *please!*" Emily begged in embarrassment.

"Ahem!" Naismith was even louder this time.

"I told you not now," his lordship said, waving him off. "Well, Toby, I'm waiting."

"I'm about to convey this innocent young lady to her bed, where she should have been kept in the first place," he said cheerfully.

"There's no need to carry me, you clunch," Emily whispered. "I can walk. Put me down!"

"Hush," he whispered back. "I'll put you down on your bed and nowhere else."

"But my lord," Naismith said valiantly, "there are—"

But his lordship wasn't listening. He was staring at his brother under knit brows. "What right have you to carry her about without her leave?" he asked his brother.

"I have every right. Since I intend to marry Miss Jessup, I intend to take proper care of her."

Edgerton, taken aback, frowned. "You intend to marry *that* Miss Jessup?"

"What other Miss Jessup is there?" Toby riposted with a grin.

"Oh, Toby, I *told* you it isn't possible," Emily said in consternation.

"Speaking of Miss Jessup," Naismith said firmly, "her parents are here."

"What?" said Edgerton, wheeling about.

"What?" Emily squealed.

"What?" Toby chortled loudly.

"Did you say that Miss Jessup's parents are here *now?*" Lord Edgerton asked.

Naismith nodded, unable to hide a slight air of smug satisfaction at the sensation he'd caused. "Yes, my lord. That's what I've been trying to tell you. Lord and Lady Birkinshaw have arrived and are asking to see their daughter. They are waiting in the rotunda."

"Well, my gracious, what's all the fuss about, Naismith?" Lady Edith asked irritably. "Tell them to come in."

"Oh, *no!*" Emily moaned as Naismith bowed himself out.

"Frightened, are you?" Toby teased. "I know. Your father is a miser and your mother is a dwarf, so you think I'll cry off."

"Dash it all, Toby," Emily hissed urgently, "stop clowning and let me *down!*"

"Really, Toby, you *are* being odious," his sister remarked. "Why don't you do as the girl wishes and set her down?"

"Not on your life," Toby grinned, lifting Emily higher on his chest. "I want her parents to see how delightfully we are getting on."

Edgerton knew he should intervene. Matters were coming to a pretty pass, and he was the only one who could sort them out. But something held him back. He wanted the fun of seeing the whole charade played out. *Confound you, Greg Wishart,* he scolded himself, *you're as bad as your brother.* But while he struggled with his conscience, Lady Birkinshaw bustled in, with the red-faced, weary Lord Birkinshaw right behind. It was too late now. With his eyes alight with amusement, Lord Edgerton stepped back behind the others to observe the unfolding of Kitty Jessup's little plot.

It was his mother who did the honors. "Ah, Lady Birkinshaw, how do you do?" she said with forced cheer, rising in queenly majesty from her chair and putting out her hand. "What a lovely surprise! We weren't expecting you for several days."

"How do you do, ma'am?" Lady Birkinshaw responded coolly. "We are sorry to break into what is obviously an intimate little revel, but I assure you we do not intend to stay. We've only come to pack up our little girl and convey her home."

"Convey her home?" Toby echoed in chagrin. "But... *why?*"

Lady Birkinshaw turned and looked him over icily. "And what business is it of yours, pray?" she asked.

Toby glanced down at the girl in his arms for a puzzled instant and then back at Lady Birkinshaw. "I should think you'd have guessed, ma'am. I'm Toby."

Lady Birkinshaw stiffened. "Toby? Toby *Wishart?*"

"At your service, ma'am."

She stared at him a moment in disbelief and then shuddered in abhorence. "I *should* have known!" she exclaimed in tones of revulsion. "Who else would greet his guests while brazenly carrying his... his doxy in his arms?"

Toby could hardly believe his ears. "*Doxy?*"

"Don't bother to act the innocent, you *libertine!* I suppose *she's* the notorious Lolly Matchin I've been hearing about." She put a shaking hand to her forehead and turned in agitation to her husband. "There, you *see* the sort of place to which you've sent your daughter? Lord only knows what depravity she's witnessed in this house!"

"Has your wife taken leave of her senses?" Lady Edith asked in amazement.

"I might ask the same of all of you!" Birkinshaw retorted, putting a protective arm about his wife's shoulder. "If you can all stand about and witness this shocking scene, you're all either demented or depraved!" He looked around until he spotted Lord Edgerton in the far corner. "I never would have believed it of *you*, Edgerton. Would've sworn you were complete to a shade. Well, this bibble-babble won't do any good. Just send for my daughter and let us go."

"*Send* for her?" Alicia gawked. "But there she *is*, right in front of you."

"Where?" Birkinshaw asked in bewilderment.

"Right there, of course," the doctor said, pointing.

"*That* one?" Birkinshaw asked, his eyes popping.

"You mean . . . Miss *Matchin?*" his wife gasped.

Emily gave a heartrending moan and buried her face in Toby's neck.

"Oh, my God!" Lady Birkinshaw muttered. "It's *not* Miss Matchin."

"Perhaps it ain't," Birkinshaw growled, "but it ain't my daughter either. I've never laid eyes on that female in my life! See here, Edgerton, what's going on here? Who *is* that imposter? And *where* are you hiding my Kitty?"

chapter twenty-five

Kitty, completely oblivious of the goings-on in the breakfast room, left her task of polishing the brass doorknobs on the upper floor (one of the few tasks Mrs. Prowne had decided she was fit to do, the housekeeper having been ordered by his lordship to keep the abigail from irritating her wounded hand) and stole down to peep in on Emily. To her surprise, she found the bed unoccupied and the room strangely deserted. She was about to leave and return to her doorknobs when she saw the note near the mirror. Closer inspection revealed her own name scrawled across the front. She tore it open with a feeling of foreboding.

Dearest Kitty, Emily had written in the neat, precise hand so carefully cultivated by the instructors at the Marchmont Academy. *Please don't be angry with me for what I have done, but I must take myself away from here before my heart actually breaks in two. I do love him so, in spite of his rowdyish ways and despicable deeds, and I could not bear to watch his love for me turn to scorn when he learns that I've lied to him all this time. I intend to borrow a curricle from the stable and make my way back to school. I've thought this scheme over very carefully; it is precisely the sort of thing you would do in my place.*

Before I go, I wish to apologize for blaming you for my misfortune. You were not at fault. You promised me an adventure, and I have had one. Even if it has left a painful and permanent scar on my soul, I think, in a way, I will always be glad I have had it. I suppose it is unlikely that our paths will cross again, but please believe that in my heart you will always be my friend. Yours, forever, Emily.

Kitty read the note with a sinking heart. The thought of Emily driving a stolen curricle through the snow all the way to

London made her sick with fear. If the girl had never learned to ride, she had probably never learned to drive, either. What if she overturned the equipage in the snow?

She dropped down on the bed to think. There was nothing to do but go after her. If she could contrive to get some sort of carriage from the stable, she could surely catch up with a driver of Emily's inexperience.

As soon as she'd worked out in her mind all the details, she leaped up from the bed and rummaged through the clothes chest until she found her reticule containing the pin money that her father had sent to her. Slipping it into her apron pocket, she flew down the hall to the back stairs. Once in her room, she began to breath easier. She was halfway to escape. Quickly she pulled from beneath her bed the wooden chest in which her clothing was stored. She took out Emily's shabby cloak and threw it over her bombazine. She searched in vain through all the pockets for a pair of gloves, but there were none. With a shrug, she took one last look at the tiny room, sighed, and closed the door behind her.

On stealthy feet she made her way to the main stairway where two footmen stood at their posts. Keeping to the shadows, she went around to the side where Jemmy stood. "Psst! Jemmy!" she hissed. "Over here!"

The footman looked around. "Here!" she whispered. "Behind the stairs."

With a suspicious frown, the footman approached her. "What're ye doin', ye jingle-brain?" he asked, looking at her cloak in amusement. "Goin' fer a ride in a sleigh?"

"Hush! Do you want someone to hear? I need your help."

"Well, y' ain't goin' t' get it. You been nothin' but trouble t' me, an' trouble's what I don't need."

"Do you need ten guineas?" she asked, showing him the coins.

"Ten—? Say, where'd ye get those? I'd go bail ye've stole 'em."

"Then you'd lose. Miss Jessup gave them to me. Do you want them or not? If you don't, I'll ask Charlie to—"

"Never mind Charlie. What do ye want me t' do?"

"I want you to get me a light carriage and two horses from the stable and bring them to the kitchen door."

"Oh, right-o!" the footman sneered. "I suppose old Reeves'll let me 'ave 'em, just like that."

"There's ten guineas for him, too."

"Even so. A carriage and two horses . . . they ain't trifles. Ye can't tuck 'em in yer pocket. An' they very likely'll be missed."

"Just tell Reeves I'll see that they're returned in two days' time. Word of honor."

Jemmy rubbed his chin. "Are ye sure you know what y're doin', Emily? There's more'n a foot o' snow out there, an' it's still comin' down. This could mean a good deal o' woe."

"Don't worry, Jemmy," she assured him with a confidence she was far from feeling. "I mean to take very good care of myself."

chapter twenty-six

"Well, Edgerton, I asked you a question! Where is she?"

Lord Edgerton sighed, shrugged, and came forward. "I suppose it's time to straighten out this tangle," he said, half regretful that the masquerade was about to come to an end. "Find Naismith, will you, Randolph? And tell him to send Emily Pratt to me at once."

Dr. Randolph nodded and left the room.

"Emily Pratt? Who the devil is Emily Pratt?" Birkinshaw asked irritably.

Lord Edgerton looked at Emily, still being held in Toby's arms. "Put the girl down, Toby," he ordered. Toby, shaken and confused, did as he was told. "Well, my dear," Edgerton asked her gently as soon as she was on her feet, "do you want to tell him yourself?"

"You *know?*" she asked, wide-eyed.

"Yes. For quite some time. But I believe everyone else is still in ignorance. Don't you think you ought to say something to them?"

She lowered her eyes and twisted her fingers behind her back. "Yes, I suppose I must." She turned and faced Toby. "My name, as you've surmised by this time, is not Kitty Jessup. I'm Emily Pratt."

"Yes, yes," Birkinshaw put in impatiently. "We've surmised that, too. But who *are* you?"

She kept her eyes fixed on Toby's face. "I'm Kitty Jessup's abigail."

There was an immediate hubbub. Everyone spoke at once. Alicia and Lady Edith exclaimed loudly that they didn't believe it. Lady Birkinshaw looked at her husband with dismay and muttered that this must be Kitty's doing and that she should have known the girl would play some sort of prank.

190

Lord Birkinshaw roared that if this *was* Kitty's doing he'd wring her neck. Only Toby remained silent, staring at Emily as if he'd never seen her before.

Finally silence fell. Everyone turned to observe the couple standing in the center of the room as motionless as if they'd been turned to pillars of salt. "Is that *it?*" Toby asked her at last. "Is that the whole of it?"

She licked her dry lips. "Isn't it enough?"

"Idiot girl! Did you think it was your *name* I loved?"

Her wide, dark eyes became enormous and filled with tears. *"Toby,"* she breathed, "you *can't—!*"

He held out his arms, and after a moment's hesitation she gave a choked little cry and fell into them. "Yes, I can," he murmured into her hair.

"But . . . there's your brother's promise to Kitty," she reminded him, nuzzling her head into his shoulder. "And the settlement . . ."

"I never promised. And I don't need a settlement. I can find a post somewhere."

"No, please," she murmured into his shoulder. "I'm nobody. I'm merely a maid-of-all-work at Miss Marchmont's school."

"Not such a nobody, I believe," Edgerton put in. "You're a trained teacher, I've been told. And a most talented musician. And never have I seen anyone exert so benign an influence upon this family."

Emily lifted her head and gaped at him. "Are you saying you *approve,* my lord?"

"Yes, I am. Although it seems that my brother doesn't care whether I approve or not. I've never before heard him offer to look for a post. I think, Miss Pratt, that your benign influence on *him* is the most remarkable thing of all."

Two vertical dimples appeared on Emily's cheeks. "I think so, too, my lord," she said.

"Now that it's agreed by all and sundry that you're going to make a new man of me," Toby said, lifting her up in his arms again, "I'm taking you up to bed." He carried her to the door and over the threshold with tender care. As they disappeared from sight, the others in the room heard him laugh. "If anyone had told me a week ago that I'd fall in love with a *teacher,"* he chortled, "I'd have told him to put his head under the pump!"

Lord Birkinshaw watched them go and then turned to his wife in irritation. "Is that your *lecher?*" he demanded. "He didn't seem so to me."

Lady Birkinshaw sank down upon a chair. "I seem to have made a hideous mistake," she said, humiliated. "I hope, Lady Edith, that you will find it in you to forgive me for the dreadful things I said about your son. I seem to have been terribly misinformed."

"Think no more of it," Lady Edith said graciously. "You were no more misinformed than I. To tell you the truth, I don't understand anything that's passed here this morning. Alicia, I hope you will sit down and explain things to me."

"There's nothing much to explain, Mama," Alicia said. "The only thing that's important is that Toby will be happy."

"Hmmmph!" Lord Birkinshaw grunted. "He'll be happy at the expense of my daughter. It seems to me, Edgerton, that you haven't played fair. We had an agreement, did we not? Confound it, we *shook hands!*"

"I know we did, old fellow, but the fates were against us. I don't think your Kitty wanted him."

"That remains for Kitty to say," Birkinshaw declared. "That is, if the minx ever puts in an appearance."

But Kitty did not put in an appearance. Dr. Randolph returned after more than a quarter hour had passed to report that Naismith had not been able to find the girl anywhere.

Lord Edgerton decided to search for her himself. He combed the house from the kitchen to the attic. More than an hour passed before he gave up. He returned to the breakfast room, where the Birkinshaws were being served a makeshift luncheon, and glowered at Kitty's father in disgust. "Damnation, Birkinshaw," he exploded, "what do you think your blasted daughter is up to now?"

"Easy, old fellow," the doting father responded, calmly chewing away on a buttered muffin, "I ain't blaming you for her disappearance. Kitty's harder to keep hold of than an eel. But she'll turn up."

"Turn up? Is *that* all you have to say?"

"What else *can* I say? She's undoubtedly up to some mischief, but there's no use making a to-do about it. You won't find her 'til she wants to be found."

This fatherly response made Edgerton sputter in fury. Birkinshaw might take this latest calamity with equanimity, but Edgerton could not. What if the girl had had an accident? What if she'd fallen down a secret stair that he knew nothing of and was lying senseless in a pool of her own blood? What if she'd slipped down the coal chute? What if she'd learned that her parents had come and was hiding somewhere in a dark corner of the house with rats gnawing at her feet? He was going out of his mind with worry, and he didn't know what to do about it.

But before he completely lost his head, Toby appeared. "I say, Greg," he said, his brow knit with concern, "I may have a clue here." He held out a crumpled piece of paper. "Kitty . . . I mean Emily . . . says that you should look at this. We just noticed it on the floor of Emily's bedchamber. Emily wrote it early this morning, meaning to run off herself. She thinks that Kitty found it and may have decided to rescue her."

Lord Edgerton ran his eye rapidly over the note. "Of *course* that's it! It would be just like her, the maddening wench! I'm sorry, Birkinshaw, to describe your daughter with these insulting epithets, but she does set my blood to boil!"

"Oh, don't apologize, old man," Birkinshaw said cheerfully. "I've used worse, myself."

"I'll go after her, naturally. I assume you'll want to come along with me. If so, you'd better ask Naismith to fix you up with a thick pair of boots."

"Come along with you? Through all that snow? You must be touched in your upper works, old fellow. *You* may go chasing after her if you wish, but I'll be content to wait right here at a nice fire with a glass of your good madeira in hand."

Edgerton blinked at him, shook his head in disgust, and went off to quiz the staff. Someone must have seen her, he reasoned, and could provide him with information to make his search easier. It didn't take long for the information to come. As soon as the news spread among the staff that his lordship was making inquiries about the abigail, Jemmy came forward and confessed. Troubled about her safety, his conscience would not permit him to keep silent. He revealed which carriage and horses he'd provided for the girl and the direction he'd seen her take. The only thing he did not reveal was the existence of the ten guineas he'd hidden in his mattress. Naismith wanted to sack the fellow on the spot, but Edgerton, both frustrated at and grateful to the fellow, postponed devising a punishment until he'd brought the missing abigail back home.

Lord Edgerton ordered the curricle to be brought around and ran upstairs to his dressing room to change. Dampler, his valet, was pulling on his boots when there was a timid tap at his door. Dampler admitted a very nervous Emily. "May I speak to you, my lord?" she asked shyly.

"Yes, of course," he said, masking his impatience to be gone. His boots on, he rose from his chair and gave Dampler a signal to take himself off. "Do sit down, Emily. Is something amiss?"

"It's about Kitty . . . Miss Jessup," she said, perching on the edge of the small room's only chair. "When you find her, my lord, please don't be angry with her. It's all my fault that she's run off. If I hadn't been so impetuous—I was trying to be like her, you see—this never would have happened."

Edgerton frowned. "What do you take me for, Emily? Do you think me some sort of monster? What did you think I'd do to her when I found her? Strangle her? I may *wish* to choke the exasperating creature, but I think I can restrain myself."

"I'm sorry, my lord," she said in discomfort. "I didn't wish to offend you. But Kitty is my friend, you see. I wish only to make you understand her. She really isn't so exasperating. She's changed a great deal since we first came here. She's become very kind and thoughtful, and I'm certain that she's only run away because she was worried about me. About my safety. She knew I don't know very much about horses, and she probably wanted to protect me. You can't be angry at her for that, can you?"

"Yes, I can. If she was so worried about you, why didn't she come to me?"

"To *you?*" she repeated in surprise. "Why would you expect her to come to you? You're the head of this magnificent estate, and much too busy with more important concerns than those of a housemaid. It isn't as if she was *acquainted* with you."

"Is that what she told you? That she isn't acquainted with me?" he asked curiously.

Emily searched his face wonderingly. "We didn't speak of you very often. I assumed that your path would not cross that of a mere abigail. Was I wrong? *Is* she acquainted with you?"

"Yes, she is. And she ought to have known that I would have gone to search for you if she'd asked."

"Oh, I *see*," Emily said, blinking her wide eyes in surprise. "You *did* say that you've known the truth about us for some time. I have been wondering how you discovered the truth. Was it *she* who told you?"

"No. I guessed. She has no idea that I'm aware of her true identity."

"And yet you say you are acquainted with her. Is it . . . *well* acquainted?"

Lord Edgerton turned away. "Well enough."

It was dawning on Emily that there had been a great deal that Kitty hadn't told her. Could there possibly have been something between Kitty and this rather formidable gentleman? With Kitty, anything was possible. Whatever the truth was, it was evident that his lordship did not need any further explanation of Kitty's behavior from *her*. She rose from the chair. "Then there's nothing more I need to say. Thank you, my lord, for listening to me."

His lordship walked to the room's small window and stared out at the snow. "Before you go, my dear," he said to her without looking around, "I wish you'd tell me why Miss Jessup embarked on this insane masquerade. It couldn't have been a dislike for Toby, for you evidently began the deception before either of you had laid eyes on him."

"Yes, that's true. It wasn't a dislike of Toby. It was a dislike of marriage."

He looked around in surprise. "Of marriage? *Any* marriage? Why was that?"

"She is very young, you know, and has been imprisoned in school for years." Emily smiled, remembering Kitty's declaration of freedom that day in the carriage on the way to Edgerton Park. "She wanted time to be free, she told me. Free to go to parties and dances and routs. Free to meet all of London's eligible men . . . *hundreds* of them, she said . . . and break all their hearts. I remember her saying that wedlock was a fate worse than death."

He did not say anything for a long while. Then he turned

back to gaze out the window again. "That's all I want to know," he said quietly. "Thank you, Emily."

"You're very welcome, my lord. I hope you find her safe and well. And very soon."

He continued to watch the falling snow for several minutes. *So, my girl,* he said to himself with more bitterness than he'd believed he felt, *you want to meet all the eligibles and break their hearts. Well, you've certainly made a good beginning!*

chapter twenty-seven

The falling snow had completely covered any tracks he might have followed, and as the afternoon advanced, the horses found the going more and more difficult. Darkness fell before Edgerton had even a glimpse of another carriage. The two lanterns at the side of the curricle threw only a faint glimmer of light before him, making the search almost impossible. The road markers were few and far between, and the possibilities of a carriage wandering off the road were limitless. For a while he took to shouting her name into the darkness, but the answering silence only chilled his bones. He finally had to admit to himself that there was little point in continuing the search tonight. He'd have to find a place to sleep and start out again at daybreak.

He knew of a small inn in the vicinity, and he pointed his horses in that direction. The snow was, by this time, coming down so heavily that he could barely see ahead of him. The horses made such slow progress that he was convinced he'd passed the inn without seeing it, but suddenly he discerned a faint light ahead. It was indeed the light from the inn he'd visited once or twice before, called the Fiddle and Bow.

The innyard was almost deserted, but the light shining from the Fiddle and Bow's large front window indicated that even tonight a few hardy souls had made their way to the taproom to warm their innards with home brew. He wished, as he handed the reins to the ostler, that he could feel some pleasure at having battled the storm and succeeded in reaching warmth and safety, but his uneasiness at the possible fate of the missing girl prevented him from experiencing any relief. In truth, he was terrified for her.

He went in, tossed his beaver on the hatrack, stamped the snow from his boots, and made his way to the taproom. Only three men sat at the little tables, each one with a mug before him. Weary and depressed, he sank down at the nearest table and dropped his head upon his outstretched arms. He didn't remember ever feeling quite this low before. All sorts of hideous possibilities jostled their way into his imagination. He saw Kitty huddled in a stalled conveyance, the wind whistling wildly about her until it slowly froze her to death. He saw her lying sprawled on a snowbank, her carriage overturned nearby, the snow inexorably covering her beautiful face and form. He pictured her unhitching her horses from her snowbound vehicle and leading them with dogged determination across a seemingly endless field, the tears streaming pathetically from her eyes and freezing on her cheeks. "Oh, God," he groaned, clenching his fists, "let me find her alive."

He must have fallen asleep, for the next thing he knew someone was tapping his shoulder. "Last call," a woman said tiredly. "We'll be closing soon. May I get you something?"

"What?" he mumbled, too miserable to raise his head.

"Ale, sir? Last call."

He turned his head to the side and opened an eye. The barmaid was standing beside his table, holding her tray right at the level of his eye. Did he want any ale, he wondered? Probably not, for he didn't believe he had the strength to sit up and drink it. "No, no," he muttered. "Go 'way and let me be."

"Are you sure, sir? It's last call."

His eye, but not his brain, noted that the barmaid transferred the tray to her other hand. The hand was bandaged. The bandage looked familiar to his eye, but it took a moment longer for his mind to recognize it. When it did, the bandaged hand was already moving away with the body to which it belonged. A shiver shot through him. Was he dreaming? He lifted his head slowly. The barmaid's back was to him, but it could very well be . . .

"Kitty?" he asked, tensely tentative.

The barmaid seemed to freeze. Then her tray fell to the floor with a crash, and she whirled around. "Lord *Edgerton!*"

He jumped to his feet just in time to catch her as she flew into his arms. "You *found* me!" she exclaimed. "I *dreamed* you'd find me."

"*I* dreamed I'd find you frozen to death in the snow," he muttered hoarsely.

He held her tight, not convinced that he wasn't still dreaming. He could hardly believe that she was safe in his arms. She was laughing and crying at once, fondling his hair with eager fingers and, heartless minx that she was, calling him *darling* and *my love*. He knew he should let her go, but he was too tired, too relieved, too foolishly besotted to do it. But all at once she stiffened and drew away from him. "*What* did you say?" she asked, staring at him aghast.

"Say?" he repeated stupidly.

"When you first recognized me. You called me Kitty!"

That brought him to his senses. "Did I?" he said, turning back to the table and seating himself heavily.

She followed him. "Who *told* you?" she demanded angrily.

"No one told me," he said with a weary sigh. "I guessed it long ago."

"You guessed? Then why did you let me go on—"

"It amused me, I suppose. I shouldn't have. In that regard I've been as reprehensible as you."

She sat down opposite him. "I'm not reprehensible. I did it in defense of my life. I didn't want to marry your brother."

"Yes," he said drily. "I know."

"It seemed a good scheme at the time." She folded her hands on the table and looked down at them guiltily. "But it hasn't turned out well. I've searched for hours, but I haven't found Emily."

"You needn't worry about that. She never left the house."

"Never *left?* How can that be? I found a note—"

"She meant to go, but circumstances prevented it. Your parents' arrival, for one."

She gasped. "Oh, no! So soon? Do they know all? Are they very angry with me?"

"Not very. They seem to *expect* such behavior of you. *I'm* the one who's very angry."

She cocked her head and peered at him. "Are you, my lord?"

"Didn't you expect me to be? And you needn't 'my lord' me any longer, now that you're not a housemaid in my employ. My name is Greg."

She smiled. "Yes, I know. I often call you Greg in my thoughts. But I really don't see why *you* should be so angry with me. I didn't do you any harm."

"That shows how little you know about it!" He glared at her for a moment and then, noting that she was about to pursue the subject, held up a restraining hand. "I'm too tired to sit here bantering with you, ma'am. Can we bespeak two bedrooms in this establishment? I am desperate for a little sleep."

"I've already arranged a room for myself, but I'm certain Mrs. Watson will find a place for you. The very best bedchamber, undoubtedly, for the Earl of Edgerton."

"What do you mean, you've arranged for a room? And, by the way, what are you doing acting as barmaid in this place?"

"I'm working for my board. You see, after I'd paid your footman and stableman their bribes, I—"

"Bribes, eh? So *that's* how you managed it. Some heads will roll when I get home!"

Kitty looked distressed. "You don't mean to . . . sack them, do you?"

"That is not your concern. You are no longer one of the belowstairs staff."

"Yes, but . . . if they are discharged, it will be my fault."

"Yes, that's true. Nevertheless, I cannot have men working for me who can be so easily seduced. But go on with your tale."

She shrugged, put that matter of Jemmy and Reeves out of her mind, and continued. "Well, I hadn't gone very far when I realized I'd given away every cent I had in the world. I hadn't left myself a groat. So when I reached here this afternoon, frozen and penniless, I offered my services to Mrs. Watson in exchange for a bed." She looked up again with a mischievous grin. "When she heard I'd been an abigail at the 'great house' with *years* of experience, she was glad to have me."

He shook his head in reluctant admiration. "I'll say one thing for you, Kitty Jessup. You are intrepid. Incorrigible, but intrepid. Nothing seems to defeat you. Your father predicted you'd turn up safe, and he was right."

Her grin widened. "Then you're not so terribly angry with me after all, are you?" she asked coyly.

Something in her grin, in her self-satisfied manner, in her complete disregard of the effect her mischief had had on others, caused an explosion within him. It was as if this provoking, vexatious, troublesome creature was actually *proud* of having cause all this confusion! All the anger that had been bottled up in him came roiling to the surface. "Not *angry?*" he asked, his voice heavy with sarcasm. "You think I'm not angry?" He rose to his feet and stood towering over her. "But of *course* that's what you think. Who could possibly remain angry with the so-adorable Kitty Jessup? And, after all, why should I be angry? Everything has turned out just as you planned, has it not? And no one is very much hurt. Only your friend, who has a dislocated shoulder and assorted bruises to show for her loyalty to you. And your parents, who traveled all night through the snow to find you, only to be mortified by the trick you played on them. And the footman and stableman, who shall lose their posts because of you. And Naismith, of whom you made such a fool. And the other servants, who will feel betrayed and who will never again wish to look you in the eye. To say nothing of *me*—the first of the hundreds of eligibles whose hearts you intend to break—who's been driven to distraction trying to clean up the chaos in your wake!"

Kitty's shining happiness had evaporated with his first angry word, and she'd grown colder and paler as his diatribe proceeded. Now, almost numb with shock and pain, she gazed up at him with a face from which every ounce of color had been drained. "Please, Greg," she whispered, agonized, holding up a hand as if to protect herself from a blow, "don't go on. Don't!"

Her stricken look pierced through him. He felt like a beast, like the monster he'd told Emily Pratt he could never be. Something strong and demanding within his breast wanted to take her in his arms, soothe her, and tell her he'd never hurt her again. But his mind would not permit it. His mind warned him that he needed the protection of his anger to keep himself safe from her.

Perhaps the best course at the moment was a compromise between the two. "Very well," he said, expelling a deep breath, "I suppose that's quite enough anger for now. I'm much too tired to remember the dozens of other reasons you've given me for wrath." He walked slowly to the taproom door. "I'll have plenty to say tomorrow, when I'm refreshed enough to remember how furious with you I am, but for tonight I'm saying nothing more than good night."

She remained seated, motionless, at the table in the now-deserted room. "Good night, my lord," she said.

"I trust you'll be ready to depart by seven. It will be slow going, even if the snow has stopped, and I want to be home before dark."

"Yes, my lord," she said dully. "Seven."

Suddenly he wheeled about. "But I warn you, you vixen, that if you have any intention of running off again—and causing further consternation for your parents and turmoil for everyone else—it will not be I who comes after you. From this moment on, if you play the slightest prank or devise the simplest scheme, I'll wash my hands of you!"

chapter twenty-eight

Kitty did not attempt to run away again. She was ready at seven on the dot, waiting meekly for Lord Edgerton in the private parlor of the Fiddle and Bow. The snow had stopped falling and a hint of sunshine was beginning to be seen through the thinning clouds, but traveling would still be difficult.

She was stirring her spoon, with an obvious lack of enthusiasm, in a bowl of porridge (which Mrs. Watson insisted on serving her so that "somethin' warm and fillin' will stick t' yer ribs") when Edgerton came in. He gave her a grunt as a greeting and, after determining that she was no more eager to finish her breakfast that he was to start his, hurried her out to the innyard and into the closed, four-horse coach he'd hired from Mrs. Watson. (Three of the four horses were his own. He left only the curricle and Kitty's "borrowed" carriage in the innkeeper's care.) The hired coachman climbed up on the box and they were off.

It was slow going, and the silence in the coach made the trip seem interminable. At first Kitty made a few feeble attempts to initiate a conversation, but when she received only monosyllables in response, she ceased trying. An hour went by, during which he stared glumly out of his window and she stared resolutely out of hers.

Finally she shattered the silence with a question that shook him out of his lethargy with a start. "Do gentlemen ever offer *cartes blanches* to well-born ladies, or must the offers be restricted to opera dancers and fancy pieces?" she asked without preamble.

"What a deuced, improper question that is, especially from a young lady who has presumably been gently reared," he said with quenching disapproval.

203

"You didn't seem to mind that sort of question when you thought I was a housemaid," she accused.

"I knew who you were almost from the first, so that part of your accusation is patently false. And you have no way of knowing if I minded those questions or not." He crossed his legs and leaned back in his corner at an angle so that he could observe her more closely. "Is this the only subject you are interested in discussing, Miss Jessup?"

"It is the only subject, of several I've tried, that prompted a reaction from *you*, my lord. So there! But I shall be happy to discuss any subject you like, after you answer my question."

"The answer is that there are no rules about that sort of thing. A gentleman may offer a *carte blanche* to any woman he pleases. It is to be hoped, however, that a real lady would reject that sort of offer out of hand."

She threw him a look of scorn. "That was phrased with admirable, fatherly tact, my lord. Thank you. But if I read correctly between the lines, I might take it, might I not, that there have been ladies here and there who have *accepted* such offers?"

"Here and there. But why do you ask such a thing?"

"Well, you see, I've been sitting here wondering if perhaps you rejected my suggestion that you offer me a *carte blanche* because you knew I wasn't really an abigail. I wondered if perhaps, knowing I was Kitty Jessup, you thought I would only accept an offer of marriage."

"I certainly did. That's why I wanted Toby to offer you marriage. There are certain women to whom one offers marriage and other women with whom one makes liaisons. You, my dear, are one of the former."

"But if some *ladies* accept *cartes blanches*, how can you be sure I'm not that sort?"

The look of amusement that she'd so often seen in his eyes came back again. "Because, my little innocent, you *are* a little innocent. That's how I'm sure."

"But I shan't always be an innocent, shall I? In a few years I shall be very sophisticated. Can I *then* be one of the 'other' women?"

"No, I'm afraid not, for by then you will be a happy wife surrounded by several chubby babies."

"Dash it all, Greg Wishart, you are making this very difficult for me! What if I never marry? What if I remain single and grow to be very beautiful and worldly . . . would you offer me a *carte blanche* then?"

His expression changed abruptly, his mouth hardening and his eyes darkening with anger. "Is *this* what you've been leading up to?" he demanded, leaning forward and grasping her by the shoulders as if he intended to give her a sound shaking. "I thought I'd made it plain that this notion of yours to become my mistress was to be put out of your mind! *I* make things difficult for *you*, do I? Well, *you*, you benighted, provoking, tormenting wretch, are making things *impossible* for me! Have you no sense of propriety at all? No iota of self-restraint? Can't you, just *once*, behave as you ought?"

Her cheeks flamed in shame, her throat tightened, and tears filled her eyes. "What g-good is b-behaving as I ought," she stammered, "if it keeps me from . . . from . . ."

"From what?"

"N-never mind. You would only get *m-more* angry if I t-told you."

"I wouldn't doubt it. But behaving properly is something one does simply because it should be done. It's not done to bring rewards but for its own sake. Like virtue."

"I don't *want* to be proper!" she said, thrusting his hands away and turning her back on him. She drew herself up, dashed the tears from her cheeks, and stared, unseeing, out the coach window. "Or virtuous either, for that matter. If you wanted somebody virtuous and proper you would have married your Miss Inglesham."

"Well, that's a facer," he admitted reluctantly, feeling uncomfortably aware that he'd sounded like a pompous ass. "I didn't mean that you needed to be virtuous and proper to the point of dullness."

She lowered her head until her forehead rested on the icy window glass. "Just how proper and virtuous would I have to be," she asked in a small voice, "for you to wish to marry me?"

"*Marry* you?" He gave a snorting laugh. "Are you now going to suggest *marriage?* What brought about this change? Did you think I would be more amenable to this new suggestion because it would be more *proper?*"

"The suggestion has nothing to do with propriety. If it did,

I could never have made it. If one is being proper, the *gentleman* has to make the offer."

"Does he indeed?" his lordship said drily. "I didn't think you had enough sense of propriety to realize that."

"That's just what's wrong with propriety. If I'd been proper, we'd never be speaking of marriage at all. Sometimes a lady *has* to be improper. *You* certainly had no intentions of making *me* an offer." She peeped over her shoulder at him. "Had you?"

"Certainly not. I'm much too old to be making offers to chits of eighteen. Even proper ones."

"What has your age to do with it?"

"A great deal. I'm middle-aged and you're a child."

"I don't know why it pleases you so much to keep repeating that I'm a child, but the repetition doesn't make it true. *I am of age*. And you needn't try to make yourself sound like a doddering old codger. You can't be more than . . . say . . . forty."

"I'm thirty-five," he blurted out, stung. She chortled in triumph. Greg reddened and gave an embarrassed laugh. "All right, you minx. You've made another point."

She turned around and faced him. "Then, if the age objection has been dispensed with, what else keeps you from making an offer?"

"Good God, what a persistent wench you are! Why are you bringing up the subject of marriage at all? I thought you found wedlock to be worse than death."

"Who told you that?" she asked, surprised.

"Miss Emily Pratt told me. The *real* Emily Pratt."

Kitty fumed. "She had no right to do so! And if I *did* utter such a foolish statement, it was before I fell in love with you."

The words sent a tremor right through him. But he was too sensible to let his emotions take control. "You don't love me, Kitty," he said gently. "You only *think* you do. It's a girl's infatuation, that's all."

She shook her head. "You can't know that. You don't know what I feel."

"I know enough. I know you'll feel this way for many young men before you settle down. You'll break many hearts. You yourself predicted it. Hundreds, wasn't that your own estimate?"

"I suppose Emily told you that, too. Well, *that* isn't true any more either. But I don't suppose you'll believe that, any more than you believe anything else I've said to you. Oh, well," she sighed, "none of it matters, anyway, since you don't love me. Not that I blame you. How could you love someone as benighted, provoking, troublesome, and childish as I?"

"I have no idea. But I do."

Her hands flew to her mouth, smothering her gasp. *"What* did you say?" she asked when she'd recovered her breath. "You can't mean it!"

"I *do* mean it, worse luck! I think I've loved you ever since you first forced yourself on me by demanding protection from a rat that wasn't there."

"Oh, *Greg!"* she breathed, a glow suffusing her entire face.

"There's no need to grow ecstatic, girl, for I don't intend to marry you, however much it hurts to deny myself the joy of it. You are eighteen. You have years ahead of you to enjoy before you settle down. You told Emily you wanted the flirting, the dancing, the romances, the blessed freedom that you'd dreamed of all the years of your growing up, and you have every right to—"

She leaned toward him and put her hand over his mouth. "Why won't you believe me? None of that means *anything* to me now."

He took her hand from his mouth, kissed it gently, and laid it down in her lap. "But it will, as soon as this infatuation of yours passes. Then I will become the first of those hundreds whose hearts you'll break."

"But, dash it all, I don't *wish* to break any hearts! Yours most of all."

"Don't concern yourself, my dear. At my age, broken hearts are rarely fatal."

The finality of his tone chilled her through. She turned back to the window in despair. "But what if they are fatal at mine?" she asked sadly.

He didn't answer. And she, her spirit wounded by his repeated rejection of every offer of love she'd made, succumbed to defeat and stared in silent misery at the passing landscape until the carriage arrived at Edgerton Park.

Before the carriage came to a halt, Greg tapped her on the shoulder. "The whole household must be aware, by this time, that you're the real Miss Jessup, so will you *please*, my dear, *try* to behave appropriately. Your parents have been sufficiently embarrassed by your roguery. I trust you will refrain from further mischief, at least while you remain under my roof."

She turned from the window and fixed him with a look of ice. "I will behave with the utmost propriety, I assure you."

Naismith emerged from the house to let down the steps of the carriage, and he welcomed them both with an impassive bow. When his eyes met Kitty's, there was not a flicker of recognition in them. He turned and led them across the terrace with his usual, measured dignity. Kitty, now familiar with the methods used by the household staff to keep abreast of the doings of the family, knew that their approach was being observed by dozens of pairs of eyes, so, true to the promise she'd just made, she paraded alongside his lordship with as dignified a step as the butler himself.

As she and Greg followed several paces behind the butler, Kitty realized that this might be the very last time she'd be able to exchange a private word with him. Despite her promise to behave herself, she could not let this final opportunity escape her. "If I promise *on my honor* always to behave with propriety, would you reconsider—?" she whispered urgently.

Greg was as aware as she that they were undoubtedly being watched. "No," he hissed between clenched teeth, staring straight ahead of him.

"If I *swear* I'll never concoct another scheme or play another—"

"No!"

They were approaching the door. "I know I'll never be able to prove to you that I'll never love anyone else, but couldn't you take a *chance* on it? Isn't it worth a little risk to—?"

"*No!*" he exploded, throwing up his arms in exasperation, perfectly aware of but completely disregarding all the watching eyes. "Kitty Jessup, if you don't stop, I'll wring your *neck!*"

He stormed off ahead of her, but she would not be deterred. She hurried her step to almost a run and caught up with him. "There's nothing really worthwhile in life that can be achieved without risk, isn't that so?" she demanded, trotting alongside him.

He burst into the Rotunda. *"Birkinshaw,"* he shouted at the top of his voice, "come down here! I've brought your damned daughter home! Come and take her off my hands, I beg you, before I lose what's left of my dignity, my disposition, and my *sanity!"*

chapter twenty-nine

Everyone converged on the Rotunda to give Kitty the noisiest and most enthusiastic greeting she'd ever received. Her mother cried and laughed, berating her for her "naughty tricks" while embracing her with unusual affection. Her father clapped her on the back and called her his "shameful little puss." Alicia, fully dressed and as rosy-cheeked and healthy as Kitty had ever seen her, kissed both her cheeks and presented her to her "betrothed," the beaming Dr. Randolph. And Lady Edith flitted about from one to the other of the assemblage, attempting to close the clasp of her necklace while urging everyone to go to the Blue Saloon for refreshments.

The last to greet her was Toby Wishart. "So *you're* the chit I was supposed to wed," he said, appraising her with a brazen leer. "I would have been quite pleased with the prospect a fortnight ago. But, now, alas . . ." He sighed with mock disappointment as he drew her arm through his and pulled her to the stairs.

"Alas? Why alas? And where are you taking me, sir?"

"To see someone who was too shy to greet you before all the others. And alas, because, alas, it is now too late for us."

"Is it really?" Kitty asked archly. "Why is that, sir?"

"*She* is why." He pointed to a young woman standing shyly at the foot of the stairs. "Miss Jessup, I'd like you to meet my betrothed and beloved Miss Pratt."

"*Emily!*" Kitty exclaimed in astonishment. This was the one bit of news Greg had neglected to tell her. "Is this *true?*"

Emily nodded wordlessly.

Kitty could see at once, in the sparkle of those large dark eyes, that Emily Pratt was happier than she'd ever been. "I'm so glad for you!" she said, choked. "If you didn't have your arm in that sling, I'd hug you for joy!"

"My shoulder can stand it," Emily said, laughing in relief as they embraced. "I was a little fearful that you wouldn't approve," she whispered in Kitty's ear.

Kitty stepped back and eyed her friend suspiciously. "Approve? Why shouldn't I approve?"

"I think she's afraid you might still change your mind and wish to marry me," Toby explained smugly.

"Hah!" Kitty snorted, slipping an affectionate arm around each of them and starting toward the Blue Saloon. "Let me assure you, Toby, old fellow, that I never even liked you. In truth, it's only now that I discover you had the good judgment to shackle yourself to Emily instead of me that I'm willing to credit you with some sense."

Later, on instructions from her mother that she was to change from the hideous bombazine she'd been wearing to some clothes of her own, Kitty found herself following Naismith down the hallway to one of the guest bedchambers. The butler was still treating her as if he'd never seen her before, and Kitty was determined to break through his reserve. "I don't suppose you've missed me a bit, have you, Mr. Naismith?" she asked, catching up with him.

He allowed himself to meet her eye. "It is only the staff that must address me as Mr. Naismith," he said coldly. "To family and guests, a simple Naismith will do."

"But some part of me will always be staff," she said, "so I'm afraid you'll always be Mr. Naismith to me."

He emitted a tiny sigh. "As you wish, miss."

"You don't approve, do you?" she giggled. "I can tell. You're going to turn away and look to the skies and ask the heavens why you've been saddled with such a tormenting guest as I. Am I right?"

A tiny twitch showed itself in a corner of his mouth. "Quite right, miss. Here is your room, miss. I hope it will be satisfactory."

"Thank you, Mr. Naismith. It seems to be a great deal more satisfactory than the other one I occupied in this house." She looked about the room for a moment and then turned back to the butler, who stood waiting in the doorway to be dismissed. "Dash it all, Mr. Naismith, admit it. You do miss me belowstairs, don't you?"

He relented and showed a real smile. "You were a terrible

abigail, miss. Really dreadful. But you tried. And, to tell the truth, I do miss you. We all do. Will that be all, miss?"

"I don't suppose I can convince you to stop calling me miss. Couldn't you call me Kitty?"

He rolled his eyes heavenward. "Certainly not, miss."

She giggled. "Well, I suppose that would be going *too* far. But thank you, Mr. Naismith, for going as far as you did."

"You're welcome, miss. Will that be all?"

"Yes, thank you. If you'll please send Miss Leacock to me, that will be all that I require." And with a brazen, triumphant wink, she let him go.

Miss Leacock entered a few minutes later, shy and very uneasy. "Ye wished to see me, Miss Jessup?" she asked, a nervous tremor in her voice.

"Yes, I did. I want to apologize, Miss Leacock, for not keeping my part of the bargain we made."

"Bargain?"

"You know what I mean. You told me your secret, but I never told you mine."

The abigail began to relax. "You needn't a-pol-o-gize, Miss Jessup," she said in a more normal way. "At least you never *revealed* my secret to anyone."

"Goodness, you didn't think I *would*, did you?"

Miss Leacock smiled. "I wouldn't have confided in you if I did."

"Thank you for that. But I am sorry that I wasn't the one to tell you my true identity. I really owed you that."

"It's all right, Miss Jessup."

"It's not all right. I really meant to tell you. I even tried to find you the day I ran off. But I was afraid someone might see me, so I gave up. But I hope this gift will in some measure make up for it." She took Miss Leacock's hand and dropped the strand of pearls her grandmother had given her into the palm.

Miss Leacock gaped down at the necklace in awe. "Oh, *Emily!* I mean, Miss Jessup, I *couldn't*—! They're too bea-*ut*-i-ful! There's no need . . . I don't deserve—"

"You *do* deserve them. You were the only one who stood my friend when I really needed one. You helped me, and you guided me, and you trusted me. Please take the pearls, Miss

Leacock. It would give me much pleasure if you accepted them."

Miss Leacock, although sincerely moved, hesitated. "Oh, dear. I don't... I never...! Oh, my! Oh, I *will*...if you really wish me to. It is the most won-der-ful gift I've ever in my life received." It took a moment before she was able to look up from the necklace. "But you know, Miss Jessup," she confided, "I was not your only friend belowstairs. There were many who liked and respected you."

"Thank you for saying that," Kitty sighed, "but they won't feel that way when they hear that his lordship is sacking Jemmy and Reeves because of me."

"No, you're wrong there. Lily was telling me all about it when ye sent for me. His lordship didn't sack Reeves. It seems that Jemmy never gave Reeves any money. He kept the money you gave him for Reeves all to himself and told Reeves that Miss Jessup had ordered the carriage. Reeves never knew he'd done anything wrong, so his lordship saw no reason to sack him. His lordship is always very fair, you know."

"Is he?"

"Yes. Always. Everyone says so." She peered at Kitty interestedly. "Don't you agree?"

Kitty shrugged. "I suppose so. But Jemmy may not feel that way."

"I wouldn't worry about Jemmy. None of us'll miss him. Nasty and underhanded, Jemmy was. And with your twenty guineas in his pocket, he'll be a great deal better off than he deserves."

"You even know how much I *gave* him? Amazing!"

Miss Leacock giggled. "There isn't much we don't know downstairs. There's even a wager among the footmen that *you'll* be...but perhaps I shouldn't say..."

"No, please. I love gossip. *Tell* me."

"Well...the wager is—for and against, you know— that'll ye'll be marrying his lordship soon."

Kitty hooted. "However did they come to wager on a tale like that? More likely the snow outside will turn to sugar! Take my advice, Miss Leacock, and put your money on the other side."

Miss Leacock smiled as she went to the door. "I won't bet against it. Sometimes we see things clearer downstairs than you up here. Thank you again for the beautiful pearls. I shall wear them always."

"You're welcome, Miss Leacock."

At the door, the abigail hesitated. "Ye know, Miss Jessup, I don't mind if ye call me the ... the name. Only ..."

Kitty hugged her. "I know, Thisbe. Only in private."

Kitty had barely buttoned up her dress when Mr. Naismith came again to her door with a message from her father to go down to the drawing room at once. When she entered she discovered both her parents sitting on a sofa near the fire, facing Toby and Lord Edgerton who were ensconced on matching easy chairs opposite them. An air of tension seemed to permeate the room, which was not dissipated even when the men rose at her entrance. "Is something amiss?" she asked.

"I should say so!" Lord Birkinshaw said with a touch of asperity. "Something's very amiss, and only you can settle it. Edgerton and I had a bargain. It was made in all good faith. We *shook hands* on it. And now I find it has been breached. Seems to me that something must be *done*."

"You're making a fuss over nothing," his wife snapped. "But if you're going to persist in this, at least let the child sit down."

Toby drew a chair to the side of the sofa and helped Kitty into it as the other gentlemen took their seats. "I'd like to know what on earth you expect me to *do*," Greg said calmly. "Forge ahead with a marriage nobody wants?"

"That's just what we're here to determine," Birkinshaw said stubbornly. He felt that he'd somehow been swindled, and he craved satisfaction. "We don't *know* if nobody wants it."

"Well, *I* certainly don't want it," Lady Birkinshaw muttered. "Never really did."

"I ain't asking you!" her husband barked.

"And *I* don't want it," Toby said promptly, "but I suppose nobody's asking *me*, either."

"No, we ain't," Birkinshaw agreed. "When your brother and I shook hands, your acceptance was *implied*. It isn't my fault that you went and entangled yourself with another female."

"Well, if it comes to that," Toby pointed out, "I *met* the other female through your daughter's machinations. If she'd played by the rules, I might be quite happily betrothed to her at this moment. Since she chose to substitute another female for herself, I would say that she herself invalidated the contract."

"Oh, you would, would you? Well, since you ain't one of the makers of the contract, and since nobody's hired you as an advocate, your interpretation ain't worth the paper it ain't written on."

"Let's stop this brangling," Greg suggested, "and get to the point. Since Toby has betrothed himself to someone else, a wedding between him and your daughter is out of the question. The only thing remaining is to determine if your daughter feels herself injured. If she does, then I as the co-signer, so to speak, of the contract will have to make some sort of restitution. Agreed, Birkinshaw?"

"Very well. Agreed." Birkinshaw turned to Kitty. "Well, my love, tell us. Do you feel yourself injured?"

Kitty, glancing at Greg, was struck with an idea. It was one of those wonderful, bubbly ideas that always set off an explosion of mischief. "Are you asking," she inquired of her father, "if I feel myself injured by *Lord Edgerton?*"

Greg, having become familiar with certain inflections in her voice, leaned forward and peered at her suspiciously.

"I suppose, legally speaking, you can put it that way," her father said importantly.

She sat erect and faced Greg with a tiny smile. "Then I say yes. Yes, I feel injured by Lord Edgerton."

"Ha!" her father chortled, slapping his knee in glee and turning in triumph to his wife. "What did I tell you?"

"This is ridiculous!" Toby said in irritation. "She told me in so many words that she didn't even like me."

"No, the girl is right, Toby," Greg said. Kitty, watching him closely, immediately recognized the familiar gleam of amusement flash into his eyes. "She's been deprived of a husband. She has a right to restitution."

"She certainly has," Birkinshaw agreed cheerfully. "Now all we have to do is determine the amount."

"I think that we should let Kitty do that, don't you?" Greg suggested, fixing his eyes on her.

Birkinshaw looked dubious. "Well, I don't know. She's

only a child, after all, and can't be expected to know the value of—"

"Please, Papa, let me decide. It *is* my injury, after all."

"Very well, then," her father agreed. "But don't be too modest."

"Well, miss," Greg prodded, eyes alight, "go ahead and tell us what restitution I should make. I suspect it will not be modest at all."

Kitty threw a gloating glance at him. "I think, Papa, that his lordship already knows what I would like as restitution."

"He does? Well, Edgerton, what is it?"

Greg got to his feet. "If I haven't mistaken your vixenish daughter's mind, Birkinshaw—and I warn you, I don't think you'll like this one bit!—she wants me to offer her a *carte blanche.*"

"Good God!" muttered Toby, his eyes popping.

"Kitty!" squealed her mother.

"That's a damnable lie!" Birkinshaw shouted, leaping up. "I ought to call you out for that! Kitty, don't just sit there! Set the blackguard straight!"

"Sorry, Papa," Kitty said calmly, keeping her eyes locked on Greg's, "but his lordship is exactly right."

"Kitty Jessup, stop this!" her mother demanded. "It is *not* amusing. Birkinshaw, I blame *you* for this. Such vulgarity cannot have come from *my* side of the family."

"Confound it, Kitty," her father roared, "must you always stir up a to-do? Admit that you're up to your usual tricks and have done."

"But it's not a trick, Papa. Lord Edgerton has spoken nothing but the truth. I am only waiting for him to say he agrees to the terms."

"But this is *insane!*" Birkinshaw's face was turning purple. "If you *like* the fellow, why don't you insist on *marriage?*"

"I've *offered* her marriage," Greg put in, struggling to keep a straight face, "but no, she *insists* on a *carte blanche.*"

"Greg!" Kitty choked. "You *beast!*"

"I *say* Greg," his brother said, his brow clearing, "is there something going on here that we've been missing?"

Lady Birkinshaw looked at her husband dazedly. "Did he say he wanted to *marry* her? Edgerton *himself?*"

Birkinshaw sank into his chair and mopped his brow. "I don't know *what* is going on. This is all beyond me."

"Well, Miss Jessup," Greg said, crossing to her chair and pulling her to her feet, "you are the injured party. It's all up to you. Are you willing to accept my compromise?"

She threw her arms about his neck with shockingly unlady-like alacrity. "Do you *mean* it, my love? You're willing to risk it after all? Please think about it, Greg. If you're to wed me, I don't want it to come to pass because of a silly trick."

He cupped her face in his hands. "It will come to pass, my love, because I can no longer live without you."

Bedlam broke out around them. Lady Birkinshaw shed tears of joy. Toby did a wild dance around the room. Birkinshaw went to the door and shouted for everyone to come down and hear the news. The commotion brought Naismith scurrying to the drawing-room doors in alarm. Through it all, Greg and Kitty stood immobile, merely smiling foolishly into each other's eyes. After a while, Kitty glanced over her shoulder and caught a glimpse of the butler gaping at them. Half the household staff were crowded behind him, their faces agog. Kitty, although she turned back to her beloved, called to the butler. "Mr. Naismith, do I have permission to speak?"

He rolled his eyes heavenward. "Yes, miss, you know you do."

"Then may I ask your opinion on a delicate matter?"

"Yes, miss."

"Can you tell me if it is proper behavior for a gentleman to kiss his betrothed before dozens of onlookers?"

"Very *im*proper, I should think."

"In that case, since his lordship and I are a couple who are very concerned with propriety, I would be very grateful if you would clear the room of all these onlookers in ten seconds, because I have not yet been kissed, and ten seconds is all I intend to wait."

BESTSELLING TALES OF ROMANCE